1.00
B

Doris J. Seymour

THE EPISODE AT TOLEDO

Books by Ann Bridge

ANN BRIDGE

THE
EPISODE
AT TOLEDO

McGRAW-HILL BOOK COMPANY

New York   Toronto   London   Sydney

THE EPISODE AT TOLEDO

"WELL, there's the post at last," Mrs. Reeder said, coming into the library at Glentoran with a huge pile of letters. "Ronnie says the bus had a breakdown." She threw the mail onto a big oak table in the middle of the room, and sorted it into piles: "Philip, me; me, Philip." It was only when the last was in its place that she handed their post to her waiting guests, who sat in deep arm-chairs in front of a sputtering fire of logs. "Two for you, Mrs. H.; four for Julia—one from your Philip, I see." She picked up the biggest pile of all and carried it away to her husband's business-room next door; then she returned and took her own heap over to a large workman-like desk under the west window, against whose panes rain was beating savagely, borne on an Atlantic gale.

Julia—now Mrs. Philip Jamieson—and old Mrs. Hathaway, her godmother, seized on their letters and read them; Mrs. Reeder, seated at her desk, tore open envelopes, flung them into a capacious waste-paper basket, and placed most of their contents in wicker trays variously labelled "Bills", "Receipts", "House", "Dairy", "Tradespeople". The busy wife of an active landlord who farmed his estate in the West Highlands himself, the bulk of her correspondence was not of a personal character. Having finished her task she lit a cigarette, slewed round on her desk chair, and asked—

"Well, any news?"

"Mine are not very interesting," Mrs. Hathaway replied mildly—in fact the correspondence of old ladies is not normally particularly absorbing. Julia Jamieson, however, had something of interest to report.

"Yes, I've heard from both Luzia and Hetta—and I can't quite make out what goes on."

"Luzia—now she's that Portuguese Duke's daughter, who came over to be your bridesmaid, isn't she? Has she got engaged yet to that old peer's boy, who lives at Pau?"

"How clever you are to remember!" Julia said, in her slow tones. "No—Nick hasn't gone to 'renew his addresses' yet. But Richard and Hetta have just been to stay at Gralheira, and now Luzia is with them in Madrid."

"Now just let me get Hetta right," Edina said. "The Hungarian refugee girl, who ended up by marrying an English diplomat?"

"Yes, Richard Atherley; he was Head of Chancery in our Lisbon Embassy then, and met Hetta; later they got married. Now he's Counsellor in Madrid."

"Right. Carry on."

Mrs. Hathaway needed no briefing about Countess Hetta Páloczy, now Mrs. Atherley; their first meeting had been unforgettable. When a car rammed her taxi in a Lisbon street, some years before, she had looked into it and seen a girl, unconscious and with a gag in her mouth, lying on the back seat; she had fetched the police, taken the girl to her own hotel, and brought her round from the overdose of drugs which the Communist thugs who were abducting her had administered. Later they stayed at Gralheira, the Duke of Ericeira's country home, where Hetta and Richard became engaged; later still, when Atherley put in a spell at the Foreign Office, Mrs. Hathaway had seen a good deal of the young couple in London, and renewed her first affection for the Hungarian girl. She regretted it when Richard was sent to Paris, as an understudy to the English Nato representative, and then on to Madrid.

"Julia, might I see Hetta's letter?" the old lady now asked.

"Of course, Mrs. H.—I was going to ask you to read it, and see what you make of it."

Mrs. Hathaway read the letter through twice, carefully; then, still holding it, she spoke.

"If Hetta is asking whether Philip—*your* Philip, Julia—or Hugh Torrens could come out, there must be something serious going on, or likely to go on. Hetta is no fool. And who is this person Luxworthy, the important American?"

"No idea," Edina said. She glanced at her watch. "Mrs. H., I must go down to the farm; would you like me to drop you off at the Stalker's House for a little? Then I can bring you back to lunch."

"Oh thank you—it's time I saw that poor little woman again. I'll just get a coat."

The interior of the Stalker's House, to which Mrs. Hathaway was admitted after tapping on the door, was not in the least characteristic of the normal West Highland cottage. Copper cooking-pots, polished to a high degree of brilliance, hung from nails on the kitchen wall; more stood on the stove, emanating smells of a foreign deliciousness. In the little sitting-room to which this surprising stalker's wife led her guest—after carefully lowering the heat under her pots—the tables and chair-backs were covered with exquisite drawn-thread work, totally unlike the hideous coloured embroidery, on stereotyped patterns, native to the place.

"Well, Madame, how does it go?" Mrs. Hathaway asked in French, sitting down.

"Sufficiently well, *chère Madame,* I thank you. I have acquired twelve young hens, and a cock, so in the spring I shall have chickens; also I have bought some ancient fowls—one of them is in the casserole at this moment. My husband is making houses for the chickens; imagine, at the saw-mill they ask him nothing for the wood!"

They talked on. Presently Mrs. Hathaway asked the French-woman if there was anything that she wanted?

"Madame, *yes.* In this shop in the village the woman—very amiable *du reste*—has never heard of a round embroidery frame! If Madame could procure one for me I should be infinitely thankful."

Struck by curiosity, Mrs. Hathaway allowed herself to ask why Madame Bonnecourt wanted a wooden embroidery frame?

"But for the *mouchoirs* of Madame Reeder! *Voyons,* Madame, sometimes I help in the laundry, and I see that Madame's *mouchoirs,* though of good, pure linen, have no monograms on them; only these small red letters, sewn on little tapes. If I had an embroidery frame I could put pretty monograms, 'E.R.', on all her *mouchoirs.* I have experience as a *brodeuse,"* the Frenchwoman said.

Mrs. Hathaway could well believe it, given the exquisite needlework all about her in the room. She promised to have a frame sent from London; just then Edina's car-horn hooted outside the door; the old lady put on her coat and hurried away, promising to return soon.

"Does she seem to be getting on all right?" Mrs. Reeder asked. When her cousin Julia Jamieson had written to suggest that since Glentoran was short of stalkers, they should give employment to the Pyrenean climber and hunter, Bonnecourt —whose promptitude had saved Julia's life and that of her child by driving her down to Pau in the middle of the night from the mountain village where she was marooned, alone, during a premature labour—Edina had agreed at once; but she had become slightly anxious when it was presently explained to her that Madame Bonnecourt, who unlike her husband spoke no English, would presently join him. In fact Philip Jamieson—so tiresome that both their husbands should be called Philip, Edina often thought—had brought Madame Bonnecourt over, complete with her earthenware casseroles and her copper cooking-pots, by sea from Bordeaux; the weight of her *batterie de cuisine* made flight quite prohibitively costly. But so far it had all worked out better than Edina had expected. Madame Bonnecourt helped in the dairy, and made beautiful butter; also in the laundry, where her treatment of Mrs. Reeder's pretty underclothes seemed a special and unconvenanted boon to her new employer. Many British country ladies, outwardly clothed in hard-worn tweeds and weather-stained Burberrys, derive a secret solace from delicious "undies"; Mrs. Reeder did, and found the French-woman's handling of these objects a delight.

"Yes, she seems quite happy," Mrs. Hathaway now replied. "She's going in for chickens; she's bought a dozen pullets and a cock."

"Oh, good. Well, let me know if you find out anything she wants."

Mrs. Hathaway decided to keep the monograms a secret, and said no more.

Philip Reeder came in for lunch; he was getting burly in figure, and silver threads were beginning to show in the bushy brown beard which he had worn all his life in the Merchant Navy. Man-like, he was full of his own concerns, and after carving slices off a haunch of venison for everyone he sat down, took a pull at a tankard of ale, and began to talk.

"Julia, I really am grateful to you for sending us that fellow Bonnecourt. He's practically the best stalker we've ever had; he's out at all hours, and I don't believe he ever misses a shot."

Julia said she was glad. "It was very good of you to take him on; his life was in danger in France then, after that mix-up with the O.A.S."

"Yes, I was a bit nervous before he came; a foreigner, and all—you never know. It was a risk, but it's paid off. And Mac-Hale tells me that he's interested in sheep too, and very clever about them; he's brought in three cast ewes already, that MacHale had missed. He's getting on, poor old boy; he doesn't get about the hill as much as he used to—or ought to—I think he relies rather too much on Bonnecourt's activities. I hope to

· 5 ·

God British Intelligence—through your brother," he turned on his wife, "or *your* Philip, Julia—don't go snatching him away from Glentoran."

Julia and Edina both laughed.

"Philip, it was in the contract that if Intelligence wanted Bonnecourt at any time, they were to have him," Julia stated firmly. "You needed a stalker, urgently, for your autumn tenants; well, you got a very good one. But I made it perfectly plain to Edina, from the start, that this was a cover-job, and that he would have to go whenever he was summoned by the Office."

"Don't like that word 'cover-job'—it doesn't fit in with this sort of life," Philip Reeder said, with a dissatisfied expression.

"Well, that is what we gave him, expressly," his wife said. "Julia writes very lucid letters, and Colin explained it to you, all over again, when he brought the man up. Don't pretend that you didn't understand at the time, just because you don't want to lose him now, since he's being so useful," Edina pursued, with wifely frankness.

"Oh, *Colin!*" Reeder muttered into his beard. Like many other people he rather despised Colin Monro, his wife's brother.

After a divine cheese soufflé, prepared by Edina's Spanish cook Olimpia, they all repaired to the library for coffee. Here Edina once again asked Julia what was bothering Hetta Atherley? "I simply *had* to get down to the farm—I couldn't wait to hear it all. What goes on?"

"She doesn't say—people brought up in Communist countries get so cautious. Only that there might be some danger; possibly to this important Yank."

"What Yank?" Philip Reeder asked, handing a cup of coffee to Mrs. Hathaway.

"Oddly enough she gives his name—Admiral Luxworthy. But I've no idea who or what he is," Julia said, folding Hetta's letter up again.

· 6 ·

"My poor Julia, maternity seems to be impairing your I.Q.!" Reeder said. "Do you never read the papers?"

"Well, not much," Julia admitted. "I'm too happy!"

"Luxworthy—Henry P. Luxworthy—is top brass in the Pentagon," Philip said. "Surely even you must have seen that the U.S. is cutting down on her Saceur airfields, and concentrating on her naval bases for Polaris submarines, like our Holy Loch?"

"What does 'Saceur' stand for?" his wife interjected. "These made-up names are so muddling and tiresome."

"Strategic Air Command Europe. You're as bad as Julia," Philip replied impatiently.

"Well, why are the Yanks reducing these Saceur places?" Edina pursued. She was not in the least intimidated by her rather formidable husband.

"Because now submarine-launched missiles have practically superseded plane-launched ones," Philip said. "Less detectable, and much less vulnerable." He was quite happy to expatiate on a subject which interested him. "So America needs fewer bases, especially airfields; but the naval ones, which she still does need, she needs *more*. So she is tremendously keen on Rota, that huge place close to Cadiz, where the Americans have a vast maintenance staff."

Mrs. Hathaway here broke in with a question.

"Philip, are the submarines from these bases going to launch *nuclear* things?"

"Yes, Mrs. H.—at least that is their purpose." Even Philip Reeder was never impatient with Mrs. Hathaway.

"How appalling!" the old lady said. "I believe Lord Rutherford was a very clever man; but why he wanted to go and split the atom, and open the door to all these horrors, I can't think! He would have done much better to try to find out how to cure cancer."

"He was a physicist, not a doctor, Mrs. H.," Philip said, pacifically.

· 7 ·

"Agreed. Well, now go on, Philip—since you seem so well-informed," Edina said, half-mockingly. "How does good Admiral Luxworthy, who seems to be so much on Hetta's mind, come into the Rota set-up?"

"I can only speculate about that," her husband replied. "That he is about to go to Spain—may have already gone—I do know; it was in the papers, and on the wireless. And I conclude that one of his main concerns will be with Rota, since Washington regards it as so important. Franco has been most co-operative about the place, and the Americans, in their turn, have gone out of their way to be the same—for example strictly limiting how much per month their staff may spend out of their *enormous* dollar salaries, so as not to disrupt the local economy; and enforcing most careful respect, by the same staff, of Spanish social and religious customs. No wolf-calls to girls in the streets—heavy penalties for that."

"Goodness, why couldn't they have done all that at their air-bases here!" Julia exclaimed. "Franco must have something, to get rules like that enforced by the Yanks."

"I think it's really the Spanish people who have something, rather than the old Caudillo himself," Philip answered her. "On the whole the English are very tolerant; the Spanish are thoroughly *in*tolerant, and someone must have tipped Washington off to watch their step if they wanted to keep Rota. Anyhow, things have gone quite well, so far."

"Then why Luxworthy's friendly call now?" Julia asked. "Just to cheer everyone along?"

"Not entirely, I don't think." Philip paused. "Here I fancy we come up against our old friend de Gaulle, and his anti-Nato theory of *'l'Europe des Patries';* in fact his general anti-Americanism. And for some time past he has been plugging these ideas, really to quite a dangerous extent, in Spain: France and Spain, the last two right-wing *Patries* left in Europe!—with poor Portugal, of course, tagging along too."

"I can't see Portugal 'tagging along' with anyone," Julia exclaimed briskly. "She has her own ideas; mostly very sound

ones, *I* think, and defends them by herself. But what does the
General think to gain by plugging his anti-American ideas in
Spain?"

"I should like to know that too," Edina put in.

"Not very internationally-minded, are you?—either of you,"
Reeder replied, mockingly—"in spite of your family connections with Intelligence!"

"Well, go on and tell us, clever one," his wife replied, with
equal mockery. "We may be too happy, like Julia, or too busy,
like me, to keep *au fait* with foreign affairs; but we both like
to know about them."

"So do I," Mrs. Hathaway added, with slight severity in her
voice—she occasionally thought that Philip Reeder was becoming rather the heavy husband. That gentleman now drew
in his horns a little, sensing the old lady's unexpressed disap-
proval.

"Well, some of this is speculation, but not wholly, and not
mine," Reeder said. "After the cattle-sale at Falkirk last week,
in the Club in Edinburgh I ran into a man I used to know,
who's in Colin's, and your Philip's"—he nodded at Julia—
"line of business. He'd heard somehow that you were staying
here, Julia, and asked after Philip; I suppose that opened his
mouth a bit to me—he knows Colin, too."

"Name of?" Julia asked.

"Watherston."

"Never heard of him. Never mind. What did his semi-
speculation amount to?"

"Just that de Gaulle would be only too glad to detach
Franco from his good-relations basis with the Americans, and
drag him back into the *Patries* camp, especially since his own
failure with Germany after Erhard came to power, replacing
his old chum Adenauer."

"So what?" Julia asked. "Why should de Gaulle's propaganda in Spain be dangerous?"

"Because the situation he's trying to create there is a *gift* to
the Communist bloc. If they could exploit it by any happen-

ing which roused the Spaniards violently against the Americans, or the Americans against the Spaniards, and threw Spain back into de Gaulle's arms, it could disrupt the Western Alliance—for quite a time, anyhow. And Rota is vital to the whole Atlantic bloc, for defence purposes."

"But what sort of happening?" Edina asked. Julia, who had long experience of Communist activities in many countries, was quicker.

"Oh, do something nasty to the good Luxworthy somehow, while he's in Spain, come merely to give a loving paternal glance at the good-working of the Rota base! Yes, that could be a real spanner in the Nato works—and the row and the recriminations would go on for ages! Thank you, Philip—this clears up a lot. I quite see why Hetta is worried."

"What does she say?" Reeder asked.

"That Luxworthy is about to come to Spain, and that she wondered whether my Philip, or Hugh Torrens, would be free to come out to help keep an eye on him. She didn't say more than that, but the letter sounded quite urgent."

"Couldn't our Embassy in Madrid lay on any help of that sort that they wanted, themselves? Or the Americans, for that matter?" Reeder asked.

"I suppose so, if all you've been telling us is common knowledge. But common knowledge so often seems to escape the Foreign Office," Julia said, unkindly. "My guess is that Hetta has had some sort of scare."

"I shouldn't be surprised. She seems to be pretty well informed, anyhow," Reeder replied. "What shall you do?"

"Well *my* Philip can't go—he's in the Middle East. I've no idea where Hugh Torrens is".

"Why not try to get hold of Torrens?" Reeder asked.

Julia hesitated—Edina frowned at her husband for this tactless suggestion; Major Torrens was one of what she privately called "Julia's cast-offs".

"Well, at a pinch I suppose I might," Julia said, determined not to let her own feelings stand in the way of the job. "What

I should really like to do is to get hold of Richard Atherley; he must have some idea of what's going on, and why Hetta is worrying."

"Well, ring up Madrid tonight—it's cheaper after six, though that doesn't really matter," her wealthy host said cheerfully.

"I'm not at all sure that that will help you much," Mrs. Hathaway observed.

"Why on earth not, Mrs. H.? I must have some idea of what goes on, or might go on, if I'm to bother Hugh Torrens about this—and surely Richard would know?"

"The official facts and dates, of course; but if Hetta has some *private* reason for being worried, I'm not at all sure that she would have told her husband."

The three young people stared at her.

"Goodness, Mrs. H.!" Edina exclaimed—"Aren't she and Richard on good terms?"

"The very best, as husband and wife. But Hetta's background, brought up in a Communist-dominated country, is quite different to Richard's—he *is* rather Foreign-Office-y, don't you think, Julia?" That young woman nodded, thoughtfully. "If Hetta thought that he would pay attention to what is troubling her, and get appropriate action taken officially, why did she write to *you?*" Mrs. Hathaway ended.

Philip Reeder lit another cigarette, got up, and walked about the library.

"Well, it looks as if you've got a point there, Mrs. H.," he said. "Why indeed? You remember what you said just now, Julia, about 'common knowledge' and the F.O.? This Hetta may have the same idea."

"No. Hetta's idea will be quite an individual one," Julia said. "I must think what to do."

She went off to feed her baby son.

On the way upstairs she made a resolution not to think about Hetta's letter while she was nursing the Philipino, as they called him, but she was only partially successful. When she left the nursery she went to her own room, and did some intensive thinking. Reluctant as she was to tackle Hugh Torrens, her discarded suitor, she decided to do exactly that; it was probably the best way of getting Hetta the information she wanted.

Philip Reeder, practical man, had installed bedside telephones in every room in Glentoran; they were mostly used as a form of "inter-comm" with the kitchen and the other rooms in the huge house—a small typed list gave the internal numbers. But by pressing a button one could be connected with the outside world, and a red switch cut one off from the rest of the household, making a call completely private. Julia used both these appliances, and then put through a personal call to Major Hugh Torrens at the Office number in London. She didn't wait for the cheap time after 6 P.M.—Hugh might be gone, and Philip Reeder was rich.

Torrens was in. "Who is that?" he asked; Julia had carefully refrained from "having her name passed", in the English telephonist's phrase.

"Julia—me—talking from Glentoran."

"Oh my dear, how *are* you? How good to hear your voice."

"I'm splendid, thank you. But Hugh, listen carefully, and be as smart as you can."

"I'll try—though you know I'm never as smart as you!"

"Well do your best. Listen—is anyone in the Office at all concerned about this high-powered Yank who's just going to Spain?"

"Oh, I know who you mean. No, it all seems quite straightforward. Ought we to be concerned?"

"I think so. I've just had some private information which is a bit worrying."

"Where from?" Torrens' voice sharpened on the two words.

"Spain—from what's usually a very 'well-informed and reliable source'. But you don't know a thing, I gather?"

"Julia, don't be nasty. You know you always beat us to it, but we do our best! I suppose you wouldn't like to tell me who your clever informant is? Not the little Countess, by any chance?"

This time Hugh Torrens was being much smarter than usual—Julia was pleased.

"Yes, it *is* her. After all, she has her own sources of information. Whatever you do, don't go aboard that stuffed seal of a husband of hers! But I do need to know what goes on, so that I can answer 'the little Countess'. That's quite a useful phrase. She calls herself 'Mrs.' now."

"I know, tactful little thing."

"Well anyhow she *is* worried, and I want to be told the form, if you can find anything out. So ring me back, will you?" She rang off.

2

SOME DAYS before that conversation at Glentoran took place Mrs. Parrott, the wife of the American Naval Attaché in Madrid, was giving a cocktail party in her flat. The flat was perfectly adequate for such a purpose, since it was one of those huge ones, covering nearly a quarter of an acre each, off the Martinez Campos; the object of the party was the entertainment of Admiral Luxworthy's wife and nineteen-year-old daughter. Spain had carefully been put last on his list of visits, and as he obviously could not drag his family all round Europe with him, he had parked them in Madrid; he knew his Ambassador there rather well, and with his concurrence had arranged it like that. But this naturally involved the American diplomatic staff in "doing something" about the female Luxworthys, in fact doing quite a lot—they had got to be shown round, they had got to be amused, they ought to meet people. Hence the party.

Nell Parrott was a warm-hearted little creature, but rather feather-brained, and an incurable chatterbox; Madrid was her husband's first post abroad, and she found diplomatic life puzzling and difficult. She was always making mistakes which she couldn't for the life of her see were mistakes when her Walter, patient but troubled, pointed them out to her. "But *why* shouldn't I have said that about the Prado to the Minister of

Education? He's a bore, anyway." One of Commander Parrott's main preoccupations, in fact, became to secure help for his Nell in any major piece of entertaining, and with the presence of the Atherleys in Madrid much of this work soon devolved on Hetta; Walter Parrott's I.Q. was much higher than his wife's, and he and Richard soon became firm friends; this, diplomatic life being what it is, involved Hetta in assisting Nell, frequently, in her uncongenial tasks.

This evening the little American, whose great asset was her extreme prettiness, was fussing round the big rooms, examining the huge trays of elaborate cocktail edibles, and shifting vases rather restlessly, when in the distance a bell rang; a moment later a Spanish maid, dressed in black and wearing white cotton gloves, announced—

"*La Señora* Atherley."

"Oh darling, there you are! How lovely of you to come along early. Now take a look round and see if everything is okay. Are the flowers all right?"

Hetta walked leisurely round the rooms, carefully inspecting the vases.

"Not this one," she said. "These are faded; you had them here last week." She lifted the vase off the table, and handed it to the maid, who still hovered about. "Remove it, please," she said in Spanish.

"That will leave a gap," Nell said.

"Better a gap than shabby flowers," Hetta replied. She went across to a shelf and lifted down a little polychrome statuette of St. Anne, and put it in the place of the discarded vase. "There—now your gap is filled."

The Parrotts had rented the flat, fully furnished, from its Spanish owners, whom in fact the Atherleys already knew; to reap the rich American rent they had retired to their cigarral (country house) outside Toledo.

"Be careful of that statuette—it is of great value," Hetta now said. "After the party, be sure to put it back on that high shelf."

"How do you know all these things?" Nell asked. "I haven't a clue as to what's valuable and what isn't, in this house."

"We had beautiful things at home," Hetta said. "Papa was learned about *objets d'art,* and tried to teach me about them. So they still interest me."

"What became of your family stuff?" Nell Parrott asked, with typical thoughtlessness.

"Oh, the Russians took it all, when they came into Hungary —they stole everything," Hetta said. "I was at school, of course—but we heard later." Her fine dark brows drew together in a little frown; less at the loss of her family possessions than at Nell's careless failure in tact. Her unhappy story—a story typical of so many Central European families —was no secret in Madrid; least of all in American circles, since her Mother, Countess Páloczy, was herself an American, and had returned to Washington three or four years previously. (The old Count had died in Portugal, whither the parents had escaped, long before.) But Hetta, though she was by now accustomed to Nell Parrott's scatter-brained lack of memory and careless tongue, could never quite reconcile herself to them; such a lack of attention, of consideration, seemed to her a failure not only in good manners, but in charity. But her Richard was devoted to Walter, so part of her duty was to help Nell, and not allow herself to be annoyed by these lapses.

The bell rang again; another maid, also in black and white-gloved, opened the door and announced *"El Teniente* Ellington." Mrs. Parrott greeted him warmly. She could always be warm; she needed no thought for that.

"Oh Jim, that's fine! You've come early too. Do you know Mrs. Atherley?"

"Yes indeed," the young American said, shaking hands with Hetta.

"Well, we're just looking round. Hetta's passed everything so far, except one lot of flowers!"

"Nell, what we should now decide is in which room you will receive, and where you will stand," Hetta said practically.

"This room, I thought; it's nearest to the hall."

"I agree. Then should you not stand *here?*" Hetta said, placing herself about four yards inside the door, close to the right-hand wall. "And Mrs. and Miss Luxworthy can stand beside you, so that you make the introductions. Shall you know everyone's name?"

"Not the Spaniards'. I'm bad at faces, and their names are so difficult."

"Who will announce?" Hetta asked.

Lieutenant Ellington weighed in at this point.

"Mrs. Atherley, there's a man laid on for that, who knows every face and name in Madrid; we fixed it with Captain Parrott. But the Captain thought it might be as well if his Former Number Two, Commander Mansfield, who's been here for years and speaks perfect Spanish—as well as knowing everyone —should stand on Mrs. Parrott's left and help with the introducing." He paused, and turned to his hostess. "Didn't your husband mention that?" he asked her, very courteously.

"Why yes, so he did—only I forgot," Nell Parrott said. "Will Commander Mansfield be along soon? He'd better be on hand before they start streaming in."

"He will be here in five minutes," Ellington said, looking at his watch—"and the Luxworthys five minutes after that."

Hetta looked at the young American approvingly. Here was an intelligent, well-bred young man, she thought. He had been to their house for drinks two nights before, and Richard had explained to her afterwards that Lieutenant Ellington had been specially detailed to act as A.D.C. to Admiral Luxworthy during his European tour, because his Mother was French, and he had been brought up partly in Europe. Anyhow, Richard had said hurriedly, North Carolinians remained much more European than most Americans—except the people from New Orleans, with its long history of Spanish and French occupation. But the Admiral had decided that his A.D.C. would be better occupied in shepherding his wife and daughter during their sojourn in Spain than in accompanying him to Germany, France, and England—countries which he felt well able to handle himself. He had been in them all during World War II; but not in Spain—which anyhow was the most important, just now.

After another distant tinkle of a bell Commander Mansfield was announced, this time loudly and clearly by the Spanish butler who had been laid on so carefully for the occasion. Hetta recognised the servant, and was relieved; he really *could* pronounce names of any nationality—so essential for this sort of party—as not all the *Madrileno* hired butlers could. After several years of marriage to an English diplomat, the once un-couth little waif from Hungary had turned into an extremely competent hostess; she still rather despised the whole social and diplomatic set-up, but it was now her job, and she had mastered it. The four people in the room all knew one an-other, so no introductions were necessary; but Hetta still ad-mired Commander Mansfield for having adopted the custom of the country where he now lived by preference—he had retired from the Service—of kissing the hands of married ladies. He was a tall, strongly-built, grey-haired man, with one of those deeply-lined, ravaged faces so common among Bostonian intellectuals—the ravages caused not by any per-sonal tragedy, but by a profound preoccupation with human life, and its expression in art. In Spain Mansfield had found both of these at their highest point, in his experience; so after his retirement he continued to live in Madrid, refus-ing further promotion—a boon to all diplomats.

Like the rest, he turned his mind to the practical organisa-tion of this almost military operation, the party for the Lux-worthys.

"Mrs. Parrott, shall you receive in this room?"

"Well, we thought so—but you'd better ask Mrs. Atherley and Lieutenant Ellington. They have it all worked out."

Mansfield turned to Hetta, who explained her ideas. "And you on Mrs. Parrott's left. But the Captain? When does he come?"

"I should have said that sooner. He's held up; a little trouble about Cuban refugees. He'll be along as soon as he can—we just carry on till he comes." He agreed with all Hetta's positioning, except for having the receiving group two yards further from the door—"Otherwise you may get quite a block. And where shall *you* be, Countess?"

"Oh, flitting about!—to lend a hand when it's needed." Hetta's command of English had improved greatly during her years of marriage—Mansfield laughed.

"Well, for God's sake let's have a drink to support us before the trouble starts," Nell Parrott said—as she spoke she went over and poured herself out a whisky. But before the others could follow suit the Spaniard again flung open the door, announcing "Madame et Mademoiselle Luxworthy."

Ellington was beautifully efficient. He crossed the great room swiftly, greeted the two American guests, led them over to where their hostess and Hetta were standing, and made the introductions. "Commander Mansfield I think you know already." Hetta noticed with amusement that Mansfield tactfully refrained from kissing Mrs. Luxworthy's hand; that would merely have embarrassed her. She was a well-educated middle-aged Middle-Westerner; but this was her first visit to Europe, and marooned in Madrid by her husband, she was already finding some things puzzling. As well as her beautifully-permed, blue-rinsed hair, and the inevitable orchid on her left shoulder, she had a kind, intelligent face, with a lovely natural complexion; Joy, her nineteen-year-old daughter, was very tall, dark-haired and tawny-skinned, and plainly spurned any form of make-up—in fact her rather large nose was distinctly shiny. Apart from this careless defect she was extremely good-looking, with lambent light-brown eyes, and a lively mouth.

To Ellington's relief, Hetta promptly took over.

"Mrs. Luxworthy, a little drink, no? In a few minutes the guests arrive, and you cannot have a glass in your hand! Miss Luxworthy, what do you drink?—a dry Martini? You too must meet so many people, who are eager to encounter your Father's daughter!" Hetta had instantly realised that Joy was going to be the difficult proposition on this occasion.

Both the Luxworthy ladies took a drink; then, once again forewarned by the distant bell, under Mansfield's and Ellington's supervision they set down their glasses and took up their appointed positions, now six yards inside the door, on the right of their hostess; Mansfield stationed himself on her left.

Of course the diplomats came first; punctuality is one of the duties they learn. Marchant, the British Military Attaché, and his tall absent-minded wife Maud, with her long drooping hands, came with their Ambassador, a stout benign bachelor; after a suitable exchange of small-talk with Mrs. Parrott and her two principal guests, he went on to talk to Hetta.

"Where's your husband, my dear?"

"Sir Noël, you should know that better than I!" Hetta said briskly. "Is it not always you who delay him?"

The Ambassador laughed—he enjoyed Hetta very much.

"Is that what he tells you?" he asked, taking a cocktail from a tray proffered by one of the Spanish maids.

"Well, did you not recall him from Portugal just now? We had hoped to be much longer at dear Gralheira."

"Oh, I must get to see that place sometime," His Excellency said. "I hear the house is quite lovely—and such marvellous partridge-shooting. I did meet the old Duque once—couldn't you coax him to invite me?"

"You had better arrange that with his daughter—she comes to stay with us tomorrow."

"Does she now?—the beautiful Luzia? I must certainly give a party for her."

"No, not a big party; they are *en deuil de famille*—for a most tiresome old Uncle or Aunt. Ask her to a small luncheon, and make up to her!" Hetta said, with a fearless mocking grin.

"Really, Hetta!" the diplomatist said. "I thought she was half-engaged to one of those Heriot boys from Pau?"

Gossip knows no frontiers, at least in Europe; Hetta was not in the least surprised by this remark, but took occasion to make the position clear.

"There is an admirer, yes; he was coming to Gralheira to meet her Father, and—well, to see if matters could be arranged. But with this mourning, it has had to be postponed— and this gives on her nerves! So I asked her to come to us, to give her some distraction. Your Excellency might help to distract her!"

"You really are a little monster, Hetta!" the Ambassador said, still amusedly. "Putting temptation in my way! Well, bring her to luncheon; I shall be discreet, as I always have to be; but if I can't secure an invitation to shoot partridges at Gralheira it won't be for lack of trying!" He paused. "I was sorry to drag you and your husband back," he went on, "but you see he's been so closely in touch with Nato in Paris, so recently, that I felt I really had to have him on hand for this visit—which is pretty crucial. And personal background knowledge is so essential, especially when one is dealing with Americans; somehow they have such a personal approach."

"Quite true—of course I know this, as my Mother is an American," Hetta said.

The Ambassador actually blushed slightly—an unusual phenomenon. He had quite forgotten, damn it, that Countess Dorothée Páloczy, who was now cutting rather a figure as a hostess in Washington, and very much in touch with the White House, was in fact Hetta's Mother; his Counsellor's wife always seemed to him so wholly European. He took her hand.

"My dear, forgive me! I have been clumsy. But look," he went on, relinquishing her hand and deftly changing the subject—"Why does the postponement of the boy-friend's visit upset her so much? Has she *des doutes,* the poor child? Of course long engagements are very trying, for both parties."

"I think Luzia could put up with an engagement of twenty

years!" Hetta averred. "But you see they are not yet engaged. This is tedious for her." She was mollified by his penitence, and a little ashamed of the remark which had prompted it.

A man in chauffeur's uniform now approached, also with a tray of cocktails; as he took the Ambassador's empty glass— "Might I fetch a whisky for His Excellency?" he asked, in admirable English.

"Yes, do, Luis," the diplomat said. "Excellent fellow, that," he went on, as the man went off. "The Parrotts are lucky to have him. He can turn his hand to anything, as well as being a first-rate chauffeur."

"Where did they get him?" Hetta asked.

"Took him over from the Peabodys when poor Peabody was taken ill, and had to go home so suddenly."

Hetta knew about the sudden departure of Parrott's predecessor.

"And where did the Peabodys get him?" she pursued.

"They brought him with them from Washington when they came," Sir Noël said, slightly surprised by her interest in a colleague's chauffeur.

"Ah. So he is not Spanish?"

"I really don't know. He speaks it like a native. Why?"

Before Hetta could reply the man came back, bringing a small tray with a syphon and decanter; the Ambassador helped himself, and again thanked the useful Luis. When the man had gone the Ambassador in his turn pursued his question. He was puzzled by Hetta's enquiries.

"Why do you want to know his nationality?" she asked.

"It is just an idea I had," she replied, rather evasively. "Certainly if he came from Washington with the Peabodys he would hardly be Spanish." As the French Ambassador came up to them she returned his greeting, and presently drifted away, leaving Sir Noël puzzled.

By now the room was filling up; the Spaniards, belatedly, were beginning to arrive, and he moved about performing his social duties with easy skill; Hetta was doing likewise, and he had no further opportunity of catechising her. But more than once he noticed his Counsellor's wife glance at the Parrotts' chauffeur with an expression of distaste and uneasiness. What idea could she have got into that little dark head of hers? There must be something; Hetta usually had a very sound reason for anything she said or thought.

The puzzle remained with him, and when the party began to thin out, and no more arrivals were to be expected, he left; Commander Mansfield's duties were over too, and the Ambassador offered him a lift home. If anyone would know the answer to Hetta's question it would be Mansfield, who had been so long in Madrid. In the car—

"Do you know anything about that chauffeur of the Parrotts?" he asked casually.

He was not disappointed.

"Luis? Yes. He's a Hungarian," Commander Mansfield replied, without the smallest hesitation.

"A Hungarian! Then what on earth was he doing in Washington?" Sir Noël asked, surprised.

"A refugee from the 1956 rising. We took quite a number of them in—not all that soon!" the other replied, rather sardonically—"but in the end we did have several thousand at Camp Kilmer."

"Then how did he pick up his job with the Peabodys?"

"Oh, we absorbed as many as we could; he was a good mechanic and a good linguist; he made his way to Washington, and got employment with some Latin-American diplomats— the Colombians. I think Peabody said. And then Peabody took him on when he was coming here; he'd already picked up a fair amount of Spanish, and Peabody thought that might be convenient, as indeed it was—and is."

"I should have thought it might have been a little complicated," the Englishman said thoughtfully. "What papers has he got? Hardly Hungarian?"

"Oh no. After they'd been screened the ones who passed as reliable were given green cards entitling them to permanent residence in the States, and a couple of years later Congress passed an act allowing them to become American citizens at the expiry of five years. So by the time he came out here with Peabody he had regular U.S. papers."

"Very convenient for him. Is Luis his real name?"

"No, he must really be Lajos—that's the Hungarian version." Mansfield in his turn was a little surprised at the Englishman's interest in the Parrotts' chauffeur, but he prudently asked no questions. And the Ambassador, saying "A ghastly business, that rising," turned the conversation. But over his solitary dinner he went on speculating about Mrs. Atherley. Some trick of manner, undetectable by a person of another race, might possibly have led her to spot the man as a fellow-countryman, but why the expression of discomfort when she looked at him?

Hetta was particularly glad of Luzia's presence during the next few days, when she and Nell Parrott and Mrs. Marchant were intensively occupied in shepherding the female Luxworthys. Hetta already had a baby girl of thirteen months; she was ten weeks gone in pregnancy with a second child, and did not feel at her best in the mornings. But the Portuguese girl knew Madrid well, and could always be relied on to give the visitors a satisfactory forenoon in the Prado, or to escort them to one or other of the very phoney and expensive antique shops, while the three married women wrote their notes and occupied themselves with their households; in the afternoons there was Balenciaga's dress salon, which exercised a strong fascination over the two Americans, or the Escorial or some other excursion, before the evening cocktail-parties began. (The wife of their own Ambassador was down with scarlet fever, so she could do nothing for her two compatriots.) Moreover Joy Luxworthy, mercifully, took to Luzia, and hence was more amenable to suggestions from her than from the others. It was Luzia who persuaded her, with a mixture of firmness and mockery, that she really could not walk into the cocktailbar of either the Ritz or the Palace Hotel in skin-tight scarlet "toreador-pants", as *Vogue* called them.

"But I bought them back home just *for* Spain," Joy protested.

"Nevertheless you do not wish to be arrested by the police as *una puta.*"

"What on earth is a *puta?*"

"A disreputable woman. Such are arrested here if they make themselves conspicuous in public places," Luzia said with finality. "Why not wear that pretty red silk dress?"

Sir Noël lost no time in giving his luncheon for Luzia; as Hetta had insisted, it was small—only one other couple besides the Atherleys and the Marchants.

"I didn't ask the Luxworthys—they're coming to dinner the day after tomorrow," the Ambassador told Hetta on the telephone. "I want to be able to concentrate on your lovely friend." He did—Hetta sat on his right, Luzia on his left; they got on famously. But Sir Noël did not forget that he wanted to pass on Commander Mansfield's information about the chauffeur to Mrs. Atherley, and over coffee he invited her to come into a small morning-room to look at a new picture he had bought—she went, cup in hand. They discussed the picture for a moment or two; then, still standing in front of it, he said—"I found out about that man Luis, the Parrotts' chauffeur. He's a Hungarian—he came out in 1956, and went to the States as a refugee."

Hetta continued to stare at the picture in front of her for several seconds, with an expression of frowning concentration; then, suddenly, she gave a small start—the coffee-cup slipped sideways in the saucer, and some of the coffee was spilt on the carpet.

"Oh, I am so sorry!" she exclaimed. "Do excuse me." As he took the cup from her she moved to a chair and sat down; the Ambassador rang the bell. When he turned back to her it struck him that she was looking rather white, beyond her normal clear pallor. "I am so sorry," she repeated mechanically.

"It doesn't matter in the least," Sir Noël said. "Please don't think of it." He gave an order to a footman who answered the bell, and turned to her again; she was still staring at the picture, frowning a little, but he got the impression that she did not really see it, but was concentrating on something else. As servants came in with a bowl and cloths to clean the carpet she got up, and again apologising, returned to the other room.

Almost at once a secretary appeared to say that the Ambassador was wanted on the telephone from London; excusing himself, he went and took the call. When he returned to the drawing-room Hetta was talking to Maud Marchant about more plans for the Luxworthys, and Luzia turned to him with some question in a laughing argument that she was having with Colonel Marchant—"Excellency, you shall arbitrate between us!" There was no chance for him to speak to Hetta alone before they left. But when his guest had gone Sir Noël speculated long, and rather uncomfortably, about why the knowledge that the Parrotts' chauffeur was a Hungarian should have disturbed his Counsellor's wife so much, if that really was the reason why she had given that little start—and he thought there was a connection; he did not believe that he had imagined it. He must try to get hold of her again and find out.

But in fact it is not so easy as might be supposed for the head of a Mission to arrange a meeting in private with the wife of one of his staff; some opportunity must occur, or be contrived. Diplomats never use the telephone for possibly tricky conversations. Sir Noël had to let it go for the moment.

But he had not been imagining things. The human memory works in curious ways, taking one so far and no further, or leaving unaccountable gaps. For a long time now the face of the Parrotts' chauffeur had seemed vaguely familiar to Hetta, and in some unpleasant context; but there she stuck. At Nell's party she had asked the Ambassador about him on an impulse, wishing to clear up this teasing uncertainty; when she stood looking at that picture in the small morning-room at the Embassy, and heard that the so-called Luis was a Hungarian, her memory suddenly raised a shutter on the past. Yes, she felt certain that she knew where she had seen him before. He had been one of a group of A.V.O. men, the Communist Secret Police, who had come suddenly to close down her convent school in Budapest, forcing the nuns to leave their home and abandon the habit, and dispersed them to scrape a living as best they could, in such civilian clothes as could be mustered for them. That was twelve years ago; the man was older and stouter; he had shaved off his moustache, his hair was now closely cut, and altogether he was smartened up almost out of recognition—but when that shutter went up she felt sure that he was the uncouth young man who had been so particularly rough with the old beloved nuns, horrifying her by his brutal words, and still more brutal laughter at their confusion and distress.

When the Atherleys left the Embassy, Richard announced that he had got to go back to the Chancery—"And what are you doing, darling?"

"There is a cocktail at the Italians, but I think perhaps I do not go. Luzia is going—the Marchants will be there."

"Quite right, I should have a rest," her husband said. He knew about the pregnancy, and desperately wished that all should go well; he wanted a son this time.

"You come back when?" she asked him.

"In time for dinner—I may look in and bring Luzia back. I'm going to play squash with Marchant first."

At home Hetta went to her room and lay down, but made no attempt to sleep; instead she thought intently. In her own mind she now had little doubt that Luis, the trusted factotum and confidential servant of the unsuspecting Parrotts, with free access to the American Embassy, was a Communist agent —she knew all about their trick of infiltrating spies among genuine refugees; several from the 1956 exodus had been spotted and caught already, in other countries. She must do something about it; but first she must decide what, carefully —it was no good acting in a hurry. And yet there was an element of hurry, or might be; Admiral Luxworthy was said to be due to arrive in Spain in a few days now. Hetta knew all about the Rota base and its importance; Richard had told her a certain amount, and Nell Parrott had of course chattered freely. Since the American Ambassador was in quarantine for scarlet fever the Admiral would be staying with his family at their hotel, and though an Embassy car and chauffeur would certainly be placed at his disposal, it was more than probable that much of the time he would go about with his Naval Attaché, actually driven by an enemy agent. Hetta, her wits sharpened by years spent under a Communist regime, and living now in the higher ranks of diplomacy, both in Paris and Madrid, was fully aware of all the considerations attaching to de Gaulle's preoccupation with *L'Europe des Patries,* and the openings which his propaganda might afford for some Communist manoeuvre in Spain.

But to whom should she pass on her disagreeable information? Richard? After some consideration she thought perhaps not; Richard had already begun to show signs of brushing aside some of her ideas as the curious fancies of a woman in pregnancy. The Parrotts? Definitely better not; Walter would persist in talking, so ill-advisedly, to Nell, and this sort of thing ought always to be handled with absolute discretion. The Ambassador would be the best person; but it was even more difficult for her to get hold of him, especially without Richard's knowledge, than for him to get hold of her for a talk in private. Then who?

Oddly enough she decided in the first place to speak to Luzia. When she herself had been kidnapped and drugged in Portugal on her way to Gralheira, soon after her escape from Hungary, Luzia, then not really out of the schoolroom, had played a major part in outwitting the principal Communist agent, who in his turn had been drugged and captured by a member of the English Secret Service at Gralheira itself, and handed over to the Portuguese authorities. If only he were here now! And what was his name? She couldn't remember, she had seen hardly anything of him; but Luzia would certainly know, and she was absolutely reliable and discreet. She rang the bell, and sent a maid to ask if her guest could come and see her?

Luzia came at once; she too had been resting, and appeared in a floating white wrapper. Hetta asked her to bring her towel from the bathroom, and wrapped its thick folds over, under, and round her bedside telephone; then she switched on her small transistor.

"Sit close to me; we must speak low, but the music helps," she said.

"Something goes on?" Luzia asked, obediently drawing up a chair.

"Yes, I think so—and one never knows where there may be microphones—put the lamp over on that other table." These precautions taken, she told her friend what had happened at the Embassy.

Luzia listened attentively.

"You are absolutely certain that this Luis is the Secret Policeman you saw in Budapest?" she asked.

Hetta pushed up her dark hair, with a worried expression.

"It came to me that he was, then—that is why I spilt my coffee. I was frightened. But it was twelve years ago, and I only saw him on that one day; he had a moustache then. It would be—awkward—to have made a mistake. I do not think I have, only Richard would so much dislike it. . . ." She left the sentence unfinished.

"Still, you cannot leave it as it is," Luzia said firmly, "if there is even the possibility that this Luis is an agent."

"No. Someone should make enquiries. I was wishing that this Intelligence person who was at Gralheira were here now, but I forget his name."

"Torrens—Major Torrens. He was in love with Miss

Probyn!" Luzia said, with a mischievous smile. "Yes, it would be good to have him here."

"But how could one find him?"

"Oh, I have no idea. And I think it would be of no use to write to him ourselves. Write to Julia; either she will know, or she can find out. Or her husband might come—this would be better, if he is not abroad."

"Where is she?"

"In Scotland with the baby, still I think for some weeks. I give you the address. By airmail she should get a letter in two days—no, in Scotland perhaps three. Write now, while I dress —then I will post the letter myself at the Centrale on my way to this cocktail."

"How much should I tell her?" Hetta asked. Luzia's clear-headedness and decision were being a comfort to her—why did being *enceinte* seem to take away both one's mind and one's resolution?

Luzia reflected.

"No details, I think; not now. Just that there is a possible danger—and to ask if Colonel Jamieson or Major Torrens could come. Miss Probyn will do whatever is sensible. Is this your writing-case?"

So while Luzia dressed for her party, Hetta wrote the letter which was to arouse so much speculation and concern at Glentoran a few days later; Luzia made time to dash off a hasty corroborative note herself to Julia Jamieson, and posted both with her own small white-gloved hand at the Central Post Office, to the dismay of the Atherleys' well-trained chauffeur.

At the Italian Embassy Luzia more or less joined up with the Marchants—Hetta had told Maud that she was not going herself. But she knew plenty of people in Madrid, and was by no means at a loose end. Presently Sir Noël came up and greeted her.

"Where is your pretty hostess?" he asked presently.

"At home—she decided not to come, but to rest a little."

"She isn't unwell, is she?" the Ambassador asked. His Counsellor's wife was normally unfailingly dutiful in her attendance at such events.

"No, just a little *surmenée*," Luzia said.

Sir Noël was slightly disconcerted. He did not yet know about Hetta's pregnancy, and her absence confirmed his impression that something really had upset her at lunch-time—something to do with the Hungarian chauffeur. He wished she had told him about it, but she was a stubborn little cuss, he said to himself affectionately, and did as she chose. As it was, he was left to his rather uncomfortable speculations.

Heads of missions seldom take any action themselves that can properly be delegated to their staff; it works better that way. Possibly Sir Noël would not have done what he did that evening if on his return to the Embassy he had not happened to run into the local member of British Intelligence. On an impulse—"Come into my study, Ainsworth, if you've got a moment," he said. In the study—"Have you got anything on your files about that chauffeur of the Parrotts, Luis?" he asked.

"Not that I know of."

"Well, you might check. He's a Hungarian, you know."

"I didn't know. I thought the Peabodys brought him with them from the States."

"They did, but he was a Hunk refugee, all the same." He went on to repeat what Mansfield had told him.

"Ah, I see. So all the screening he'll have had will have been done at this Camp, Kilner or whatever it is. In that case we should hardly be likely to have anything, if they gave him American papers."

"Just so."

Major Ainsworth looked rather hard at the Ambassador, whose face remained expressionless.

"Well, they must have his record, such as it is, over there," the Major said. "No good talking to my opposite number here, the chauffeur man has been here so long. Might it be as well, Sir, for me to make a signal to Washington, and have it looked up?"

"Yes, I think so. Or do it through London, and let them pass the enquiry on—whichever is simplest. It ought to be a *full* report, to be of any use."

"Any hurry?" Ainsworth asked. He was dying to know what had prompted this enquiry, but knew the Ambassador too well to ask.

"The sooner we hear the better, certainly," Sir Noël said, evenly.

"Right. I'll see to it at once. Goodnight, Sir."

"Goodnight, Ainsworth. Thank you. Let me hear what you get," he added, with the slightest emphasis on the word "me", as he got up.

Now why, the Major wondered, as he went back to his office, was the Old Man being such a clam about this? But he did exactly as he was told, peculiar though it all seemed to him.

3

THE REPORT from Washington was rather slow in coming in, and when it did it was completely neutral: Lajos Pánay had been screened at Camp Kilmer in the ordinary way, along with scores of others, with negative results; he had therefore been given a green card, and set free to earn his own living. But what Major Ainsworth found even more peculiar was that a few hours after he received this report another telegram arrived from the office in London; decoded it ran: "Are you fully satisfied about security arrangements for Luxworthy? Not really your pidgin but we have had tip-off from usually sound source about some risk." It was signed Torrens.

Now it so happened that Ainsworth had managed to catch the Ambassador and deliver the Washington message, as instructed, to him personally almost at once—Sir Noël had put the slip of paper away in his safe, and thanked him with a brevity that amounted to a dismissal. The Major hesitated whether he ought to go and bother him again? He fully realised the connection between security for Admiral Luxworthy and the reliability of the American Naval Attaché's chauffeur, but it was curious that London should be worrying about the security angle too. Was there a connection, or had Torrens got some other idea in mind? He did telephone through to ask the private Secretary if H. E. was available, but he had gone out, and in the end Ainsworth decided to leave it alone—the Old Man didn't like to be bothered for nothing.

Luzia, like most women, was less inclined than men to leave things alone. While she and Hetta awaited a reply to their communication to Mrs. Jamieson, the girl occupied herself in cultivating Lieutenant Ellington; if anything had eventually to be said or done he, she decided, would be much the best person to deal with. Since he was dancing attendance on Joy and her Mother she met him constantly, and it was not difficult to get onto confidential terms with him—in fact the young man was in the early stages of a heart-fall for this lovely creature, and impressed by her knowledgeableness, not only about Spanish art and architecture, but about the European situation, which she discussed as readily as American girls of her age discuss frocks and boy-friends. It seemed quite natural to him that she should ask if he himself knew the Rota base— he didn't.

"But when the Admiral goes you go also?"

"I imagine I'll have to."

"Shall you fly? It is a very long drive."

"I fancy that will depend on how much time the Admiral has in hand. He prefers going by automobile, to see more of the country; but the Ambassador would rather fly, and if he's out of quarantine I presume he will go along."

"Ah, so then they will go in one of the Embassy cars. That is good; for a long, hot drive in a very *big* car is important—one gets less tired."

Luzia passed this on to Hetta.

"They would do better to fly," Mrs. Atherley said. "Couldn't you persuade this nice Ellington to arrange it? He seems *épris* with you."

"I could try. I wish Miss Probyn would write."

But when Julia Jamieson's letter came it did not help them very much. She carefully began with news of Mrs. Hathaway and the baby, mentioning, as a family item, that her husband was in the Middle East. "As for Luzia's old acquaintance at

Gralheira, I spoke to him on the telephone, and passed on your message, and he said he would make enquiries. I haven't heard since."

"This is tiresome," Hetta said impatiently. "She does not say if he comes—Torrens, I mean. I wonder what we should do now?"

"Of whom do you suppose Major Torrens makes his enquiries?" Luzia speculated.

"I imagine there is someone from Intelligence here," Hetta said, frowning. "But I do not know who it is." (In fact British Intelligence tends rather to keep itself to itself abroad.)

"Would not Richard know?"

"Yes—but then he will ask why I wish to know, and say I am fancying things," Hetta said, frowning more than ever.

"Let us think about it till tomorrow. Admiral Luxworthy does not come for a few days yet, Ellington told me. Come,"—looking at her watch—"we ought to get dressed. Joy and Mrs. Luxworthy asked us to come in good time."

To return so much hospitality Mrs. Luxworthy was giving a cocktail party in their hotel, the new Castellana-Hilton beloved of American visitors because, as Richard Atherley said, practically the whole staff not only speak, but think in American. Rather reluctantly, Hetta went to dress, still uneasy in her mind. She was never one for postponements.

The Castellana-Hilton is as functional and impersonal as any other international hotel—bright, glittering with chromium and mirrors, giving no hint, inside, of what country it is in. The party was being given in a large private room, and since Ellington was largely in charge of the arrangements, the same man had been hired to announce the guests as had functioned at the Parrotts' own cocktail—Commander Mansfield was also in attendance. Very few people had arrived when Hetta and Luzia walked in except the Parrotts themselves.

"Well now aren't you nice, to come along in good time," Mrs. Luxworthy said warmly to Hetta; Joy greeted Luzia, and drew her to one side.

"D'you like this dress? I got it all in a hurry, this afternoon; Balenciaga had just got some new things in, and everyone had seen all my others so often."

"Turn round," Luzia said. The dress was a vivid tangerine, long and full-skirted; it suited the girl very well, with her dark hair and complexion.

"Yes, I like it very much, Joy. Tomorrow you can take it back and make them alter it a little—the waist could fit more closely, and it dips the least bit at the back."

"But it's all right for tonight?"

"Oh yes. The colour is perfect."

Captain Parrott came up to them, a tall pale man with the peculiar American look of being almost antiseptically clean.

"Good evening, Countess. Joy, I think your Mother would like you to go and stand with her—people will be coming along in a minute."

Joy went over to her Mother; Captain Parrott took Luzia to one of the buffet-tables and gave her a champagne cocktail.

"You've been terribly good to that child—in fact you've done so much for both of them," he said. "It could have been a little awkward, with the Ambassadress laid up, and Nell so new to everything. I don't know where we'd have been, but for you and Mrs. Atherley."

Luzia asked how Mrs. Packer was?

"Not all that good. It's a nasty thing, scarlet fever. The Ambassador is getting a bit worried about her. It couldn't have come at a more awkward time, either, with this visit. It puts a lot on Nell."

While Luzia was sympathising with him a very young man from the American Embassy hurried up.

"Will you excuse me?" he said politely to Luzia; as he spoke he took a slip of paper from his pocket. "This has just come in, from Paris," he said to Parrott. "I thought you ought to know at once, and Mrs. Luxworthy too."

Also excusing himself, Parrott unfolded the paper.

"Well, for mercy's sake!" he exclaimed. "He'll be here to-morrow! But that means the whole schedule will have to be re-arranged! I'd better get started right away. Does the Ambassador know?"

"Yes, I rang through to him before I came along here. He was pretty upset—he says he'll still be in quarantine."

"Why in tunket did he have to go and change everything this way?" Captain Parrott exclaimed—and then checked himself. "If you'll excuse me," he said to Luzia, and hurried over to where his wife stood with Mrs. Luxworthy. His news brought a general stir and exclamations.

"Well, isn't that too bad! If only he'd come today, he could have been at the party!" Mrs. Luxworthy said, with genuine regret.

"I'll have to leave you, Mrs. Luxworthy," Parrott said—"I'm terribly sorry, but there's a lot to arrange. Please pardon me."

"Oh Walter, you can't!" Nell protested. "Not twice over!"

"I have too," he replied brusquely, and hastened away.

Hetta was talking to the Italians, politely regretting that she had missed their party—she didn't hear this interchange. Nor did Ellington; he was seeing that the Moroccan envoy and his wife and son were being supplied with soft drinks, as befitted devout Muslims, instead of any form of alcohol—it was the sort of thing he had been sent to Europe to do. Luzia drifted in his direction, greeting people as she went; presently he noticed her, and as she had expected, as soon as he could he joined her.

"I think it's going all right," he said. "Do you?"

"Yes." The room was beginning to fill; people were eating, drinking, and some already even smoking; as the noise of voices increased everyone was talking louder, sure sign of success at a cocktail-party. There were a few chairs and small tables arranged round the walls—"Let's go over and sit down for two minutes, where we can talk," the young man said. "I think I rate that much for myself!"

"Do you dislike such parties?" the girl asked, smiling a little.

"Not in moderation. But there has been quite a lot of it lately, you must admit! And one can never be quiet and talk to the people one wants to talk with," he said, looking rather meaningly at her.

"We are talking now."

"Yes, Heaven be thanked! But either my conscience, or Walter Parrott or someone, will hunt me out of this chair in no time, you'll see!"

She laughed at his rueful expression.

"It will not be Captain Parrott, because he has just left," she said.

"Left? Why in the world?"

"Because Admiral Luxworthy returns tomorrow."

"How in all the earth do you know that?" he asked, staring at her.

"I was with Captain Parrott when a young man from the Embassy brought the message. So now he goes to see about altering the time-table."

"But *why* is the Admiral doing this? It's a hell of a thing," Ellington burst out, looking aghast.

"Perhaps he wanted to see his wife! Captain Parrott was vexed also."

"I'll bet he was vexed. It's a hell of a thing to do," the young man repeated—"with the Spaniards of all people." He got up. "Didn't I tell you Walter, or my conscience, would soon hunt me out? We've had no time at all."

"Sit down again for one moment," Luzia said. As he did so—"Your Ambassador will still be in quarantine for some days, will he not?"

"Yes—and that's another hell of a thing!" Poor Lieutenant Ellington was thinking of all the various complications ahead of him—the meetings with Ministers, the dinners, the luncheons—as well as the vital trip to the South.

"So when the Admiral goes to Rota he will wish to go by car?"

"He'll surely do that." He glanced at her curiously.

"Ellington, will you listen to me? I have something to say to you," the girl said earnestly. "Will you promise to listen?"

"Of course. What is it?"

"You should arrange that on this trip Luis does not go with you."

He stared at her. "Luis? Do you mean Walter's chauffeur?"

"Yes. Leave him behind."

"But why?"

"I cannot tell you the reason now. But it is important, this."

Luzia felt that she had gone quite as far as she ought without consultation with Hetta; she seized this chance of catching Lieutenant Ellington before he went off to see to the readjustment of the Admiral's programme, as she guessed he would wish to do—if she had waited she might have been too late. She got up as she spoke; so did he, and caught her by the arm.

"Look, this is silly! You've got to tell me the reason."

"No, I have not. You promised to listen," she said reproachfully, looking at him with her immense grey eyes. "You cannot need him; there are endless Embassy cars to use, and bigger ones. Do not take him, and do not speak of it." Determinedly, now, she moved away, and began to talk to the French Counsellor. As soon as she could she made her way to Hetta, whose expression showed that she too now knew of the Admiral's unexpected return even before she said, "He comes back tomorrow."

"I know. Let us talk in the car. How much longer must we stay?"

"Only a short time," Hetta said. "We cannot leave just yet."

They separated; but when the guests began to leave Luzia rejoined her hostess, and they made their farewells together.

"Now, what do we do?" Hetta asked as soon as they were in the car.

"I have done something already." Luzia reported what she had said to Ellington.

"You did not tell him why?"

"No, though he pressed me. I thought I had better speak to you first."

Hetta reflected. "Do you think he will act on this, what you have said?"

"I believe he will," the girl said. "It was a clear warning. Why should I say such a thing without a reason? Ellington is not stupid."

"No, but will he be able to make others do as he says? We ought to be certain. When do they go to Rota, now? Before all these functions, perhaps, instead of after? That would be much simpler; only one item to be changed, instead of several, and with their own people," Hetta went on, considering the thing from the diplomatic angle.

"I do not know."

"Ellington may think of this—poor Walter probably not!" Hetta said, with a faint smile.

"But how do we find out?" Luzia asked.

"Oh, I shall talk to Nell. She will tell us anything she knows!" Hetta said with assurance.

In fact the manifest advantages of advancing the date of the Rota visit, and letting the other official fixtures stand, had occurred to Lieutenant Ellington as soon as he heard of the Admiral's change of plan; after Luzia had left him he slipped out from the party and rang up Captain Parrott at his office from the hotel.

"Walter, what you you trying to fix? I can't get away just yet, but don't you think the best thing would be to switch Rota only, and leave the rest the way they are?"

"Yeah. The Ambassador said that just now. I was about to get through to them."

"Fine. Well, just warn them that it will be sooner than we said; we'd better not try to fix a hard date till the Admiral's actually here. Goodness knows what other idea he may get into his head! Right—I'll be seeing you."

"Wait! They'll be wanting to know down there if it's to be plane or car," Parrott said.

"Tell them to wait till tomorrow—we'll settle all details then. I must get back now, Walter." He rang off.

It was easy for Luzia to avoid Lieutenant Ellington for the next forty-eight hours, as she had decided to do; he was fully occupied with Admiral Luxworthy. Both she and Hetta were enormously relieved to learn, through Nell's "careless talk", that the Rota party was going in two of the Embassy cars— "Lieutenant Ellington says it may still be pretty hot down there, and they'll be cooler in those big saloons. Anyway now I can keep Luis—I just hate being without a car."

"So he did pay attention to what you said," Hetta observed later. "You were quite right."

"Yes, *grâce à Dieu!* So now all is well."

"No, all is not well. For this particular occasion, yes; but when the Admiral is gone, we must do something. I think perhaps I speak to Sir Noël."

Admiral Luxworthy's visit ran its course smoothly: the trip to Rota, then the official functions at high level, finally a polite call on the Caudillo. It emerged in the course of it— through Nell Parrott, of course—that the Admiral had hustled through his other European visits in order to see, and show his family, something of the "real old Spain". Nell consulted Hetta. "He doesn't want to see more of Madrid, and I guess Mrs. Luxworthy and Joy are getting sick of this town. What would you say?"

"But certainly Toledo—it is quite near, and full of wonderful things: all the Grecos, and also the Alcazar."

Nell looked doubtful.

"Yes—but where will we eat? That huge garden restaurant place outside the gates is so American now; you hear Kansas

City at the very next table! And there's not much in the town. Anyhow you'll come along to show them round, won't you?"

"When do you go?"

"On Sunday."

"On Sunday I cannot—we are going out to lunch with the de la Torres at their cigarral."

"But that's right *at* Toledo!" Nell exclaimed. "Oh Hetta, *couldn't* you get them to invite the Luxworthys too? That really would be something for them to see!—so few foreigners ever get inside one. I've never been to a cigarral myself; we barely know the de la Torres," the little American added wistfully. "I suppose you couldn't coax them to let us come along?"

"I must ask Richard," Hetta replied. She was always very scrupulous about consulting her husband's feelings on such matters, arousing a certain envy in Walter Parrott. "I will let you know, Nell, if it can be done."

"Well, I don't see why not," Richard Atherley said, when she put the point to him at lunch-time. "It's in the Spaniards' interest to butter up the Americans, and the Admiral is quite a figure, after all. I like him; he's very quick at the uptake. Ring up Pilar and see what she says."

The Marquesa de la Torre said Yes—she even displayed a certain enthusiasm for the idea. "Pepe will be very much interested to meet him. The wife and daughter come too, of course? Anyone else?"

"I'm afraid so," Hetta said, with her usual regrettable frankness—diplomatic life had not quite cured her of that yet. Pilar de la Torre laughed.

"Well, how many?"

"Certainly his Aide-de-Camp, Lieutenant Ellington; and I think also the American Naval Attaché, Commander Parrott, and his wife, should come; she has been looking after the daughter and Mrs. Luxworthy before the Admiral arrived, and indeed since."

"Yes, they cannot be omitted. Well, it may have to be a

buffet luncheon, but that does not matter," Pilar said serenely. "Very well, *ma chère*—we shall expect you all at half-past two. *Au revoir.*"

Walter Parrott was even more pleased than his wife when this plan was unfolded to him; he came round to the Atherleys to thank Hetta. "The Admiral's delighted to be getting into a proper Spanish country house," he told her. Then, unlike his wife, he proceeded to discuss the practical details.

"Now you say lunch is at 2:30. That will give us quite a long morning to look at the town—he's all set on that. But you are to say what we're to see, and where we're to meet. How early can you start? They get up at all hours."

Hetta felt that this occasion demanded a special effort, and said she thought she could start at half-past nine. "Then we shall be there by eleven, or a little before—that will allow time to see a few things."

"Well, you say what." Parrott took out a note book. "The Alcazar?"

"I think *not*—not to go into. It is all so rebuilt since it was shelled in the Civil War; it no longer seems old. We could drive past, to see the exterior, and also just look into the old town, on foot—and then go on to the Cathedral; that is essential, it is such pure Gothic. That is already on the way to San Tomé, which is essential also, and one can drive on to El Greco's house and the little museum. There it is not so far from the Puente San Martin, which we cross to go down to the cigarral."

Walter was writing busily.

"Sure that's enough? It's really only three main things."

"If we see them properly we shall certainly not have more time than we need. And do you not imagine that Mrs. Luxworthy and Joy will want constantly to stop and look at shops, and to buy damascened paper-knives?" Hetta asked, laughing. "Also this route takes one through most of the city."

Walter agreed.

"Then where do we meet up?"

"I think really best outside the city, at the Tavera—that large church on the right, beside the main road. Then we will go ahead, and you can all follow us."

The most striking thing about Toledo, apart from its situation, is its colour. The river Tagus washes its foundations on three sides; within this green boundary the city is piled up on a hill, buildings above buildings, all of the sandy gold of a lion's coat. A whole city the colour of a lion, rising from a lion-coloured countryside, is an astonishing spectacle; well did Shakespeare write of "tawny Spain". Within, it has kept its mediaeval character to a surprising degree; the steep narrow streets, cobbled or paved with uneven flag-stones, are lined with ancient houses, their stone or plaster fronts of the prevailing sandy-golden tone. In fact the streets are so narrow that many are impassable for a large car; Hetta, who did not want to walk more than she could help, had carefully worked out their route so that they could drive most of the way.

On the Sunday morning the three cars duly gathered under the high, rather gloomy walls of the Tavera Hospital; Captain Parrott, troubled by his inability to answer the Admiral's innumerable questions about everything he saw from the windows, there suggested that Luzia should go in his car, and let Luxworthy ride with the Atherleys—this change-over made, they drove on into the town. Richard was driving; he had left his chauffeur at home, to impose a little less on the de la Torres. The Parrotts had been less thoughtful—Luis was at the wheel of their Chrysler, an Embassy chauffeur drove the car provided for the Luxworthy party.

The Admiral was delighted with this arrangement. Hetta showed him the old Arab walls on their left as they approached the Puerta de Bisagra; she could even give him dates—the Moors wresting the city from the Visigoths in 711 A.D., hence "Yes, the walls are eighth-century." They pottered a little on foot in the old city, with its curious arched doorways, giving onto courtyards with here a glimpse of greenery, there a fountain, or occupied by men who plied their various metallic trades: black-smiths, wheel-wrights, workers in wrought-iron, and above all the *damasquineros*, inlaying bronzed steel with delicate threads of gold with exquisite skill —the visitors were entranced. The Admiral was a little disappointed not to go all over the Alcazar; to his mind its siege during the Civil War was of much greater interest than what was left of its Moorish architecture. But when Hetta said she could sit in the car and wait for them he contented himself with a hurried look round, and then obediently rejoined her.

"Where now?" Richard asked.

"The Cathedral."

The problem which confronts all experienced visitors to the Cathedral at Toledo is how to find room to park in the shade.

"Damn! It's practically full up already," Richard said, slowing down in the open square, and looking round for a space; the other two cars pulled up behind him. A policeman, in one of those shiny broad-brimmed black hats turned up at the back, which make the Spanish police so picturesque, approached; when he saw Richard Atherley he saluted smartly, and came up and greeted him through the window. "Let the Señor come with me—I find a place." Richard indicated the other two cars, also seeking shade; with calm authority the Spaniard walked over, shifted a market-cart, and told a bus-driver to move his machine; soon they were all accommodated. As they got out the man again saluted, and smiled at Hetta.

"Friend of yours?" Luxworthy asked Richard.

"Well, he knows us. When he isn't being a policeman here he's the baker in the village near the de la Torres; he brings bread to the cigarral in a sort of wicker wheel-barrow," Richard said, grinning.

The interior of the Cathedral at Toledo is much earlier than the façade, and as Hetta had said, of an astonishing purity, but her guests were too unfamiliar with Gothic to be much impressed by this, so she led them to the sacristy to see the pictures, especially the Goyas and the El Grecos; Mrs. Luxworthy however preferred the alleged Bellini. She had timed their visit carefully with a view to the Treasure being open to public view, and did at last score a real success with the Cross which surmounts Isabella the Catholic's colossal monstrance—this, as she explained, is made out of the first gold brought back from the Americas by Christopher Columbus.

"Well that *is* something to see!" the Admiral exclaimed. "Now what else have you got for us, young lady?"

What Hetta had got next for them was Greco's enormous masterpiece, "The Burial of Count Orgaz"; they drove on to Santo Tomé to see it. "Here in Toledo one must concentrate on El Greco," she said to the Admiral; "he lived and worked here so much that he and the city always seem to me to be inseparable; and here one sees him as nowhere else. And one must see *much* of his work to appreciate it."

This theory is sound enough, but probably a single morning is too short for the wholly uninitiated to come to an appreciation of this strange genius—El Greco left the Luxworthys relatively cold. "I don't see why all his faces have to be lengthened out that way," Joy said frankly, staring at the enormous canvas, rising almost to the roof above the Count's tomb. "They look hardly human to me."

Richard laughed.

"He's rather an acquired taste, like caviare, Miss Luxworthy. But you couldn't go home and say you'd been to Toledo *without* seeing that picture—and the others. Where now, Hetta?"

"I had thought his house, and the little museum by it," Hetta replied. She looked at her watch. "But should we perhaps go and have coffee at that place in the Square? We have plenty of time."

Everyone liked this idea, and they went and sat in front of the shop which serves not only coffee, but curious twisted cakes of ground almonds and honey.

"They're terribly sweet," Joy observed.

"Yes—but here one must eat them," Luzia said firmly.

"They are a feature of Toledo. They have them also in Morocco; there they call them *Cornes de Gazelles.*"

"How on earth do you know that, Hetta?" Atherley asked.

"Miss Probyn—Mrs. Jamieson—told me; she ate them in Marrakesh, and heard there that they have them here also."

"That's very interesting," Admiral Luxworthy said, taking another bite at his rather sickly sweetmeat. "Moors in both places, of course."

"Yes, that is what Torrens told her; he knew Spain also."

Refreshed by the coffee, and the comfort of sitting down, Hetta persevered with her plan of completing the Greco cycle, in spite of the Luxworthys' lack of enthusiasm; she saw to it, however, that the two ladies bought some damascened objects on their way. She was getting tired, and felt rather unwell; it was very hot. But once in El Greco's actual house, so small and simple and contemporary, her enthusiasm revived, and communicated itself to her hearers; it has in fact been rearranged with the utmost skill to show what a sixteenth-century Toledan residence was like.

"And he loved the cat—come and see how often he painted it, and his pretty wife," she said, and led them to the small museum. Indeed it is difficult to escape the feeling of coming very close to the great painter in those two small buildings; even Joy bought several postcards of the cat and its young and pretty mistress, still so alive and vivid, as El Greco painted them nearly three hundred years ago. Then they got into the cars again, and Richard still leading drove across the Puente San Martin and out along the road leading to the cigarral.

§§§§§§§§§§ 4 §§§§§§§§§§

THE CIGARRALS of the environs of Toledo derive their pretty name not, as one might suppose, from the ceaseless shrilling of the cicadas, or *cigales,* in the olive-groves whose silver foliage diversifies the tawny landscape, but from the groves themselves —"cigarral" is an Arabic word meaning "the place of trees". Some are large, some quite small, but an essential feature for all of them is a certain simplicity, within as without; people go to them to enjoy the country, and refuse an elaboration which would contrast too strongly with the peaceful austerity of the countryside and its life. The cigarral belonging to the de la Torres lay right on the Tagus, a couple of miles downstream from Toledo; from its terraces, overhanging the steep cliffy banks of the river, one looked back at the golden city on its hill against the fierce blue of the sky—the sound of the water contended with the whirring of the cicadas in the olive-trees on the landward side. Once a convent, it had long stood empty and derelict, the chapel at one end—dedicated to the Holy Archangels—bare and deserted, doorless and with broken windows; this, like the house itself had been devoutly restored by the de la Torres when they bought the place, and now served the small village for Mass on Sundays, saving the country-people, including the baker-policeman, the hot trudge into the city. A few old trees still shaded, here and there, the terraces at both ends of the long building; the new owners had planted shrubs and a few modest flower-beds among the stone benches on which nuns had once sat; a denser screen of shrubs shut off the garage, a new addition, from the wide open space beyond the chapel.

Inside, the long cool rooms seemed rather bare, the pieces of fine furniture stood so far apart on the tiled floors; such rugs as there were, were concentrated in front of the open hearths, now filled with pots of flowering plants; the chairs and settees were mostly of wood, and rather severely upright, a few cushions offering the only concession to comfort—except in Pepe's study and Pilar's own little sitting-room, where there were some easy-chairs. The few pictures were all of religious subjects, so were the small pieces of polychrome sculpture which stood here and there in the big bare rooms; the conventual atmosphere was almost completely preserved, in all its tranquillising restfulness. There were all the modern requirements in the way of bathrooms and so on, but mostly upstairs, and even there carefully kept away out of sight—a nun's cell, Pilar often explained to strangers, was just the right size for a lavatory, while two knocked into one made a small bathroom very nicely.

To this unusual place the Atherleys, on that hot Sunday, brought their party, who looked about them in surprise as they were being introduced, in the first of the series of rooms, to their host and hostess. Pilar de la Torre was tall, with the auburn-russet hair that some Spanish women possess, and a pale, matte complexion; she was not exactly beautiful, but her fine, rather mediaeval-looking features, and a certain stillness about her, made her very striking; Pepe, her husband, was a short, dark little man, rather rotund, with a merry face and an endless flow of spirits—the greatest possible contrast to his stately wife, who promptly led her women guests upstairs to that concealed plumbing, leaving Pepe to look after the men. Then they all went out to have drinks on the terrace, where some canvas garden-chairs were disposed in rather scanty patches of shade; the de la Torres eschewed the vulgarity of gaudy sun-umbrellas. Hetta sat down at once; she felt tired and rather unwell, after the early start, and all the trailing round sight-seeing; but the Parrotts, the Luxworthys, and Lieutenant Ellington, drinks in hand, went over with their host to the low parapet, looking down on the swift river below them, looking up at Toledo, lion-gold cubes of buildings piled up against the sky. The Admiral soon came back to where Pilar sat with Hetta.

"I do just hope you aren't too tired," he enquired anxiously. "Mrs. Atherley has been marvellous, Marquesa," he said to his hostess. "She seems to know everything, and she worked out a wonderful round for us, showing all the most important things in such a short time. I'm afraid some of us were pretty dumb about a lot of it—El Greco takes a bit of getting used to." Pilar agreed politely about El Greco; Hetta said what was necessary about never seeing too much of Toledo.

Ellington was seizing the chance of talking to Luzia; they moved a little away from the others, and leant on the stone parapet.

"Oh, see!" the girl exclaimed suddenly—"there are people walking along below us. Can there be a path?"

"Must be, if people are walking! I'd have thought it was too steep," the young man said, leaning far out and peering over. Indeed he too could catch glimpses of figures moving along between the growth of bushes which clothed the face of the cliff.

"I wonder where they are going?—and how they get down to it?" Luzia speculated. De la Torre heard her, and came over.

"They are people from further down the river," he said. "They have been to Mass in the chapel this morning, and they will have gone to the village afterwards, to drink wine and see their friends. They like the river path; it is shady, and not so hot as the road."

"But how does one get down to it?" Luzia asked.

"There is a path down, nearer the village, and we have

made some steps near the garage also," he said. "It is a pleasant walk, so close to the water."

Pilar de la Torre now summoned them all to come and eat. "You must be starving," she said to Mrs. Luxworthy. "Alas, we have only rather a picnic for you."

The picnic was in fact an ample buffet-luncheon, set out in one of the further rooms nearer the chapel end of the house; enough chairs had been mustered for everyone to sit down if they wished, with little tables near them, but except for Hetta—and Mrs. Luxworthy, whose feet ached—most of the company obstinately remained on their feet. The men helped the women, and then themselves—Pepe went round with a large flagon of chilled white wine, filling glasses. The food, though cold, was rather rich; Hetta, offered chicken, accepted, only to find that it was coated in a thick white sauce, and that a very oily Russian salad covered the rest of her plate. She did her best, but she felt increasingly sick; she signed to Ellington to take away the unfinished plate. Pepe noticed him, and came over to her. Re-filling her glass—"You do not like this? Let me bring you one of our specialities. Lieutenant Ellington, would you bring another plate?" Eager as a boy, he went across to one of the long trestle tables, and returned with a dish which he set down beside her. "Sucking pig in aspic!" he said, triumphantly, and proceeded to carve a slice.

Anyone who has ever seen a cold sucking pig in aspic will remember that it bears a quite horrifying resemblance to a dead baby, its small legs, tucked in under it, hiding the little pink hoofs. As her host cut neatly through the tiny carcase and brought out a slice, stuffed with forcemeat and truffles, Hetta almost shuddered—this completed her *malaise*. She managed to thank her host, and took up her fork; but when he had gone on to display this culinary masterpiece to Mrs. Luxworthy at the other side of the room, she got up and slipped quietly out. She knew that there was a passage leading from the house directly into the chapel, and took it, but she must get into the air; she hurried through the old building, where the scent of incense still hung, and with a hasty genuflexion towards the altar pushed aside the heavy leather curtain, and passed out into the open space before the doorway. There she stood for a moment, breathing deeply; this was better. But she felt that she really was going to be sick, and stepped over to the parapet above the river and knelt there, her elbows on the cold stone; if she was sick into the bushes on the cliff it would not matter. All the same she struggled with her body, swallowing down the hot saliva which constantly welled up in her mouth, and trying to master the impulses of her stomach—and after a few minutes she was successful. She continued to kneel there, deeply relieved, and thankful for the sweet air, coming up fresh from the flowing water below; soon she must go back, but she had better wait till she was quite sure of herself.

Presently she thought she heard voices below her, but she paid little attention; she had been so often to the cigarral that she knew all about the river path and the steps down to it, and its use by the peasants on Sundays—only wasn't it rather late for them to be going back? Then, suddenly, she was all attention—surely the unseen speakers were talking Hungarian? Now she strained her ears to listen, but it was hard to catch the words above the sound of the river; they were just too far off. Noiselessly, crouching down under the parapet, she crept along a few yards in the direction of the sounds, and then knelt and listened again. And now she could catch some of the words.

"It will be at seventeen hours?"

"About that. You have plenty of time." Then some words she could not catch, and the second voice again. "How do I know in which car? But all must slow down for that bend by the bridge; and near the ruined building where there are the *obras* cars can only go singly." More inaudible words, and again the second voice. "But you have seen him at the Cathedral just now—you cannot mistake his grey hair. Now you had better go—soon I must get out the car."

The last words sent Hetta hastening noiselessly back to the

· 52 ·

chapel. There she sank into a seat, greatly agitated. One of the speakers must be Luis. All this could only mean that something was being plotted against "him"; and "him" could hardly be anyone but the Admiral. She must get hold of Walter or Richard quickly, and tell them—but would Richard, anyhow, believe her? He was so fond of teasing her about seeing spies everywhere, and telling her that she must grow out of it.

Her agitation brought on the feeling of nausea again, but she dared not go out now. She heard what sounded like a motor-cycle start up and go off, and then cars being driven round to the front door. Distracted by the immediate fear of being sick in the chapel, she ran into the house, up the back stairs, and made her way into one of those lavatory cells just in time.

Being thoroughly sick brings a certain relief, but it also leaves one panting, perspiring, flushed, and with streaming eyes; also it takes some time. When Hetta had stopped retching she managed to find a servants' bathroom; there she washed her face in the basin, rinsed out her mouth, combed her hair, and put on some powder; as she went through into the front of the house she heard Pilar calling her—"Hetta, where are you?"

"Here—I am coming," she called, as she hurried downstairs.

"We thought you lost!" Pilar said.

"I felt a little unwell—I went into the air. I am sorry if you had to look for me. But where is Richard? I want to see him."

"Out here—the Admiral says he must get back early. Such a pity!" The Marquesa studied Hetta's face as she led her out to the front door. "You are all right now?" she asked. Hetta said Yes.

At the door everyone was grouped about the cars, preparing to depart; Richard was already seated in his, with Joy beside him, and Ellington and Luzia in the back; Mrs. Luxworthy and Nell Parrott, who had made their farewells, were getting into the Embassy car allocated to the Admiral, who stood waiting with Walter Parrott beside the latter's car; at the wheel sat Luis.

"We've done a little re-grouping, as you see," Walter said. "The Admiral wants you to ride with him and tell him about everything." He held open the door of the car for her.

Hetta looked about desperately; Richard, seeing her, started his engine.

"There you are at last!" he called to her—not unamiably. "Good—now we can go." He drove out of the arched gateway.

Hetta's heart failed her. Must she make a scene now, in front of all the others, and with Luis within earshot? She felt unequal to it. She must try to get Walter to take a different road home as they went along. She kissed Pilar Goodbye, apologising again as she thanked her and Pepe, and got into the car.

"Oh, but my bag!" she exclaimed.

"I will fetch it—is it in the dining-room?" Pepe asked, and started indoors without waiting for an answer.

"No, I left it upstairs," Hetta said to Pilar. "I will find it" —and she began to get out.

"Tell me, and I will get it," her hostess said. "You should not run about." She knew all about Hetta's pregnancy, and thought she looked far from well, and disturbed about something into the bargain.

"It was in the bathroom—but in one of the servants' bathrooms," Hetta said, ready to cry with vexation at her folly. "Let me find it, please."

"No, I find it," Pilar said, and went off, wondering why on earth Hetta should have used a servants' bathroom? Something very peculiar must have been happening.

The Embassy car now drove off; the Admiral looked furtively at his watch; Walter waited. Pepe came out, waving empty hands, and saying that he had looked everywhere, but everywhere!—Hetta apologised afresh. After what seemed to her an age Pilar returned, calm and unhurried, bringing the bag and a flask of smelling-salts. "Take these with you," she said; "I have plenty." And with a final warm embrace to Hetta she let the party go.

Admiral Luxworthy did not find that delightful Mrs. Atherley such a lively and informative companion as she had been in the morning—once or twice she hardly seemed to hear what he said, and replied briefly, almost at random, when he repeated his questions. Hetta was of course trying frantically to remember exactly where on the way out they had passed the *obras* (road-works) where there was single-line traffic; and when she thought she had placed the danger-spot, about half-way to Madrid, she cracked her brains trying to think of some church or village which would serve as an excuse for a detour—it would have to be a *good* excuse, with the Admiral in a hurry; and she could think of nothing. She prayed, desperately, for help:—for clearer wits; for resolution, if the worst came to the worst, to stop the car and get out and tell Walter the position; that she might not faint, which she felt very near to doing. She sniffed at Pilar's smelling-salts, answered another question of the Admiral's and prayed again. There must be *some* village to see, some form of help.

Her prayers were answered—but as so frequently happens, the answer took a form quite different from anything she had either thought of, or asked for. Once clear of Toledo Luis began to drive very fast indeed; with the delay over the missing handbag it was nearly twenty to five when they left the cigarral. Good driver as he was, he took one bend too fast; the car encountered a pot-hole at the edge of the tarmac, burst a front tyre, and went completely out of control; it hurtled off the road, over the low verge, and somersaulted into the dusty yellowish field beyond—ending up, as cars, curiously, so often do, right side up. All the occupants were flung about pell-mell; Hetta, light and small, was catapulted over from the back seat into the front. In the shock she cried out, in Hungarian—when the car finally came to rest she found herself looking up at Luis, the chauffeur, and saw, only a few inches away, the expression of mingled rage, astonishment, and fright which came over his face at her words. It was gone in a flash—but at that instant she knew, now with absolute certainty, that he was the former A.V.O. man whom she had seen in Budapest.

Astonishingly none of them were seriously hurt except Hetta, who had fractured her left wrist; the men merely had bruises, and cuts from the broken windows. One set of doors would still open, and they scrambled clear and lifted Hetta out after them, laying her on the ground; in the open air she fainted clean away.

She came to the next morning in a pretty room in one of Madrid's nicest clinics, full of sunshine and flowers; Luzia was sitting by her bed.

"So—now you are awake! How do you feel?"

"Oh, my head aches!" she said as she tried to sit up; a Spanish nurse made her lie down again. "Where am I?" she asked, dazedly. "And what is the matter with my hand?" She noticed now that her left hand and arm were in plaster.

"In the Isabella Clinic—you broke your wrist in the accident, and they gave you morphine."

"Is the Admiral safe?" Hetta asked, suddenly alert.

"Yes, perfectly. He sent you these this morning," Luzia replied, a little surprised, as she brought an enormous vase of pink carnations over to the bed.

"Oh, that is good! How did he get home?" Hetta asked eagerly, ignoring the flowers.

"In the ambulance with you—so did Commander Parrott!" Luzia said, laughing a little.

"And the baby? It did not miscarry?"

"No, thank God."

Hetta looked more relaxed.

"I should like some coffee," she said, "and to sit up more— just a little." The nurse put another pillow under her head, and went to fetch some tisane—not coffee just yet, she said; meanwhile Luzia told Hetta what had happened.

"Commander Parrott stopped a car on the road—the Admiral would not leave you!—and got the people to drive him back to the cigarral; there they telephoned to Toledo for the ambulance, the doctor and a machine to tow the Parrotts' car home, and then rang up the Embassy. Oh the concern!—we heard almost as soon as we got in. Richard was terribly upset, and this poor Nell *quite* lost her head! But the de la Torres were so good—they drove out themselves to the place, with the doctor, and saw you safely into the ambulance, and then rang up again to say you were all on your way. So Richard arranged this room, and had the surgeon waiting for you, to set your wrist."

The tisane came, and while Hetta sipped at it thoughts chased one another through her aching head; she had an enormous bruise on her forehead, which she fingered gingerly. Thankfulness that the child was still safe, deep thankfulness that the Admiral had not left her alone with Luis—which would certainly have meant the end of everything for both of them!—and though much was still blurred, between the shock and the morphia, she kept a clear recollection of the expression on the chauffeur's face, so close to her own, and her complete certainty about him at last, after these months of disquiet.

The doctor came in while she was finishing her tisane, and prescribed more sedatives, and complete quiet. "I except the Condesa; she is as good as a nurse!"

"My husband too, I hope?" Hetta said, smiling faintly.

"Naturally—but few visitors. Calm, repose, quiet! Remember the infant—he too has had a shock."

"You are *sure* he will be all right?" Hetta asked, pleased at the pronoun "he".

"So far as we can tell; when you are stronger we will have an X-ray. For the moment, repose and calm."

Then Richard came in, full of affection and concern; Luzia slipped out. Presently—"The Admiral wants to look in later on to say Goodbye," he said. "I suppose you could see him for a couple of minutes? He's terribly upset about you; he somehow feels responsible."

"Yes—but only *he,* please, Richard! Make my adieux to those ladies; the doctor says I should see very few people, except you and Luzia—to keep the child calm."

"I'll arrange that—they'll understand. Now you rest, darling. I'll be in this evening."

Hetta was dozing when a nurse came and said that "this American Admiral" wished to see her; the woman propped Hetta up a little, combed her hair, and held the compact while she put on powder with her one hand; then she brought Luxworthy in. He asked anxiously how she was feeling, and whether her wrist hurt her?

"No, not much, thank you. They give me sedatives."

"I feel awfully about it," the Admiral said. "If I hadn't been so selfish about wanting your company, you'd have been safe in one of the other cars. Anyway, I'll call the Countess up the moment I get back, and tell her you're all right. She'll be glad I've seen you."

Hetta thanked him, and sent her love to her Mother; now that she was safely married, free and independent, and half the world away, she was able to feel more affection for her rather difficult and ultra-social parent.

"I'll surely do that. And I'll never forget all you did for my wife and Joy; you've been kindness itself to them. You gave *me* a marvellous time, too, yesterday—something else I shan't forget, young lady!" The greying head bent down as in a most un-American fit of gallantry he kissed Hetta's undamaged hand—a hovering nurse shooed him out. It was only when the kind man had gone off to Barajas airport that Hetta remembered that she had never thanked him for his flowers.

Richard had arranged that Luzia should go in Hetta's place to see the two ladies off at the airport; Nell and Walter Parrott of course were also there, and poor Mr. Packer—"Just out of quarantine in time to say Goodbye, Admiral!" There were troops of Spanish officials, too; during the more formal leave-takings Lieutenant Ellington managed to snatch a word with Luzia.

"Well, Condesa, I suppose it's over. I wish it wasn't, but it was good while it lasted." Then he surprised her. "Maybe you were wise to tell me to keep that chauffeur out of the Rota trip. If I'd been smarter, I might have had him left behind yesterday as well."

"You should have him dismissed, now," the girl said. "He is not a safe person for Embassy personnel."

"You still won't tell me why?"

"Can it be necessary, after this?" Luzia had not yet been told of what Hetta had overheard at the cigarral, but had jumped to the same conclusion as Ellington, that the accident to the Chrysler was perhaps not an accident.

There was a stir; people were moving towards the plane.

"I must go. Maybe I'll get myself posted to Lisbon!" Ellington said; he wrung her hand and rejoined his party. After the plane had taken off Luzia drove back with Nell and Walter in one of the Embassy cars; to her great satisfaction Commander Parrott told her that he was afraid the Chrysler would be out of action for several weeks. She asked to be dropped at the clinic, but Hetta was sleeping; she took a taxi back to the Atherleys' flat and had some sleep herself; she had not left Hetta all night.

When Richard went in to see his wife later that afternoon he found her much more wide-awake. On rousing up she had demanded tea and sandwiches, and hidden her sedative tablet under her pillow instead of taking it; now at last she was determined to tell Richard everything, and she must be completely clear-headed to do it. He gave her a kiss, asked if her wrist hurt her, and frowned at the huge bump on her forehead.

"Anyhow it's better than a cut would have been," he said; "It won't leave a scar."

"No—but now, Richard, never mind about me—sit down and listen. There is something you must know."

"There's nothing wrong with the child, is there?" he asked anxiously. "Santana said it was all right."

"So he told me. No, it is this chauffeur of the Parrotts'. I ought to have told you sooner, but I wanted to be quite sure before I spoke, so that you should pay attention."

"Can't think why he did such an idiotic thing yesterday," Richard said, lighting a cigarette. "He's usually a frightfully good driver."

"So he may be. But as he is also a Communist agent, he is not a very good person to drive important Americans about," Hetta said crisply.

"What on earth do you mean? Do you think he drove off the road on purpose?" Richard asked, the dreaded look of incredulity appearing in his expression.

"That I am sure he did not! He was driving too fast because he was afraid of being late for an ambush which he had concerted with other Hungarians, further up the road, where there are the roadworks, and cars must go slowly. It was to be at five o'clock, and our car was late in starting, because I was unwell—and then I mislaid my bag."

"But are you sure of this? How can you know?"

"Because I heard them planning it all—in Hungarian!—at the cigarral. I went out to be sick—this *awful* baby pig!—and then I heard people speaking on the path below me, and when I caught Hungarian words I crept nearer, and listened. They settled the time—seventeen hours—and the place, near that bridge where cars can only go singly, and they asked in which car, and he—it must have been Luis—said how could he tell, but they had seen him at the Cathedral, and would know him by his grey hair, whichever car he was in."

Now she had Richard's full attention.

"Did you *see* Luis?"

"No—they were below among the bushes, and I did not wish to be seen. But who but he could have pointed the Admiral out to them at the Cathedral, and know all our plans, and speak in Hungarian?"

"I didn't know he knew Hungarian," Richard said.

"But of course, since he is a Hungarian."

"How do you know that?"

"The Ambassador told me. And then I thought I recognised him as a member of the Secret Police, whom I had seen in Hungary ages ago."

"Why didn't you tell me that at once?"

"Because you would have laughed at me, and said I must stop seeing spies behind every bush!" she retorted vigorously.

"Well, yes—perhaps," Richard admitted. "But yesterday, when you had just heard of this ambush—why on earth didn't you tell us at once?"

"Because then I *was* sick," she replied flatly. "I had to find a lavatory—and afterwards I had to wash and tidy myself in one of the servants' bathrooms. And when I came downstairs you were all wishing to start, and the Admiral in a hurry, and Luis sitting in the car listening—it was too difficult!"

"But you couldn't have let the Admiral drive into an ambush, if you were so sure of it?"

"No, of course not. I was trying to think of something to show him that would take us off the main road before we came to the place, and I *couldn't* think, and he kept talking all the time—it was frightful! And then, thank God, we had this accident."

Richard almost laughed.

"Tell me," Hetta went on rapidly, "Did you see a motor-bicycle anywhere near those *obras?*"

"Yes, as a matter of fact I did, when I had to pull up—a motor-bike with a combination. It was in a small side-road just between the bridge and a little tumble-down building; I noticed it because there was no one in it. Why?"

"Because I heard it drive off from the cigarral. Of course the men will have been hiding in the building, ready to shoot; I heard them speak of it."

Somehow this detail, and the fact that he had seen the empty motor-cycle combination himself while he waited to pass through the one-way lane—a sitting shot, if ever there was one—dispelled the last of Richard's doubts about Hetta's story. He looked grave. But there was one point he wanted to get quite clear.

"You say you thought you recognised Luis as someone in the Secret Police, whom you had seen in Budapest. But what made you think, there, that he was in the Secret Police?"

"Because he came, with many others of the A.V.O., to close our school, and turn the nuns out. But he was the worst—he laughed when they cried!" Hetta said angrily. "Of course he was younger then; and much less tidy," she added.

"But you weren't positive it was the same man?"

"Not till yesterday. *Then,* I was," she replied, with absolute conviction.

"Because of what you had overheard?"

"No, it was when the car turned over, and I was thrown across into the front, right on his lap! I cried out, I suppose in Hungarian, and I saw his face—only *inches* from my own! I shall never forget how he looked."

"How did he look?" Richard asked, falling into her idiom.

"Astonished—frightened—furious! Oh, he looked at me so wickedly!" she exclaimed with a shudder. "Then I knew him without any mistake. He should not be here with the Parrotts; it is not safe."

Richard was inclined to agree with her. He did his best to soothe her; she was trembling all over now.

"It is all right; I have a tablet," she said, feeling under her pillow.

"What a curious place to put it!" he said smiling, as she swallowed it with a sip of water.

"I pretended to take it, and then hid it instead," she said, now smiling a little too.

"Why?"

"So that I should be fully awake, and able to make you believe me."

Richard felt rather ashamed. It was true that he had often

teased her about her suspicions, not always remembering that she had been a prisoner in Communist hands herself, when in Portugal.

"I do believe you, my darling," he said. "But you are safe here. Rest now—I will see about it."

"Tell the Ambassador," she said, urgently.

In fact Richard intended to do precisely that, and at once; but on his way out, in spite of what he had said to Hetta about her safety in the clinic, he saw the matron, and gave strict orders that no one was to be allowed to see his wife but himself, the doctor, and the Condesa. He did not at all like the idea of Luis knowing that Hetta was a Hungarian, even though the man could have no means of knowing that she had overheard his plans.

At the Embassy he was lucky enough to catch Sir Noël, just setting out for a cocktail party—the car was at the door.

"Could I possibly see you for a moment, H.E.?" he asked. "It won't take long," he added, seeing his chief glance at his watch.

"Very well. Come into the study. How is Hetta?" Sir Noël asked, as they sat down.

"Getting on very nicely, thank you. But she has just told me something that I thought you ought to know at once."

"About yesterday?"

"Yes."

"Does she think that chauffeur-man of Parrott's drove off the road on purpose?" Sir Noël asked. Richard looked at him in surprise.

"No, she's sure he didn't. It was worse than that." He repeated what Hetta had overheard about the projected ambushing of the Admiral. "And when we got to the one-way traffic, sure enough there was a motor-cycle, empty, waiting in a little side-road." He went on to describe how after the crash Hetta had at last definitely recognised Luis as an A.V.O. member whom she had seen in Budapest all those years before.

· 63 ·

Again the Ambassador surprised his Counsellor.

"Ah, that's why she was suspicious about him, and was so upset when I told her he was a Hungarian by birth. H'm— well she's rather smarter than the American Security people —as one would expect!"

"How do they come into it?" Richard asked, with increasing surprise.

"Oh, they screened him at that Camp place they had for Hunks, and were so well satisfied that they gave him American papers!" Sir Noël said ironically. "One moment—I think Ainsworth had better be in on this." He raised the baize-lined lid of the box in which his desk telephone was housed, and lifted the receiver. "Mr. Ainsworth, please." A pause. "Ainsworth? Oh, good. Could you come to my study for a moment." He put down the lid of the box again, and rang the bell; when a servant answered it he ordered drinks to be brought, and the chauffeur to be told that he would not be wanted for another half-hour. "This is rather more important than drinks with the Japs," he said to Richard—"So we might as well have some drinks ourselves. Oh, I wonder if Miss Manson is still there?" Again he uncovered the telephone. "Miss Manson, please. Help yourself, Richard"—as the tray of drinks was brought in. "Miss Manson? Oh, good. Could you ring up the Japanese Embassy and say that I am very sorry, but that I may not be able to come this evening. . . . Oh, an urgent cable, I think. . . . Thank you so much. Don't stay too late." Once again he replaced the baize-lined lid.

Richard was full of curiosity as to what had been going on between his chief and his wife about the Parrotts' chauffeur— clearly Sir Noël knew much more than he himself had yet been told. But before he could frame a question Ainsworth came in.

"Ah, that's right. Give yourself a drink, Ainsworth," Sir Noël said, pouring out a whisky for himself as he spoke. "Now, you remember that enquiry we had made in Washington about the Parrotts' chauffeur?"

"Yes, Sir. It cleared him completely."

"Well, now listen to what Atherley's wife has just told him. Carry on, Richard."

Richard repeated Hetta's story, still astonished that an enquiry should actually have been made in Washington. Had that been done at Hetta's instance?

"Good Lord!" Ainsworth ejaculated at the end. He paused for a moment. "They seem to have had much the same idea in London," he said thoughtfully. "Does your wife know Torrens?" he asked Richard.

"I think she met him in Portugal, ages ago," Richard replied.

"But they don't correspond?"

"Definitely not," Richard said, rather nettled at the suggestion.

"Why, Ainsworth?" the Ambassador enquired, surprised in his turn.

"Only just after we got the reply from Washington, I had a signal from Torrens, asking if we were perfectly satisfied with the security arrangements here for the Admiral."

"You never told me that."

"No, Sir. I'm sorry—I thought as this Luis had been given such complete clearance in the States, it wasn't worth bothering you again. But now I just wondered if by any chance it tied in."

"I wonder too," Sir Noël said thoughtfully.

TO CAUSE the diplomatic mission of another Power, however friendly, to get rid of a valued and trusted servant is a matter of some delicacy, and Sir Noël eventually decided to see Hetta himself; after all, the whole case against Luis rested on her *ipse dixit,* and her recognition of a man she had last seen so many years before. He trusted Hetta completely; it was a case of persuading the Americans to trust her word. There was some corroborative evidence in the fact of Richard Atherley having himself seen the empty motor-cycle combination in the precise spot indicated by his wife as the scene of the ambush, and also in Torrens' independent enquiry about security for Admiral Luxworthy from the London office; in fact what the Ambassador chiefly wanted to clear up was just how independent that enquiry had really been?—and he guessed, rightly, that he was more likely than Richard to learn this.

Accordingly Ainsworth was told to take no action that evening—in any case by this time no one would be in their offices any more—and through Richard it was arranged that Sir Noël should go to the clinic at 9:45 the next morning.

"Oh, I *am* so glad that you have come!" was Hetta's greeting.

"Are you, my dear? Well, I am very glad to see you looking so well, except for that bruise. Does your wrist hurt much?"

"No, hardly at all, unless I move it, thank you."

"That's good. Well, it seems that you were quite right in your suspicions of that chauffeur," he said, sitting down. "Tell me, did you write to anyone in London about it? Said you were worried?"

"In London, no."

"Then where did you write?" he asked.

"To Mrs. Jamieson—she used to be Luzia's governess in Portugal; I met her there, ages ago. I was so worried, and her husband is in Intelligence, so I thought she might be able to help. He is abroad somewhere. Was it wrong?"

"No—though it might have been a help if you had told *us* more," he said, smiling. "Tell me, does Mrs. Jamieson know a Major Torrens in Intelligence?"

"*Very* well—at one time he wanted to marry her!" Hetta exclaimed, laughing.

"Do you know if she told him about your—well, your anxiety?"

"That is what we *hoped* she would do!—it was why we wrote to her," Hetta said frankly.

"H'm." The Ambassador reflected. "When you say 'we', who else wrote, or knew that you were writing?"

"Luzia. She has had experience of Communists, too—in their own house, at Gralheira!" Hetta replied. "So of course I consulted her. To write to Mrs. Jamieson was her idea."

"Do you know if she spoke to anyone else about it?"

"Yes, to Ellington, this young Aide-de-Camp of the Admiral's."

"Told him that she had written to Mrs. Jamieson?"

"No no—told him that Luis should not drive anyone to Rota!" Hetta said, laughing again. "We were afraid that he might not pay attention, but he did."

"Did she tell him why not?"

"No—she just said it would not be right. But he was sufficiently *épris* with her to do as she asked." Hetta looked amused.

"H'm," the Ambassador said again. He had been thinking

that when dealing with the American Embassy it would be extremely convenient if the fact of Hetta's letter to Mrs. Jamieson could be suppressed, if it were safe to do so; that would give its full weight to Torrens' enquiry from London. Well, Ellington was gone now.

"Have you still got Mrs. Jamieson's reply to your letter?" he asked.

"Oh no—I burnt that."

"Did she write to the Condesa too?"

"No, the one letter to us both."

"Good. Well, tell your lovely friend not to mention the fact that you wrote, to anyone. I need not tell *you* that!" He paused. "Look, Hetta," the Ambassador went on, "I hope it won't be necessary, but if our American friends are—well, difficult—about getting rid of this man, would you be willing to repeat to their Intelligence people what you told Richard?"

"Of course. He ought to be got rid of," she replied vigorously. "But Nell will make a great fuss!" she added.

"I don't doubt it," Sir Noël replied drily—Mrs. Parrott's "fuss" was partly what he had in mind. "One of us will bring him, of course," he said. "Goodbye, my dear. Get well quickly."

Back at the Embassy he first saw Richard.

"Yes, both she and Luzia did write to a friend in England—a Mrs. Jamieson, who has a husband in Intelligence. But in her reply this lady never actually said that she had communicated with Torrens, so when dealing with our Allies I think we can forget that they wrote at all! Ainsworth had better go ahead with his opposite number at once. Will you tell him? Oh by the way," he added, as Atherley made to leave the room, "Hetta said she would be quite willing to tell the American Intelligence man what she told you herself, in case of need."

"I hope they won't want to bother her," Richard said, frowning a little.

"So do I. But if they do, she's the key witness. The important thing is to get rid of this fellow."

"Yes—and to get him right out of the country!" Richard said anxiously. "I don't like their even being in the same town, now that he knows she's a Hungarian. He may think back and remember *her* from Budapest, too. And the Communists are certain to have a file on her."

"Why?" Sir Noël asked, rather startled.

"Because she was mixed up in getting that Father Horvath out of Portugal. They kidnapped her there, and drugged her—it was a miracle that she escaped."

"Good Heavens!" Sir Noël said, horrified. "I'd no idea of that—you must tell me some time. Yes, certainly they'll have a dossier. Ainsworth had better lose no time."

Within twenty minutes Ainsworth, briefed by Richard, was talking to Milton Day, his American colleague. Day took the point at once, though he too expressed surprise that the office in London should have made enquiries about security for the Admiral—Ainsworth said nothing to that. Major Day also thought it remarkable that Mrs. Atherley should have recognised the man from so long ago.

"I wonder if maybe we hadn't better get a report on him from home," he observed. "He must have been screened at that Camp, before he got his papers."

"We did that."

"*You* did? For Pete's sake! Why?"

"The Ambassador realised that Mrs. Atherley was suspicious about him, and thought we'd better check; she's a highly responsible person, with a first-hand knowledge of Communists and their methods—which is more than you or I have!" Ainsworth replied firmly. "We did it through our Embassy in Washington."

"Any result?"

"No, completely negative."

"And you still think he ought to be fired? Captain Parrott

isn't going to like this at all," Day said, looking rather worried.

"Of course he isn't. All the same he'll have to lump it," the Englishman said bluntly. "He can hardly call our Counsellor's wife a liar—and don't forget that Atherley did see the motorcycle combination, empty, at the very spot where Mrs. Atherley overheard that the shooting was to take place."

"Yes—yes, that sounds like confirmation. Tell you what, Jim, will you come along with me to see the Captain?"

Ainsworth agreed, and they went together to Parrott's office, where Day said his piece. Walter was no better pleased than Major Day had anticipated at the idea of losing his chauffeur, but he was too sensible to raise serious objections.

"I just don't quite know how we'll get along," he said rather gloomily at the end. "How soon do you people want him to leave?" He looked at Ainsworth as he spoke.

"With the minimum of delay," Ainsworth answered. Richard had thought it well to stress to him that the Communists had been up against his wife once already, and would certainly be keeping tabs on her since the incident on Sunday; he rubbed this in. Parrott nodded gloomily, and reflected.

"How do we go about it? He's an American citizen; I can fire him, but I can't very well deport him, nor dictate to him what he does after he's fired, so far as I know."

Major Day grinned.

"Leave that to the Spanish Security Police! The people here had all they wanted in the way of Communists back in their Civil War; they'll see him clear out of the country, which is just what's needed. I'll see them, and fix it."

"Then maybe I needn't even fire him myself," Parrott said hopefully. It would be easier for him if it was done in that way; he wouldn't have to explain anything to Nell.

"Maybe you needn't," Day said. "In fact I think it might be better if you don't. I don't have to tell you that the fewer people know about this the better," he added—he too knew Mrs. Parrott's tongue. "He isn't working alone, and Mrs. Atherley ought not to be put at risk. The less warning he gets the better. That right?" he said to Ainsworth.

"Perfectly right," Ainsworth turned to the Captain. "Have you any idea where he's likely to be at this time in the morning?"

"In the flat, I'd fancy. The car's being repaired, so my wife was going to let him polish the floors and do the silver," Parrot replied ingenuously. "He's marvellous at those things. I don't know how she'll get along without him—we'll never get another man like that."

"Let's hope you don't—not in *all* respects," Ainsworth said ironically—Parrott gave a rueful grin.

"Well, that's settled—you'll say nothing to your wife or anyone else, and we'll get the Hispanos to see to him," Major Day said firmly. "Let's go," he added to Ainsworth.

"Hey, they won't frighten my wife, will they?" the Captain asked anxiously.

"No—some very polite Señores in plain clothes will ask to see him, and just invite him to go along with them." Day and Ainsworth took their leave and went out.

"If you're not busy maybe you'd come along, in case they ask any surprise questions," Day said in the corridor.

"Right."

But the Spanish Security Police made no difficulties whatever. When Day had explained the facts to a very senior officer this gentleman made a few notes, and then said, with a perfectly impassive face—"Do you wish him to be killed?"

"No—just put on a plane that goes non-stop to New York," Day replied, grinning a little.

"The plane will probably have to re-fuel at Bermuda or the Azores. But I will let one of our people travel with him—I assure you that there will be no trouble," the Spaniard said. "I will let you know which flight—I assume you will wish to inform your colleagues at home of his return." Day said Yes, and with ceremonious courtesy the Spanish official bowed his visitors out.

"Very co-operative people, the Spaniards," Major Day said blandly as they drove away—Ainsworth agreed, with a brief laugh.

"I'm rather surprised they didn't want to find out more about his colleagues, the actual ambushers," he said.

"Don't worry—you can bet 100 dollars they'll find out what they need to know before they put him on that plane," Day replied easily.

"Even though he's got American papers?"

"Yes. Communism knows no nationalities, for them."

"Nor for the Communists themselves, come to that," Ainsworth said. "Well, if you'll drop me off at the Embassy I'll tell Atherley—he'll be relieved to know that it's all settled."

"I'll do that. I'll let the Captain know—he won't be all that relieved!"

"Yes, it's bad luck on him."

Ainsworth duly reported to Atherley, mentioning the Spanish offer to have Luis liquidated, and Major Day's comment; Atherley too laughed, and presently passed the story on to the Ambassador.

"It's extremely convenient that they are so co-operative, as Day calls it," Sir Noël said. "And very lucky for them that your wife should have uncovered this business for them just now."

"Oh really? Why just now, H. E.?"

"With this second American visit coming off—I believe in about a month."

"Who is coming?"

"Someone very high up in the State Department; it may even be the Secretary of State himself, Packer thinks. Luxworthy dealt with the practical side—whoever comes now will tie in all the political ends, and I imagine sign the agreement, or a new agreement. Anyhow it's out of our hands now," the Ambassador said. "Give my love to Hetta when you see her."

"I will." But Richard didn't take the hint and go. "There is just one thing," he said. "As soon as Hetta is fit to travel I

should like to get her off to Gralheira, to have a little peace—
and forget about all this performance."

"Taking the family?"

"If you mean the child and its nurse, yes indeed. Or did you
count me as part of the family? Nothing would suit me better," Atherley said with a sly smile.

"Oh, I know you're due for some proper leave, Richard," Sir
Noël said, "and that I cut you short last time. But you ought
to be here when this American comes. How soon would you be
able to go?"

"That will depend on the X-ray," his Counsellor replied.

"What X-ray?"

"Hetta is expecting another child, and the doctors have an
idea that they'd better make sure that being somersaulted
about in a car hasn't done it a bit of no good."

"Good gracious me! I'd no idea of that. I *am* sorry, Richard.
Yes, of course they must find out. There's no sign of anything
wrong so far, is there?"

"No, thank Heaven—but Gralheira is at the back of beyond, so we must make absolutely sure before she leaves
Madrid."

"Well, congratulations to you both. I don't see why you
shouldn't at least take her there, if you are able to go fairly
soon, and settle her in."

"Thank you very much."

When Parrott went home to lunch his wife greeted him with
a mixture of dismay and vexation.

"Luis went off this morning, while I was out, and he hasn't
come back yet. He never asked leave, and he hasn't finished
the parquet, nor touched the silver. Did you tell him he could
go out?"

"No, I haven't seen him today," Walter replied truthfully.

"I can't imagine what's happened. He never does anything
like that," Nell said fretfully. "Manuela says some men came
and rang, and he went off with them—she was on her way to
answer the bell, but he was right in the hall, and opened the

· 73 ·

door himself, and just went with them. He never even put the polish and the burnisher away."

Walter hesitated. It was going to be almighty difficult to keep the truth from Nell, though he was relieved that the police had acted so promptly. Once the man was out of the country Nell would have to know, but the longer that could be put off the better.

"*You* didn't scold him about the accident, did you?" his wife asked suspiciously, noticing his hesitation.

"No. Except asking him what happened I never said a thing to him—he told me he'd hit a pot-hole."

"Well don't say anything to him when he turns up, either," Nell said. "There must be some good reason. Let's have lunch."

Walter knew only too well how good the reason for the chauffeur's sudden departure was, but wisely left it for the moment. He spoke Spanish tolerably well—Nell hardly knew any—and later took occasion to question Manuela himself about the men who had called. "Were they friends of his?" Manuela thought not. "He seemed surprised, and showed no pleasure; one of them picked up his jacket, which was on a chair, and another took him by the arm. I could not hear what they were saying, and two or three more closed the door after them very quickly."

"Very curious," Parrott said carefully.

"So I thought also," the maid replied. "Since the Señora was out I went through into the small salon, and looked out of the window, and saw them taking him away in a car; there was a second car, with more men in it, and they all drove away together. In my opinion the Señor Comandante would do well to take another chauffeur," Manuela said, with an expressionless face.

When Parrott returned to his office he rang Major Day, and asked if he could come round? When the Intelligence man arrived Parrott repeated Manuela's account.

· 74 ·

"Quick work!" the Major said. "I hope this hasn't worried Mrs. Parrott?"

"Well, she's fretting a bit. I haven't told her yet."

"Much better not. I've made a signal to our folks at home, telling them just what I think of their screening arrangements at Camp Kilmer! It's pretty embarrassing, the British uncovering all this—really on our behalf."

"Do you know yet when he goes?" Poor Walter was longing to be free to tell Nell, and get the whole thing over with.

"No. I'll tell you right away when they let me know."

It was after lunch the following day before the Spanish official asked Major Day to come and see him. The chauffeur was going on a night plane to New York—Day jotted down the flight number, and asked if the Special Police had traced any of the rest?

"The two Hungarians, yes; but there must be Spanish agents involved too; for those we must wait till we have—examined—the two we hold."

"Well thanks a lot."

"We too are grateful—to this English diplomat's wife in particular! We owe her much—as you do," the official said. "I trust she is making a good recovery?"

Back in his office Day sent off his cable giving the flight number; he had already had a disturbed and apologetic message from Washington. It had been agreed "at the highest levels" that American Security over there would let Luis go free, but tail him closely in the hope of uncovering further contacts in the States.

"Doubt if he'll have many over there," Major Day said to Ainsworth, when reporting all this to him. "It was here he was intended to operate."

"Yes. I'm glad they've got those two other Hunks, but I hope they'll manage to get a line on the Spanish chaps involved. Let me know when you hear any more. We don't want them to try anything nasty on Mrs. Atherley."

"Would they do that? They don't know her by sight, nor what part she played."

"Communists are good guessers, and they leave nothing to chance," Ainsworth said, as he left.

Major Day too decided to leave nothing to chance; he knew Mrs. Parrott's recklessness and obstinacy, and refrained from ringing up her husband till after the plane had left. As he rang off—"I'm almighty glad I'm not in his shoes right now," he muttered to himself with a gloomy grin.

Ainsworth had of course passed on the news of the prompt action by the Security Police to Richard Atherley, who was considerably relieved to know that Luis was under lock and key. But he still thought it advisable that Hetta should go to Gralheira as soon as possible, and Luzia strongly urged this course after she had heard in detail what had taken place at the cigarral, and still more at the time of the accident. "This is bad," she exclaimed. "Now he knows that Hetta speaks Hungarian, he and his associates will attribute anything that happens, to her. I wish they could catch these others, the actual murderers." She was not wholly pacified when Richard told her later that two other Hungarians had been caught. "They must have been in liaison with Spaniards too. We should go quickly. I telephone to Papa—I am sure it will be all right. Yes, of course the nurse and baby go also, and you as well, Richard. Thank goodness this *deuil de famille* ends next week!—so the Ambassador can come too and shoot partridges, since apparently he wants to so much!" she added laughing. "I am sure he and Papa will get on famously." (She was thinking privately of someone else who could now be allowed to come: Nicholas Heriot, whose visit had been postponed because of the family mourning; she wanted to consult Hetta as to how this could best be managed. The larger the party in the house, the less the embarrassment for the suitor who was coming "on approval".)

On the afternoon of the day when Luis was to be flown out she was sitting in the clinic discussing this knotty point. The

Duke had extended the warmest possible welcome on the telephone to the whole Atherley family—"and of course the British Ambassador too, if he cares to come. I will write to him." "But Hetta, Papa did not mention Nicholas," she said rather sadly. "He knew that he was coming, and *wished* him to come, before old Tia Ana died, and he had to be put off. And last night he did not speak of him at all."

"Perhaps he forgot."

"Possibly. I should like him to come while you are there; then you would see him. I am sure you will like him. But who should write?"

"Who put him off?"

"I did, as Papa does not know him. But this is a little different," the girl said, with a faint blush. "Should I ask Papa to write?"

Hetta considered.

"No," she said at length. "I think you must write yourself. For your Father to write might seem—well, to emphasise the matter too much. It was all arranged, and then *you* had to ask him to postpone his visit; now you write and say that the *deuil* is over, and that we are all going there. It is quite natural."

There was a knock on the door.

"Come in," Hetta called in Spanish.

Round the door came a man in a neat uniform, such as messengers from the smartest shops wear, carrying a sheaf of roses done up in cellophane. "For the Señora Atherley," he said, going over towards the bed, and staring hard at Hetta. Luzia sprang up, took the flowers from him, and almost pushed him out of the room, shutting the door behind him.

"Who are they from?" Hetta asked. But when Luzia had undone the cellophane there was no card, nor any label to indicate from which shop they had come.

"This is curious," Hetta observed. "You are sure there is no card?"

"Quite sure." The girl frowned a little as she put some flowers which were rather over into the waste-paper-basket, rinsed out the vase which had held them, and arranged the roses in that—she stood it on a table in the window. Richard had told her of his arrangement with the clinic that no one was to enter Hetta's room except her, himself, and the doctor, without his authorisation—he had telephoned personally about the visits from Admiral Luxworthy and the Ambassador. She did not want to alarm Hetta, but it was not really with any change of subject that she asked, as she sat down again—"Have they settled when the X-ray is to be?"

"In two or three days, I think."

"How slow they are! Always *mañana,* in Spain! Does Dr. Santana not think you well enough yet?"

"Yes, but the radiologist is busy."

Richard Atherley was both disturbed and angry when Luzia told him about the mysterious flowers; she slipped down to the Embassy and caught him before he went to pay his usual evening visit to the clinic.

"What fools!" he said irritably. "I told the matron most definitely that this was not to happen."

"I think, now, that she should have the X-ray tomorrow, and leave the day after—surely there must be a radiologist in Madrid who is *not* so busy?"

"There had damn well better be!" He reached for his telephone and arranged to go and see Dr. Santana at once. "Will it be all right at your end?" he asked Luzia then. But he had no real doubts about that; he had stayed at Gralheira himself often enough to know the inexhaustible capacities of that household. "And can you get her packed?"

"Oh yes—I have got Speranza with me. I warn Nannie tonight, so that she can be preparing also—and I telephone to Papa."

"Bless you," the young man said fervently. "I'm glad you're here."

Dr. Santana had rather a *mauvais quart d'heure* with the British Counsellor. The Isabella Clinic was where he sent all his richer patients, and was more or less under his control;

Richard, in spite of his anger, was careful not to give the doctor the real reason for it—he put it on the grounds of a promise made, and broken; instructions given and not observed. When he had pulverised Santana sufficiently he demanded an X-ray on the following day, and got his way—no doctor wishes to upset his diplomatic clientele, let alone lose them. Richard went on to the clinic where he remonstrated strongly with the matron; but when he went in to see his wife, and she told him about the anonymous roses, he treated it lightly. "The Spaniards are frightfully casual," he said, and went on to tell her that the X-ray was settled for tomorrow. "And after that, darling, if the X-ray is all right I want to take you to Gralheira at once."

"You come too? Oh, how lovely!"

"Yes, for a few days." He explained about the second American visitor, and how he would have to be back in Madrid for that—"So the sooner we go, the better."

The X-ray was perfectly satisfactory; it revealed no sign of any injury to either mother or child. All the same there was a delay of a further day or two. They were too large a party for one car; the Duke of Ericeira naturally sent one of his big Humbers to fetch Luzia and her maid—it was so vast that Richard thankfully arranged to let his baby and its nurse travel in that, along with Hetta's own maid. But the drive from Portugal to Madrid took a whole day, so the man had to stay a night before starting the return journey. This pause allowed time for Richard to clear up his work, before even a short absence, to his satisfaction; the Swiss Nannie could pack at leisure, and Luzia do some last-minute shopping for herself and Hetta. On the last afternoon the girl came in to Hetta's room in the clinic with a radiant face.

"I am sorry I am a little late," she said, putting down one or two small parcels. "I had to wait for a telephone call, and it was slow in coming through—not at the time they said."

"From your Father?"

"No—from Nick! I wrote to him that day when you said I should, and he got the letter today—I had written on your paper, in my hurry, which gives the telephone number of the flat, so he put in a personal call. You were quite right; he did not think it strange in the least that I should have written—he comes next week!"

"I am very glad," Hetta said warmly.

"So am I—now you will see him. He is glad too!" the girl said, with a slight blush.

Hetta didn't doubt it—with the faint colour in her pale face Luzia, always beautiful, was enchanting.

"Now here is your powder, and the Forêt Vierge, and the Worth Eau de Cologne. Can you think of anything else, before the shops shut? No?—then I think I should go and finish my packing. I come tomorrow morning early, early, to get you up and finish your *nécessaire de toilette*."

"How kind you are."

"*De nada*. Oh, there is something I nearly forgot. Would you have wished to see Mrs. Parrott? She telephoned, twice, but I said I thought you were not well enough—she sounded so cross!"

"Poor Nell! Was she cross about Luis?"

"Yes—and that everything will be so difficult for her without him. I am afraid this husband of hers must have let her know that you were in some way responsible for his being sent away."

"Poor Nell!" Hetta said again. "It seems unkind not to see her, but—no, it is wiser that I do not."

"So I thought. Tomorrow will be a long day, and you should not be worried. And no one will ever make her understand what is of importance and what is not," Luzia said sagely.

In spite of her pity for Mrs. Parrott, Hetta had to laugh.

6

GRALHEIRA in autumn is an idyllic place. The great grey baroque house, with the knott-garden of tiny clipped box hedges outlining its gravel paths extending all along the south front, stands at the foot of the pine-clad Serra in open agricultural country, stretching away to the south and west, where on clear days the horizon is the distant dim blue of the Atlantic ocean—a Virgilian landscape, then full of the country activities which Virgil loves to describe. When the Atherley party arrived the maize-harvest was just ending, and while the women sat in groups in open-fronted sheds tearing the enfolding husks off the maize-cobs, men heaped the latter in slatted wooden stores, set up on stone supports; rats could not climb out from under the stone, so the precious grain was safe. Yet other men were pulling up the maize-stalks, tearing off their leaves, and chopping the stalks into lengths to dry for winter fuel; the coarse stalk-leaves served as bedding for the oxen. Shepherds tended flocks of milk-white sheep, the ewes, newly sheared, even whiter than their nearly full-grown lambs, which still wore the thick woolly coats which gave them a curiously rounded look, faintly comical; great slow-moving oxen, their coats like burnished bronze, drew long narrow carts of manure out from the cattle-stalls, to be spread on the fields and ploughed in when all the maize-plants were lifted.

Through these tranquil scenes Hetta, Richard, and Luzia

walked in the golden autumn weather, sometimes with the old Duke, when he was not occupied with his bailiff and estate matters. Inevitably Nick Heriot's impending arrival was in everyone's mind, though most of all in Luzia's and the Duke's; the possible engagement of his only child could not fail to be a matter of the deepest concern to him. He had taken to Hetta when she first came to Portugal, years ago; on her one or two recent visits to Gralheira his original liking had grown into warm admiration and respect; he was delighted by the friendship between her and Luzia. And one day before Nick's arrival when they were out walking the thing most in his mind came out.

"This young Heriot—do you know him yourself?"

"No, I have never met him. But Mrs. Hathaway has known him and his family for years, and thinks highly of them all," Hetta replied; she was touched by his confidence, and anxious to reassure him, for Luzia's sake, as well as his own. Her mention of Mrs. Hathaway struck just the right note.

"Ah, Mrs. Hathaway! Such a penetrating person. Her opinion would always be valuable." He looked musingly up at the trees on the Serra. "We so much enjoyed her stay here. Imagine, she was interested in forestry! I wish she would return."

Nick created a good impression even before his arrival by telegraphing to the Duke, mentioning that he was coming by car "if not inconvenient," and that he proposed to arrive at five o'clock on Thursday; he could be caught with a telegram at the Grand Hotel in Salamanca on Wednesday night, if there were any change of plan.

"This is well-mannered," the Duke said to Hetta as he showed it to her. She looked at him with affectionate sympathy, remembering him on her first visit—now a little older, a little greyer, but still bearing his curious resemblance to a Scots laird, still wrapped up in his estate and the welfare of his people. She determined to do all she could to ease this meeting, so momentous to him, and exerted herself to distract his mind during the last hour or two, when the tension could be felt both in him and Luzia.

In fact Nick Heriot did everything exactly right. He arrived dead on time—he had purposely so arranged his three-day drive from Pau that the last stretch should be a relatively short one. His car was a sensible saloon, not a sports-car—which the Duke had secretly dreaded; his light tweeds were perfectly correct, his London-made shoes the exact counterpart of the Duke's own. (The Duke had dreaded suède shoes almost more than a sports-car.) Luzia, the only person he knew, introduced him to her Father, then to Hetta and Atherley—his manner of respectful ease was just right, neither too easy nor too respectful. He replied sensibly to enquiries about his drive, mentioning, almost casually, what a relief it was to get onto the Portuguese roads after the Spanish ones; he referred to the advanced state of the harvest—"I see they have begun ploughing already. Is it an unusually early year, Sir?" he asked his host—the Duke, pleased, replied that it was rather an early season. Nick mentioned, with admiration, the bronze-coloured oxen—"I'm glad they still use them for ploughing here."

"Yes, mechanisation drives the men off the land," the old gentleman said.

"Doesn't it take the heart out of the land too? I mean, if one uses tractors, where is the dung to come from?" Nicholas asked bluntly—whereat the Duke beamed, and told his new guest about the lack of straw, since they did not grow enough wheat or barley for litter, and how the maize-leaves and the coarse outer husks from the cobs were used instead.

"And the finer ones from the *espigos,* are used for filling pillows and mattresses," Luzia put in. "Papa, should we not take Nicholas to see an *esfolhada* party?"

"Yes. There will be one soon at the miller's, him they call the Ferreiro—that is quite close," her father replied.

"What is an *esfolhada* party?"

"Stripping the husks from the cobs."

"But we saw some women doing that yesterday," Atherley said.

"Ah yes, but that was not a party. When all the maize is gathered on one farm, the neighbours come in to help; all sit together and strip the cobs; they go on till the last one is done, and then have a *huge* supper, and dance till three in the morning!" Luzia said with animation. "They have such fun."

"It is what they used to call a 'shucking-bee' in America, I believe," the Duke put in unexpectedly; "the same system of going from farm to farm, and making what might be tedious work into a social occasion. But I never heard that they have our convention about the *Espigo Rei*."

"What is that, Sir?" Nicholas asked.

"Now and again someone comes on a cob which is all red, a sort of freak; that is the King Cob, the *Espigo Rei*. If a man finds one he can kiss all the girls—and if a girl finds one, she can kiss the man she prefers," the Duke said, looking a little sly.

"I should expect the livelier lads to go to the party with a King Cob in their pockets," Atherley observed.

"Oh, they do!" Luzia replied, laughing. "But people are on the watch for this—if a boy has that reputation, they look in his pockets!"

When they went up to dress for dinner, Hetta asked Richard what he thought of Nicholas.

"Oh, a thoroughly good type—as one would expect. Old Lord Heriot has done a lot for Pau; he's immensely public-spirited, I've always heard. But I wonder if Luzia put the boy up to all this talk about agriculture? I thought Mrs. Hathaway said he was reading chemistry, or physics or something at the University, and meant to work at Lacq when he was through with Oxford or Cambridge, whichever it is."

"I believe he once had that idea. But since he fell in love with Luzia, I am sure he is serious about Gralheira, and looking after the place properly. You see it all comes to her, and she told Mrs. Jamieson, when they were in Pau, that she would never marry anyone who would not settle down here, and "help Papa"."

"How do you know that?"

"She told me herself—Luzia, I mean, when we were here last time."

"H'm. I shouldn't have thought a degree in chemistry would be much use in running Gralheira," Richard said, putting cuff-links in his shirt.

"*Yes*, Richard, a great deal of use. Nicholas has very good ideas; he thinks they should use all this resin which comes from the forests, themselves, instead of selling it cheaply to other people: put up one or two small factories, down near the railway, and make varnishes and plastics and—and things you do make with resin," Hetta said with energy. "This would give employment on the spot, and be much more profitable, he told Luzia. And for such things to know chemistry would be necessary."

"Yes, well that is quite an idea," Richard said. "Anyhow, I like him. Do you?"

"So far," his wife replied. "I think he seems quite as nice as Luzia says he is. Certainly he has very good manners—and tact."

Nicholas continued to win good opinions all round. As they walked about the estate and the country outside he asked quite sensible questions, not only of the Duke, but of Luzia, or anyone else who could answer them, like a rather distant cousin, Gil de Castelo Branco, who had come up, as he often did, for the week-end from Lisbon, where he worked in the Ministry of External Affairs—a lively intelligent youth, who was a pleasant addition to their little group. He was there when they walked over the fields to the early stages of the *esfolhada* party at the miller's farm, and gave immense satisfaction to the country-people when he produced a brilliant red *Espigo Rei* from his pocket, and kissed all the prettiest girls who sat round among the older women tearing the papery husks off the maize-cobs, ending up by giving the miller's grey-haired wife a hearty buss, amid general applause.

"Gil, where did you get it?" Luzia asked as they were strolling home.

"From Elidio. When you told me last night where we were going today I asked him to get me one," the boy replied cheerfully. Atherley burst out laughing.

"Elidio is the perfect butler! You ought really to call him Jeeves!" Gil had read P. G. Wodehouse, and like Nicholas laughed too; the others had to have the joke explained to them.

Next day, at Luzia's suggestion, they drove up into the Serra; she wanted Nicholas to see the source of the resin, about which he had these novel ideas. The autumn tapping—the trees are usually tapped twice a year, in spring and autumn—was in full swing, and Hetta and Richard, as well as Nicholas, saw with interest the ingenious methods by which this important crop is harvested. Below each white scar on the trunks of the trees were fastened small earthen-ware cups, into which the sticky sap slowly oozed; here and there men with curious long-bladed axes went from tree to tree, re-opening the wound in the wood.

"Yes, they have to do that three times during the tapping, or the resin coagulates in the air, and stops the flow," the Duke said, as they moved further up the slope into the wood, between the white-scarred trees, each with a pile of creamy chips at its foot. "See,"—he went to a tree where a man was about to use his axe, and lifted a small wooden bat with a short handle from the top of the cup—"this is to keep the chips from falling into the resin."

"Neat," Atherley commented.

Further on, where the tapping had been begun earlier, it was now over; girls were going from tree to tree removing the cups and with a sharp-edged tool scraping out their sticky contents into large tin cans; as these were filled they were carried down to the edge of the wood nearest the rough track, where the resin was poured into large metal barrels, which lay about under the trees. Nick asked some questions about what became of the resin?

Most of it was exported, the Duke told him; "It is quite an important export."

"I never knew that," Atherley said. "Roughly how much a year, Duke?"

"I can give you the precise figure at home," the old gentleman said. "I do not want to exaggerate, but it runs into tens of thousands of tons."

"Good Lord!" Richard ejaculated.

"You did not learn this when you were in the Embassy in Lisbon?" the Duke asked a little quizzically.

"No—I wasn't on the Commercial side," Richard said.

"We produce between eight and nine thousand tons from Gralheira alone, as a rule," the Duke observed.

"Is it a valuable crop?" Richard asked.

"To the country, yes, but to the actual producer less so; it is bulky and heavy, and the freight charges to the ports eat up much of the profit."

Hetta looked at Nicholas at this; he said nothing. Tactful creature, she thought, smiling a little; he knows better than to rush things. He did however presently ask why all the branches were cut off the trees almost to the top?—for fuel, his host explained. "Practically all the bread in Portugal is baked with pine-boughs, even in the towns. Since we have to import coal, this also is of value to the economy, but does not greatly enrich the producer," he added, smiling. "Fortunately the railway to São Pedro do Sul runs right through the estate, and I have arranged to have one or two sidings built, so that the wagons can be loaded on the place."

Early the following week Richard Atherley had to go back to Madrid. He left quite easy in his mind about Hetta—the bruise on her forehead had gone down, the surgeon from Oporto had been to examine her wrist, and was coming over presently to remove the plaster and strap it up; she was eating and sleeping well, and was happy and in good spirits. After he had gone the others continued in their tranquil routine of walks and drives, but now as often as possible Hetta stayed with her host, so as to leave Nick and Luzia together.

"I get a good impression of this young man," the Duke said one day, watching the young couple walking ahead of them.

"Oh, I am very glad. I like him so much."

"You do? I too am glad of that—I rather wanted to hear your opinion of him. He is undoubtedly intelligent, and well-bred; I find his manners perfect, in what cannot be the easiest of situations for him," the Duke said, with a fine small smile. "Also I understand that his family are well off," he added.

"I believe so—Richard says that they have a large and valuable property in Pau, and there are only the two boys to inherit it."

"This is not the most important thing, of course," the old man went on. "But to be the father of an heiress is a responsibility!—and the more so when the inheritance is in land; the human factor becomes so important. One would not be greatly distressed if stocks and shares were not properly looked after!"

Hetta laughed.

"I believe old Lord Heriot would be exceedingly distressed if stocks and shares were ill-treated," she said. "He is Scotch, you know."

"Yes. And prudence over any form of wealth is a good thing—I agree with His Lordship there," the Duke said, smiling. "But I cannot help hoping that this boy may take a real interest in the place and the people—there is still so much to be done," he ended with a little sigh.

Hetta wondered if she should pass on what Luzia had told her about Nick's ideas for light industries at Gralheira, but decided that it would probably be better if the young man himself spoke more openly about his genuine interest in the management of the estate, now that Luzia's Father seemed to take the engagement for granted. Later she mentioned this conversation to Luzia. "Nick has been very tactful so far, but I think that now he might express his interest in everything more openly."

Luzia threw her arms round her friend's neck.

"Oh, you are good! You are a help," she said.

Hetta was amused to notice, during the next couple of days, that Nick Heriot was acting on her advice. They drove out once or twice to visit friends in the neighbourhood; in every village large wine-casks stood about in front of the houses, in preparation for the vintage, some new, cream-coloured, others streaked in brown and beige, old ones which had been trimmed for the new season. Here and there young men were rocking these last to and fro, with a loud jangling metallic sound. Nick asked his host what they were doing?

"Cleaning the inside of the casks. They half-fill them with old chains, and any odd bits of metal, along with the water, and rock them about—it cleanses the wood much better than scrubbing, and much more quickly, though it is quite hard work."

"That water looks as though the old iron had been rather rusty," Nick observed, as they passed some youths emptying a cask.

"Oh yes, the rustier the better! Rust has a very purifying effect. But some of the colour is from the lees of last year's wine, which the chains have dislodged."

Nick was amused at the ingenuity of this method of cleaning barrels. He asked the Duke when his own vintage would begin?

"On the lower slopes, in a few days, now. Tomorrow I must go with the bailiff to inspect the *adega* and see that all is ready for the ranchos. Would you care to come too?"

"I should like to very much indeed. What are ranchos?" the young man asked.

"The wine-treaders. We have not enough man-power on the place to deal with all our own grapes, especially as many are busy just then with their own vintage; so the ranchos come from places where the vintage is earlier or later than ours, or where they grow little wine. The same people come year after year."

"All men?"

"Oh no—the women come with them, for the cutting. The men do the carrying to the *lagares,* and then the treading."

"I must see this," the young man said.

"They love coming," Luzia put in. "They look upon it as a sort of holiday. They bring their guitars and tambourines, and dance in the evenings in the *adega,* while the men tread the grapes."

Next day the whole party walked out to the *adega.* It was a large airy shed with a cement floor on which were installed three square wooden troughs about ten feet across, with sides some two-and-a-half feet high, the actual *lagares;* the last of these were being scoured out, and the water run off through a pipe onto a sort of roofed terrace below—here the barrels would stand to receive the wine, the Duke explained. Outside the shed some shallow troughs, quite small and also freshly scoured, were propped up to dry in the sun; in these the men washed their feet before they began the treading. The Duke held one or two up and examined them carefully—"Yes, they are clean," he said to the bailiff, who was in attendance. Then he went to inspect the quarters which were being prepared for the ranchos in a building close by. The ground floor consisted of a large room with long wooden tables and benches at one end; at the other was a big cooking-stove, two yellow marble sinks with taps, and shelves full of gay country pottery— plates, bowls, and mugs; cupboards for the bread, and a per- forated zinc larder for the eatables. Having examined every- thing minutely, and told the bailiff that the big copper cooking-pot for the soup must be more thoroughly polished, he led the party up an outside staircase to the two sleeping- rooms above, where mattresses in tartan cotton covers lay on beds of fresh hay, a pillow at the head of each mattress, two blankets neatly folded at the foot. The Duke picked up several of these, and sniffed them—two he put on one side.

"These have not been properly washed," he said to the bailiff. "*Por favor,* tell the women to do them again, and ex- amine each one yourself."

"Most certainly, Your Excellency."

In the washrooms outside the Duke observed that there was not enough soap, and insisted on being shown the locked cupboard where the towels were kept; he said that another two dozen must be provided. "Who will be doing the cooking for the ranchos this year?"

"Esperanza and Antonia, as usual—and young Ana will help with the vegetables and the washing up, Your Excellency."

"*Muito bem.* But please see that those blankets are washed today, so that they will be aired."

As they walked home the Duke said to Nicholas—"Senhor Oliveira is really quite a good man; but here it must be known, and *seen,* that every detail is looked into; otherwise people get careless. Those women he spoke of know that I shall come and taste the food myself—but they never know when I am coming!" he added smiling. Luzia shot a gleam of satisfaction at Hetta as she overheard this. Nick asked what sort of food the ranchos would be given?

"Oh, soup—always soup! And *broa,* maize bread, and a great deal of *bacalhau;* that is dried cod, it is one of our staple foods here, and old Esperanza knows many excellent ways of cooking it. And of course salads and vegetables, and all the wine they wish for."

"What they really enjoy most is the coffee," Luzia put in. "For the country-people this is rather a luxury, or at least to be used sparingly; here they can drink it by the litre! And Papa, tell Nicholas about the *peru* on the last night."

Her father smiled at her.

"Yes, on the last night, when all the wine is made, they have a special dinner—roast turkey. This is a great treat for them."

"Why is it called *peru?* Do turkeys come from Peru?" Nick asked. "I thought they were native to North America, originally."

"That is the turkey-buzzard. The birds we eat were found domesticated in Mexico by the first conquistadors, and introduced from there, I believe. I do not know how they came by the name *"peru"*—a geographical confusion, perhaps."

"A much more reasonable one than our calling them turkeys, anyhow," said Nick laughing. "At least Mexico and Peru are in the same hemisphere."

Hetta was increasingly pleased with the way things were going. The Duke continued to tell Nick about the countryside and estate matters, and Nick to show an intelligent interest. When the old gentleman was occupied with the bailiff, or was busy in his study, Hetta as far as possible left Nick and Luzia to go for walks alone; they returned from these with such radiant faces that it was obvious their personal relationship was unclouded too. However, this involved Hetta in sometimes taking walks alone; old Mrs. Hathaway had told her that exercise was good for the baby, and it had certainly worked well for little Richenda, her first child, who was the healthiest and most cheerful of babies. At first she had walked mostly in the grounds, which were surrounded by a high wall—but she was a good walker, and as the memory of the episode at the cigarral faded, and her natural confidence returned, she began to go out through one or other of the high wrought-iron gates in the wall and stroll along the tracks through the fields, pausing to exchange greetings with the peasants working, or watching men, their trousers rolled thigh-high, treading their own grapes in those parti-coloured barrels.

One day as she approached a group of women who were beating the seed out of flax-plants onto a *liteiro,* a hand-woven bed-spread, she saw that they were talking to three men—that is to say the men were addressing them, and they were shaking their heads in non-comprehension, and laughing with bucolic glee at this fact; as she came nearer the men moved off, and were lost to view behind a patch of still-standing maize beyond the house—it struck her that there was something rather hurried and furtive about their departure. Hetta had picked up some Portuguese during her first stay in Portugal, and had increased it on her previous visits to Gralheira from Madrid.

After greeting the women she asked who their visitors were?

Oh, strangers, foreigners—it was hard to understand what they said, the women replied, still laughing; one young girl added that she thought they were looking for work, but she could not be sure.

"They were not Portuguese, then?" Hetta asked, rather surprised.

"Oh *não não, Minha Senhora.* Portuguese they certainly were not." They might have been Spaniards, the young girl added.

Hetta had not noticed the men's appearance very particularly, and in any case she had only seen them from a distance —one she thought had grey hair. She walked on a little further after leaving the women, and then took a different track back towards the house. This ran downhill to the banks of a small stream thickly bordered on one side with what the Portuguese call *canas,* a tall blue-grey reed almost twelve feet high, which the peasants cut and use for fencing; she crossed the stream by a little bridge and walked slowly along on the further bank, watching a dipper perching on stones in the water. She stood still to see if she could spot the entrance to its nest; suddenly she was aware of a movement among the reeds on the opposite bank—a hand parted them cautiously, and a face with a dark moustache peered through, and then a second face; as she stared at them they withdrew, but through the screen of reeds she clearly saw two figures moving quickly away.

This was so unlike the normal Portuguese openness and cheerful friendly behaviour that Hetta became a little suspicious; she stared hard through the reeds, and thought she saw a third figure; she could not be sure. But why peer and stare, and then hurry away? She went back to the bridge, crossed it, and looked about; a small pine wood came down almost to the stream, and she could see no one. She felt slightly uncomfortable as she walked home.

Two days later she encountered them again, as she was returning from a walk on the more hilly ground behind the house; here, close to the estate wall, the path ran through a wood where the healthy mata, the prickly undergrowth used by the peasants both for litter for their stalled oxen and as kindling for their fires, afforded a certain amount of cover. Rounding a corner of the path she saw, on a bank a little above her, a man's grey head sticking up through the dull green underbrush; he peered at her intently, and a moment later the dark moustached face she had seen through the reeds by the stream appeared beside the grey head—he too stared at her before he ducked down again. She hastened her steps, then forced herself to slacken them to her former pace—they were rude, but not more than that, she told herself. She was however somehow very glad to pass through the great stone gateway onto the smooth gravel of the drive, which several gardeners were raking; their familiar faces were reassuring. She passed the time of day with them, and was about to go up the steps into the house, when on an impulse she turned back and spoke to the oldest, a lame old fellow.

"Oh Fernando, did you perhaps see some men loitering about outside? I passed them just now in the wood."

"*Sim, sim, Minha Senhora,* I have seen them—three, one a grey-head."

"Who are they?"

"*Minha Senhora,* I do not know this; certainly strangers. For some days they hang about, watching who comes and who goes—sometimes on this side of the park, sometimes on the other. I think they are looking for someone, perhaps."

"They should be at work, at this time of the year," Hetta said, with assumed firmness.

"So I think also," Fernando replied.

Hetta went into the house rather disturbed. "Looking for someone"—Fernando's words stuck in her head. Could they be looking for *her?* Certainly they had been looking *at* her hard enough, both just now, and by the stream two days ago; and she remembered that the girl who was beating out linseed had said she thought they might be Spaniards.

If one has not only been brought up in a Communist country, but has actually been kidnapped by Communists, like Hetta Atherley—let alone have stumbled on a Communist plot to assassinate a person one knows, and that quite recently, one is apt to take even trivial things more seriously than ordinary people. Reason with herself as she would, Hetta could not resist the impression that perhaps she herself was now being spied on, even hunted. It was true that Luis had been deported, and some at least of the other Hungarians imprisoned; but they must have had Spanish associates—had they followed her *here?* She suddenly remembered the man who had brought the mysterious flowers with no card to her in the Isabella Clinic—*he* had stared at her in just the same way. True both Luzia and Richard had brushed that aside as an accident—but had it been an accident? (She had of course no idea of the fuss that Richard had made with the authorities at the clinic about that, nor how he had hurried her X-ray precisely on that account—she just remembered the man's peculiar, searching stare before Luzia had fairly shooed him out of the room.)

The result of all this was to make her decide not to walk alone any more, not even in the park. After all she had the child to think of, Hetta told herself. Greatly to Luzia's surprise she suggested next morning that she should join her and Nick in their walk, having learned that the Duke would be occupied doing accounts with his secretary; he was busy in the afternoon too, and after the siesta she again followed them out into the garden—she felt too restless to stay in the house. Things went on like this for three whole days—the Duke was constantly taken up with the estate accounts for the quarter, which he wanted to get finished before the vintage began, and Hetta stuck to the poor young people like a leech the whole time. Nick became rather exasperated.

· 95 ·

"I say, is your cousin coming up this week-end?" he asked Luzia, seizing a moment when Hetta was playing with Richenda in the knott-garden.

"Gil? I expect so. Why?"

"So that we can sometimes see one another to speak to!" the young man said impatiently. "I can't think what has got into Mrs. Atherley all of a sudden—she never leaves us for a minute."

"It is rather strange," Luzia said thoughtfully. "There must be some reason, but I cannot think what it is. Hetta would never be tactless or inconsiderate without a reason."

"Couldn't you drop her a hint?"

"No—I must wait, and find out. There must be a reason," she repeated. "It is unfortunate that Papa should be so busy just now."

Gil did come up for the week-end, so the four paired off happily again. But after those days of frustration Nick was eager to get his affairs settled, and on Sunday morning after Mass in the lovely chapel upstairs, and breakfast in one of the morning-rooms, he firmly led his beloved up into the wood behind the house, and made her sit down on a mossy tree-stump.

"We do not walk?" she asked.

"No, sweetheart—we talk! We simply must take this chance, while we can be together. Tell me—is it going well enough with your delightful parent, do you think, for him to accept me? Because if so I should like us to be engaged straight away."

"With him, I think it goes very well; you see how he shows you what goes on, and tells you about everything. But you"— she paused, and studied his face earnestly—"are you sure that you could be happy, living here and helping Papa?"

"Yes," he said firmly. "I think it could be a perfectly absorbing job. Of course I shall have to learn Portuguese, one would be sunk without that. But now that he has seen me, here, do you really think he will agree?"

Luzia began to laugh.

"You have not asked me yet if *I* agree, now that I see you here."

"Well, do you?" He put his hands on her shoulders and looked gravely in her eyes. "Luzia, you know that I love you, and I believe that you love me—enough to be going on with, anyhow. Will you marry me?"

"Yes, I will," she said, as gravely as he. "I do truly love you, Nick."

He gave her a long kiss, and then took his hands from her shoulders.

"Good!" he said. From an inner pocket he pulled out a clean handkerchief, one corner of which was knotted; he undid the knot and revealed a ring with a superb emerald, in a quaint old-fashioned setting of rose diamonds.

"Oh, how beautiful!" she exclaimed. "Nick, it is *quite* lovely."

"Try it on."

"No, you must do that."

But when he put it on her finger it was very loose.

"Oh, it's far too big. You have such narrow fingers for all they're so long. Never mind—I'll get it altered. You do really like it?"

"I love it."

"I thought I would rather you had this than a new one," he said. "You see it was my Mother's engagement-ring, and my Grandmother's, and my Great-grandmother's before that."

"And your Mother let you have it?" She was almost incredulous.

"She gave it me herself—for *you*. You know how they all love you—Father is always asking when you are coming back to Pau."

"They are darlings," the girl said, warmly; she had the happiest memories of her stay with Lord and Lady Heriot. "Papa will *love* this," she added.

"The ring?"

"Yes—so many having worn it. It is like a betrothal in itself." She took it off. "You had better keep it till you have spoken to Papa."

"I shouldn't let you wear it till it's been made to fit, anyhow," the young man said, once more knotting it into the handkerchief and stowing it away; Luzia watched him, smiling.

"Sorry there's no box," the young man said, seeing her smile. "My Mother said there was one when my Father gave it to her, but it fell to bits."

"When it fits me, it will need no box."

"Luzia, there is one other thing," Nick said, slowly.

"What is that?"

"Will your Father mind very much if I don't become a Catholic? at least not at once? Of course the children will be Catholics—I realise that. And what about you?" he added.

"Naturally I should like it if you were one, and so would he. But he knows you are not. Why do you say not at once?" she asked, a little surprised.

"I think it would rather upset my old man if I became an R. C. He understands about the children, and he doesn't really mind that; it's—well, it's a step further off. But I think he might mind about me."

"Then if this is your motive, I think Papa will approve it. I have only read a little theology, but to be a good son to one's parents must surely be right," Luzia said, with her little definite manner when she had made up her mind about anything.

When Nicholas Heriot went into the study to ask the Duke of Ericeira, formally, for the hand of his only child, he was understandably a little nervous. Curiously, the room itself gave him a certain confidence, it was so like the "business-room" in a Scottish country house, with its safe, its filing cabinets, the shelves full of agricultural books and publications, even the huge map of the estate on one wall. To Nick the only unusual feature was the array of eight telephones on the big desk, but his host had already explained the reason for them—to be in touch with the farm, the *adega,* the oil-mill, the garage, the bailiff's house and office, and so on, as well as the outside world, without the trouble of keeping someone to work a private switch-board.

Nick was very brief and straight-forward. Still standing, he said—"I greatly wish to marry your daughter, Sir, and I have come to ask if you will accept me as a son-in-law."

"Sit down," the Duke said. Nicholas sat down. "What do your parents say to this plan?" the older man asked.

"They already know and love her; they would like it above all things."

"Would they be willing for you to spend most of your time here? This will be essential, especially when I am gone."

"Naturally they realise that, Sir, and accept it."

"And you—could you be happy, content, in this sort of life? Being a land-owner entails a great deal of actual drudgery."

"Much more worth while than most forms of drudgery," the young man said energetically. "I can't think of any sort of work that I should enjoy more."

"I hoped that was so," the Duke said, smiling. He got up. "I need not ask if you love my daughter, for I am satisfied that you do. Yes, Nicholas—I shall value you as a husband for her, and a helper for myself—which I am beginning to need increasingly. You have my consent." And greatly to Nick's embarrassment, he kissed him warmly on both cheeks.

"Thank you, Sir," the boy stammered out. "May I tell her?"

"We will tell her together." He rang the bell, and bade Elidio ask the Condesa to come to the study.

Luzia had been waiting in the small breakfast-room close by; she too was a little wrought up when she entered the room—her grey eyes moved from one face to the other in silent questioning. It was an emotional moment; her Father masked it with a small pleasantry.

"Well, my child, so you have found me an assistant! I have no objection to him, except that he does not speak Portuguese."

"He will learn! He has said himself that it was essential! He will begin immediately!" Then, seeing her Father smile at her, she threw her arms round his neck and hid her face on his shoulder. "Oh, Papa!" He smoothed her hair; when she lifted her head bright tears stood in her eyes—they fell as she reached up to kiss him. Nick was considerably affected by the scene.

"Papa, we shall all be so happy together," she said then.

"Yes, I believe that we shall. Well, my children, you have my blessing. But if this is a formal betrothal, where is the ring?"

Nick took out the handkerchief and produced the ring—the Duke looked at it attentively.

"This is a splendid stone, and a very beautiful setting," he said approvingly. "It is not modern, surely?"

"It was the betrothal-ring of his Great-grandmother, and his Grandmother, and then of his Mother!" the girl exclaimed before Nick could answer.

"Your Mother's ring? But does she not wear it?" he asked Nick, in surprise.

"She took it off and gave it to me, before I came here," the young man said. "She wished Luzia to wear it also, if we could get your consent to our engagement."

The Duke was delighted. He looked again at the ring. "Yes, the setting is completely characteristic of that period," he said. "This makes me more anxious than ever to meet your Mother, Nicholas. It is something to give up one's son to a young woman," he went on, smiling, "but to surrender one's engagement-ring also!—this is generosity indeed. Very well; put it on her hand."

"It will have to be altered before she can wear it—it is too big," Nick said, nevertheless obediently slipping the ring onto Luzia's finger.

"It becomes you, my child," the old man said. "See that you live so as to become it."

7

NICK drove into São Pedro do Sul, the nearest town, there and then, and despatched a telegram to his parents; he sent it in French to facilitate its arrival at Pau, and wrote it out in block capitals. On his way back he met the Gralheira Land-Rover—he learned later that the chauffeur was taking in a telegram, similarly prepared, from the Duke to his Mother, expressing the utmost pleasure at the engagement, and warmly urging the Heriots to come and stay at Gralheira as soon as possible.

Dinner that night was a festive affair. The Duke got out some of his finest champagne; the Portuguese make a very good version, but for this occasion, he explained, they must drink French wine, since France was the Heriots' adopted country. There were toasts—everyone was very gay. Hetta in particular was delighted; in the general happiness she forgot her private worries for a little while. When the two telegrams were mentioned—"Have you telegraphed to Mrs. Jamieson?" she asked Luzia.

"No—I did not think of it."

"But you *must* let her know—after all, it was because of her that you went to Larège; otherwise you would never have met Nick!"

"This is true," their host said. "Miss Probyn must be told— you owe her very much, my child, besides your fiancé!"

"I do this; I will write the telegram tonight, Fausto can take it early tomorrow. I ought to have thought of it."

"Is there anyone else in England who should be told at once?" the Duke asked, looking at Nick.

"Only my grandparents, and I expect my Mother will see to that—she conducts the family correspondence," the young man replied.

"Then doubtless she will put the announcement in *The Times*," the old gentleman said. "This should be done as soon as all close relations have been informed, of course."

Nick was rather startled; he had not realised that the Duke read *The Times* as regularly as he did the Portuguese papers. He said that "the parents" would probably think of that.

Gil was driving back to Lisbon that night. Usually he returned early on a Sunday evening, but on this occasion he stayed for dinner, "to drink Luzia's health." During their walk in the afternoon Hetta had taken occasion to ask him, rather vaguely, about her recent suspicions and fears. She and Luzia, and Atherley himself, had settled to make no reference at Gralheira to the episode at the cigarral; her broken wrist was the result of a perfectly normal accident, as far as the Ericeira household knew—and she was not sufficiently sure of her ground to take Gil into her confidence. Still, he was in the Ministry of External Affairs, so she had sounded him out, cautiously.

"What happens if Communist agents are found operating in Portugal?"

"If they are caught, the Security Police deal with them—as they did with those who kidnapped you, Madame Atherley!"

Hetta had never heard very definitely what had happened to her captors; she had at first been too shattered by her experience, and then too busy falling in love with Atherley, and becoming engaged to him. Now, after a period in Spain, she had an uncomfortable idea of what probably lay behind Richard's easy phrase "rounded up". She put another question.

"But if they were Spaniards?"

"Then of course they would be handed over to the Spanish authorities; their Security Police are even tougher than our P. I. D. E. But it is most improbable that Spaniards would operate here. Why do you ask?" He had seemed surprised.

"Oh, it was a hypothetical question," she replied rather lamely. "Some agents were caught in Spain the other day, I believe."

"I'm glad to hear it!" the young man commented sourly— "but not surprised. Since the Civil War Spain is full of Communists who have gone underground. The situation is much worse there than it is here, where they never got much of a hold. That is why the Spanish Security Police are so tough— they have to be. And anyhow Spaniards are rather cruel, in a way our people are not. I suppose they have more Moorish blood; the Moors used to be hideously cruel."

This conversation had not helped Hetta very much; in fact all it had done was to add a further facet to her *malaise*. Even if her suspicions were somehow proved to be correct, it would be a horrible thing to have been instrumental in handing men over to certain cruelty—Gil's words about the Moors stuck like a burr in the back of her mind.

Nick and his host made an early start next morning; by seven they were out in the vineyards to see the almost ritual cutting of the first bunch. After that the women worked methodically along the rows of vines, tossing the bunches into large baskets; they examined each one carefully, pinching out any unripe or mouldy grapes, before doing so. As the baskets were filled men came along and carried the full ones off to the *adega,* re-placing them with empties; it was all done very smoothly, and with a precision which Nick admired. It was some hours before the two men returned, hot and thirsty, for long cool drinks in the morning-room.

"Yes, it is a magnificent crop," her Father said, in answer to a question from Luzia. "In fact Oliveira has been rather foolish this year—he miscalculated, and did not notify enough of our regular ranchos, so he has had to take on some strangers. I noticed at least three faces that I did not recognise. I do not care for casual labour; I prefer to employ the same people year after year."

Hetta pricked up her ears at this. Three strange faces! Might these be the men she had seen? Her disquiets returned, and it was rather uneasily that two evenings later, after an early dinner, she joined the others when they walked across to pay one of the Duke's surprise visits to the *adega*.

"Oh, but you must come and see it," Luzia protested, when she hesitated. "I expect they will have the *música* up tonight, and then it is so gay."

In fact the scene in the *adega*, when they paused in the doorway to watch, was gay in the extreme. The treading was now well under way, and the chilly masses of grapes in the granite *lagares* had been reduced to the consistency of rather runny black-currant jam, the *lagrima*, as it is called before fermentation begins. In this dark syrupy stuff the treaders, with linked arms, were prancing to and fro; they had removed their trousers and were wearing very short flowered cotton pant-ettes.

The *música* had indeed come in, to cheer them on; under the unshielded electric lights a concertina and a couple of guitars, accompanied by several tambourines, were playing a lively folk-tune, and the shed was full of men and women dancing on the cement floor, while others beat time with their hands, or sang the words of the song. Luzia took a tambourine from one of the girls and handed it to Hetta—"Beat it!" she said peremptorily, and joined the dancers. In spite of herself Hetta was caught by this gaiety; she perched on a stool and pounded on her tambourine till the ball of her thumb ached. The Duke, looking pleased, asked the foreman of the ranchos if fermentation was beginning? Yes, in the earliest *lagare*, the nearest one; he dipped a thermometer in a metal frame, such as one uses for fruit-bottling, into the liquid, wiped it with his fingers, and held it out to be examined.

"What does that tell you, Sir?" Nick asked.

"Fermentation brings on a rise in temperature; in this *lagare* it has begun. If you feel in the next one I expect you will find that it is still cold. The *lagrima* is very cold indeed."

"Where can I wash my hands?" the young man asked.

"You need not do that," his host replied, laughing a little. "Fermentation is one of the most powerful sterilising agents that exist; it eliminates all impurities."

Nick put his hand into the next *lagare*. "It's icy," he said, startled. "May I feel in this near one too?"

"Of course—but it is not very warm yet; it is only part-way to becoming *mosta*—must, one should say in English."

Nick was full of questions. How often did they take the temperature of the must? How long must fermentation go on? Pleased, the Duke continued to explain the processes of wine-making; but Hetta, still mechanically pounding her tambourine, studied the faces of the treaders. Yes—in the furthest of the three *lagares* she saw a grey head, and then the man with the moustaches who had peered so intently at her through the reeds. When she could get her host's attention she pointed them out to him—"Are those two some of the strangers?"

"The one with the grey hair is—yes, and that rather villainous-looking fellow with the moustaches."

"And do they eat and sleep with the others, in the place you showed us?"

"Certainly." He was a little surprised at her interest in some casual labourers. But Hetta was determined to find out all she could while she had the chance.

"I wonder where they come from?" she speculated; the Duke spoke to the foreman.

"He thinks they are Spaniards," he told her, "but he has no idea from what place they came. Of course we are not very far from the frontier here. Antonio does not think they are very accustomed to treading grapes," he added, smiling, "but at least they make up the team for the third *lagare*, so we are fortunate to have them." He turned back to Nick, and went on telling him about fermentation. "In the later stages it gives off carbon dioxide gas."

"Isn't that dangerous for the men?"

"Oh no; it is very heavy, and only hangs in the air a few inches above the surface of the *mosta*. But if you hold a lighted match in it, it goes out instantly."

"I *must* see that!" the young man said again—his eagerness pleased his host.

"You shall—we will come down later on. For that, it is better when the wine is being rested; then the *manta* has formed on the top of the fluid, and the gas is undisturbed above that."

"The *manta* being?"

"The stalks and skins and pips; they rise to the surface and form a sort of crust during the resting period."

Nick was amused that the Duke spoke only of the wine being rested; obviously the ranchos took their rest and food then too, but the important repose was that of their product! He asked how soon the gas might be expected to appear?

"In another three or four days, shortly before the wine is run off."

Hetta, listening idly, her thoughts elsewhere, caught his words. Three or four days more treading; so the strangers would presumably remain at least for so long. That gave her only three days for certain, to make up her mind whether to mention her suspicions to anyone. She had very little to go on, in any case; but her main concern now was less the fear of being thought foolish than of doing something from which her heart and her conscience alike recoiled. If only she could ask advice from a completely independent source—but there was no one but the old Duke, who would certainly feel involved, and probably go straight to the authorities.

Luzia noticed her friend's silence and abstraction as they walked home, as she had noticed her hesitation about going to the *adega* at all; she asked her if she was tired?

"No, not in the least."

It occurred to the young girl that perhaps Hetta was fretting for her husband, and to entertain and distract her she suggested that they might go for an expedition next day. "You have never been to Sta Maria da Trapa, have you, Hetta?" she asked.

"No—what is that?"

"Oh, it is a most beautiful place—a convent of Cistercian nuns, with wonderful buildings, and unique statues. And it is a lovely drive there over the Serra. "Papa!" she called, interrupting her Father's conversation with Nick—"Hetta has never been to Sta Maria da Trapa. Could we not go tomorrow? She ought to see it, and Nick too."

"Nick cannot see much of it, since it is a convent of nuns," her Father replied.

"Papa, do not be a tease! He can see the outer cloisters, and the Coro Baixo, and those fascinating painted statues, and the Treasure."

"Yes, he can see those. Go by all means." He turned to Hetta. "A former acquaintance of yours is there just now, whom I think you used not to care for very much in old days."

"Who is that, Papa?"

"Monsignor Subercaseaux."

"What is he doing there?" Luzia asked in surprise.

"He has not been well, and is gone there to rest and recuperate in the care of the good nuns, and to benefit from the mountain air. But you will not need to see him," he added to Hetta, with a small ironical smile.

"Do you come, Papa?"

"No, my child—I shall stay with my wine."

"I think perhaps I will ask the de Freitas to come with us," Luzia said. "They are staying at São Pedro do Sul, and their car is being repaired after that smash they had; they must be very dull, and he knows so much. We could pick them up on the way. I telephone"—and she ran off and did so.

Luzia's motive in inviting her car-less friends to join their expedition was not purely disinterested. Since her Father was not coming, an extra couple would mean that she could see more of Nick than if they went only with Hetta. But Hetta had her own reasons for hoping earnestly that the de Freitas would accept, and for thankful rejoicing when Luzia came back and said that they were delighted to come, and were bringing a niece with them. Monsignor Subercaseaux was just exactly what she had been longing for, an independent person before whom she could lay her problem; and it would be much easier to escape from a number of people than from two. It was true that when she had first known the Monsignor immediately after her escape from Hungary, she had formed a rather unfavourable opinion of him; he was her Mother's confessor, and she considered that he was not only worldly himself, but encouraged her parent in a quite excessive snobbery and concern for social success. But that was a long time ago; marriage, and several years of diplomatic life, had dissolved many of her early prejudices—she looked back with shame on the intolerance of her ill-informed judgements in those days, for which her adored Father Antal Horvath had rebuked her at the time. She remembered his very words, à propos, precisely, of the Monsignor—"And must all God's servants be cast in the mould of which Hetta Páloczy approves?" His sternness had made her cry, then; now she knew for herself that he was right, and thanked Heaven for the chance of seeing the social priest. See him she must—and before she went to sleep she composed a brief note in her room, begging him to see her immediately. She made several attempts before she found a formula which satisfied her as being sufficiently urgent, and yet not seeming hysterical. After all, he might well have disliked her, too!

Sta Maria da Trapa lies at the head of a long shallow valley on the further, northern side of the Serra; the pine-clad slopes make a dark background to the complex of grey granite or white-washed buildings. The road to it from Gralheira is rough and narrow, but the drive is a glorious one; great hills rise on either side, deep valleys sink away below. Professor de Freitas knew a great deal—Luzia was quite right about that

—and on the way, from behind his gold-rimmed spectacles, he gave the party in the big Humber some account of the convent's history. A saintly princess retired to it in the thirteenth century, reformed the dress and manner of life of its occupants, and endowed it richly on her death. Hardly anything of the original house remains; owing to the royal scale of these endowments the place was repeatedly rebuilt, and what they were to see, the Professor told them, belonged almost wholly to the seventeenth and eighteenth centuries. "But those, with us, were a *good* period, architecturally," he pronounced.

They could only agree when, on arriving, he led them into the outer cloister, a great open square surrounded by large plain arches, surmounted by an exquisitely graceful baroque pediment containing an oval window above every arch, with urns topped by flambeaux in between—the whole lime-washed to a dazzling whiteness. But when he took them over to admire the carving on the well-head in the centre Hetta slipped out and round to the entrance of the convent proper, where she pulled hard on a small chain; a thin tinkling answered her pull. After what seemed to her a long time, in her anxiety and impatience, she heard steps and the jingle of keys inside the massive door; bolts were shot back, and the door was opened a little way, revealing a very old bent nun. Hetta, in her rather uncertain Portuguese, asked for "the Monsignore" and held out her note; the nun looked doubtful, but said that she would enquire if he would see a visitor. Hetta managed to slip in past her, and said firmly that she would wait in the portress's small cubby-hole of a lodge; she was afraid that if she stayed outside she might be caught by the others, and her plan interfered with. The nun, looking more doubtful than ever, gave her a chair, and went shuffling and jingling away.

A long pause ensued. Hetta waited in a fever of nervousness. Would he see her? Would she be able to make her fears sound reasonable? She tried to compose herself, and said some prayers. At last the old portress came back, led her upstairs and along several corridors, and showed her into a typical convent *parloir*—a vase of flowers stood on a bare wooden table so polished that the sweet-peas were reflected in its shining surface, four plain wooden chairs were ranged round the walls, a large crucifix hung over the mantel-piece. Then the door opened again, and in came Monsignor Subercaseaux.

"My dear Mrs. Atherley!—this indeed is a great pleasure! Is your husband with you? Oh, he remains in Madrid? I should so much like to see him again—in the past he and I were—fellow-conspirators, let us say! I trust he is well? And you? But what have you done to your hand?"

This effusiveness was at once a relief to Hetta, and rather threw her off balance. She began by using his question about her hand, which was still in a sling, as an *entrée en matière*.

"I broke my wrist in a car accident in Spain," she said briefly. "The chauffeur was a Communist agent whom I had seen in Hungary, and recognised."

"But how came you to be driven by such a person?" He looked startled.

"He was employed as chauffeur by the American Naval Attaché in Madrid."

Now she had all Subercaseaux's attention, and she told him the whole story: her suspicions of Luis, what she had overheard at the cigarral, the car crash, and the expression on the man's face when in the sudden shock she had cried out in Hungarian. The Monsignor, looking grave, asked the questions one might expect.

"Oh yes, Luis was deported to America—he had United States papers, because he went there as a refugee after the rising; and some other Hungarians were imprisoned, I think Richard said."

"But he must have had Spanish associates. Were they also caught?"

"I think not; certainly not all. This is why I seek your advice."

"Go on, my child."

She told him of her two encounters with the strangers at

Gralheira, and what the old gardener had said about their watching "who came and who went" at the house. "They are certainly Spaniards," she said, and mentioned that they were now treading the wine. "I may be foolish, but I have the idea that they may be watching me—I am afraid now to go out alone. I am expecting my second child," she added flatly.

"I am very glad. I hope it will be a boy this time," he said warmly. "But continue. Could any of this chauffeur's Spanish accomplices know you by sight?"

Hetta hesitated; then she told the priest about the man who had brought flowers into her room at the clinic. "This *never* happened—and there was no name, or card, when we undid them. Luzia made light of it, but she was displeased, I could see; and it seemed very curious. Since I have seen these men here, I—I have wondered if he was sent to the clinic to know what I looked like."

"Have you told the Duke about this?—or Luzia?"

"No. You see I cannot be sure if the men are really agents. Also I do not wish to trouble Luzia, just now that she is engaged."

"Oh, she *is* engaged, is she? To this young Scotsman from Pau?" No one was more close to the international social grapevine than Monsignor Subercaseaux—he allowed himself to leave the main subject to ask Hetta her views on Nicholas Heriot, and how the Duke of Ericeira had reacted to the engagement? He was pleased with what he heard, especially of Nick's desire to do all he could to be useful in running Gralheira, and his determination to learn Portuguese.

"All this is excellent," he pronounced.

"Yes, Monsignor, I too think so. But you see it is very awkward; I am afraid to go out alone, and if I walk with Nicholas and Luzia, they cannot be free to get to know one another as they should be doing. I am being a raspberry!" Hetta said. The priest laughed.

"Gooseberry," he corrected her. Then he looked grave again. "You have spoken to no-one about this?"

"Not openly, no. I asked Gil de Castelo Branco, this cousin, what would happen to Communist agents, Spanish ones, if they were caught here, and he said they would be handed over to the Spanish Security Police." She went on, rather hesitantly, to explain her distaste for this—"even if they are guilty, horrible things are done to them; and if they were innocent, horrible things might still be done, before their innocence was proved. I would not wish to have that on my heart, my Father."

Her use of those words made him look very benevolently at her. He realised clearly that she had come to him, less for advice about her own safety than to resolve a problem of conscience. At first he spoke almost musingly.

"Ah, yes. 'It must needs be that offences come, but woe unto that man by whom the offence cometh'. I understand you, my child. Let me reflect."

Hetta sat quietly while he did so, looking out of the small window at the view down the long sunlit valley. She was enormously relieved to have put her problem into other hands; and his whole manner, after those first few rather gushing sentences, caused her to feel that the Monsignor was wise as well as worldly-wise, as Father Antal had told her long ago.

At last Subercaseaux spoke.

"I think you cannot keep silence about this any longer," he said. "One does not know how much is involved; others besides you may be threatened. It is important to try to establish the facts, too."

"Tell the Duke? He will act at once, and ruthlessly, I am afraid."

"Not in the first place. Tell Luzia; she has a splendid head on her shoulders, and all their people love her—she may well find out a great deal about these men, and rapidly. She can also drop a hint to the estate servants to be on the watch. This young de Castelo Branco should be told—he is in a position to have the local police put on the *qui vive,* without taking any immediate action." He paused. "You have not written to your husband?"

"No. He would be so worried, and he cannot leave Madrid at the moment, because this other important American is coming, to complete some arrangements about the naval base at Rota—and Sir Noël wished him to be there."

"Ah yes." Naturally the Monsignor knew all about the American politician's impending visit. "All the same, it might be as well if the British Intelligence personnel in Madrid knew of the situation here." He considered, tapping his fingers on the shining surface of the table.

"If only one knew whether it is a situation at all," Hetta said.

"In all the circumstances I think we must assume that it is," he replied rather gravely. "It seems very probable that the Communists, now that they realise who you are, and that you speak Hungarian, will also have made an assumption—that you were in some way connected with the removal of this chauffeur. They will have a very full dossier on you. I think—yes, I think that perhaps I had better get a word to Madrid. I have channels!" he said, smiling a little. "But do you speak to Luzia at once, and the cousin."

Hetta pointed out that Gil would not be coming up till the week-end.

"Tell Luzia that he should come sooner! She will arrange it," Subercaseaux said easily. "And let me know at once if there are any more positive developments." He gave her the telephone number of the convent. "There is an extension to my sitting-room."

"Thank you, Monsignor." She rose. "It was good of you to see me."

"No, wait a moment," the priest said. "Please sit down again." Hetta did so, wondering—she was anxious to get back to her party as soon as possible. But for some time Subercaseaux sat in silence, again drumming with his fingers on the table. At last he spoke.

"If the situation is what I suspect it to be, things may happen quickly," he said slowly. "I should wish to be able to come at once, if my help were needed. But I have no car here. However, by good fortune a young priest is with me, Father Martinez, who is acting as my secretary; he has one of those dangerous motor-cycles, on which he travels at great speed; he could be at Gralheira within an hour." He paused. "Though he is still young, he has had much experience in difficult situations. He speaks Spanish fluently," he added, almost casually. "If the need should arise, you should telephone and ask him to come at once."

Hetta was rather bothered by this suggestion. She recognised some of the implications behind the Monsignor's words, but was not sure that she understood them all, or that she liked what she did understand. But her usual ingrained caution at once asserted itself.

"If he is to come and take any part in dealing with these people, I ought to see him," she said.

"Why?"

"But Monsignor, can you ask? To recognise him, of course."

He smiled then.

"Ah yes. You are right. I remember that you went to the airport in Lisbon to recognise Father Horvath when he was flown out from Spain." He drew out a very thin gold watch from the belt of his soutane, and looked at it. "How long can you stay here?"

"Perhaps half an hour; it depends on the others."

"And where can we find you?"

"I do not know—I left them in the outer cloister when I came to you. I had not spoken of this, even to Luzia. I know Professor de Freitas wished us to see the Treasure, and the Coro Baixo," Hetta said worriedly.

"Ah, de Freitas is in the party? A wonderful guide! Well, I shall try to have Father Martinez found at once, and send him to you. If this fails, he shall ride over to call on you tomorrow morning. In either case he will be advised that he may be sent for, and I shall inform him about the whole situation."

He rose. Hetta, to her surprise, found herself taking an almost affectionate farewell of a person she used to dislike so much; unasked, he formally gave her his blessing for herself, and for the child she was carrying. Comforted and reassured, she went out into the corridor, and managed to find her way downstairs to the entrance, where the old portress, still jingling her keys, let her out. She made for the church, which, since it now serves the village as well as the convent, is accessible from the road; the Treasury must adjoin it, she guessed, so the others would be somewhere there.

She found them in the Coro Baixo, really the nave, outside the grille which enclosed the nuns' choir, the Coro Alto; Professor de Freitas was showing them the splendid eighteenth-century organ, and the carved stalls on both sides. Luzia saw her first.

"Are you all right?" she asked, hurrying to her side. She remembered how Hetta had once before slipped away at the cigarral to be sick.

"Yes, perfectly. I will tell you afterwards," Hetta murmured. She looked about her, looked up. "Oh, but how glorious!" she exclaimed.

Luzia too raised her eyes towards the roof. Looking down on the choir from niches on both sides were tremendous statues, more than life-size, of nuns in their habit—but *painted;* under the black folds of their granite veils the faces showed with faultless and life-like naturalness. The Professor overheard Hetta's exclamation, and also came over to her.

"Yes, they are the great glory of this place," he said. "Are they not wonderful? Eighteenth-century, of course, and unique." As the others gathered about him, eager to miss nothing—"You would hardly credit it," he went on, "but some years back the Commission of Ancient Monuments seriously proposed to take the paint off them."

"But why?" Hetta asked.

"Why indeed? The same insane urge for simplicity which has ruined so many of our churches, stripping them of the accretions of centuries of piety. Here these gentlemen wished to leave the lifeless stone, instead of this inspired marvel!" He spoke with actual passion. "Mercifully it was prevented," he added more calmly, and went on pointing out the perfection of the carved habits of the statued nuns, so stylised and so dignified.

"I wish you had seen the Treasure," Luzia said to Hetta. "It is marvellous. And imagine—it was the country-people round about who preserved it! When the convent was about to be dissolved, in the last century, they came in and took it away and hid it, out of devotion to the Saint; and when the nuns were allowed to return, it was all brought back—but *all!*"

"In some cases the original rescuers were already dead, so their children brought it back," Nick put in. "Isn't that a nice touch?"

"Very." Hetta thought it a nice touch in Nick himself to be so pleased with that part of the story and so, judging by her happy glance at him, did Luzia.

A certain amount of discussion and consulting of watches now took place. The Professor wished them to drive on a few kilometers down the valley to see another church, with a very rich and peculiar baroque façade, including elaborately-dressed figures on the roof; Nick on the other hand wanted to take a different road back over the Serra, in order to pass through what the Duke had described to him as "a Stone-Age village", full of extremely primitive houses; Luzia was afraid that to do either might take too long, and risk making them late for luncheon—she was well broken in to her Father's mania for rigid punctuality at meals. Hetta too looked at her watch, for a different reason; she had told Monsignor Subercaseaux that she could remain at the convent for half-an-hour in order to see Father Martinez, and there were still twelve minutes to go—her one wish was to delay their departure. She drew Luzia aside, meaning to ask her help about this, when a little side door in the grille separating the nuns' choir from where they stood suddenly opened, and a very small figure in a black soutane came out through it.

"Ah, that will be he! Do just keep them for a moment,"

Hetta muttered to Luzia, and walked over to the little priest.

Luzia could always be relied on to do as she was asked at once, and leave questions till afterwards; she did so now, putting some query about the organ to Professor de Freitas. Hetta went up to the little priest, more than ever struck by his extreme smallness. "Father Martinez?" she asked.

"Yes. Is it Madame Atherley?" he replied, in tolerable French.

"The same. I am very glad to meet you," she said simply. Certainly he would not be easy to impersonate unless one dressed a child in a soutane, she thought—and smiled at the idea. The little priest smiled back at her.

"So now we know one another by sight," he said easily.

"Yes. Thank you for coming to find me. I will not delay you now—indeed I think my friends are about to leave. Goodbye, Father."

"Or possibly au revoir, Madame," the little man said; he bowed, and went back into the inner choir, locking the small door after him.

8

IN THE END the party did no further sight-seeing, but took the de Freitas' back to lunch at Gralheira. Hetta managed to snatch a moment alone with Luzia, while Madame de Freitas and the niece were washing and tidying themselves up, and asked her to telephone to Gil and ask him to come up at once. "Could you not do it now, before lunch? I will take care of these ladies."

"He will be coming up on Saturday," Luzia said.

"That is not soon enough. Monsignor Subercaseaux said he must come at once."

"Oh, it was he you strayed away to see?"

"Yes—he said you would be able to make Gil come. But do *hurry*, Luzia!" She spoke urgently—Luzia, without asking any more questions, went downstairs and put her call through, not from her Father's study, but from an instrument outside the pantry, mostly used by Elidio. As they all reassembled in the drawing-room—"He will drive up tomorrow morning," she said in a low tone. "But really, Hetta, must we wait till he comes to hear what goes on? I think I shall explode!"

"No no," Hetta replied laughing. "I tell you when they have gone," with a glance in the direction of the guests.

After luncheon, accordingly, they settled down in a small morning-room which Luzia had more or less appropriated to her own use—she had installed shelves to hold her books, and a writing-table with pigeon-holes, which she kept as meticulously tidy as her Father did the huge desk in his study. "Does Nick come and hear also?" she asked.

"Oh yes—after all, he is now part of the family."

However, Nick's presence rather slowed matters down, since so much that was common ground between the two young women had to be explained to him. Hetta began by telling Luzia of her two encounters with the strangers, and her sense of being spied on—"Also old Fernando said he had seen them, and thought they were watching to see who comes and who goes at the house. And when I learnt that they were Spaniards, I was—well, frightened to go alone."

Luzia gave a long "Aah" of comprehension. "Did I not tell you that she would certainly have some good reason for wishing to walk with us?" she said, wheeling round on Nick—the young man blushed at being given away. "But do you know for certain that they are Spaniards?"

"Yes, because now they tread the wine with the ranchos"— she explained having recognised them at the *adega,* and what the foreman had told the Duke.

"Why does their being Spaniards matter so much?" Nick asked.

"Oh, because Spaniards were probably mixed up with the Hungarians who tried to assassinate that American Admiral on the road from Toledo," Luzia flung out hastily. "This is how Hetta's wrist was broken, when the Hungarian chauffeur drove too fast to try to keep his appointment with the assassins, and had a smash, you see."

"I *don't* see, but I suppose I shall in time," the young man said resignedly.

"The Admiral and Hetta were in the same car," Luzia said impatiently, as though that made everything clear.

"Good God!" Nick exclaimed, horrified.

"Yes, well never mind now, Nick. But Hetta, these men should not stay here, working at the vintage—they must be sent away at once," she said energetically, getting up.

"No—wait, Luzia; sit down again, and hear what Subercaseaux said."

"Oh well he probably has good ideas, the old fox!" She sat down again. "So what did he say?"

"First, bad news for you and Nick!" Hetta said, half-laughing. "The old fox, as you call him, says I am not to walk alone."

"Is this why he makes me send for Gil? I do not believe it!"

"No, that is not the reason." Hetta spoke seriously again now. "First he wishes you, Luzia, to arrange with your people on the place to keep an eye on these men, and learn all you can about them—because really we know nothing for certain."

"This I can do without Gil!"

"Of course. But Gil is also to arrange something."

"What?"

"To have the police up here told to keep a watch on them, but not to *do* anything until—well, until they have instructions. The Monsignor said that Gil would be in a position to have this arranged."

"Oh yes, of course—through Colonel Marques, of the Security Police," Luzia said briskly. "He knows this house; he came here before, when you had been abducted, to collect the agent whom I found in the kitchen, and whom Nannie Brown drugged for Major Torrens. That *was* fun!" She was full of animation at the recollection. "Oh, *why* did not Miss Probyn send Torrens this time?—he did all so energetically. Ah well, I suppose we must manage without him. And what is the dwarf for?" she asked suddenly, turning to Hetta.

"The dwarf?" Nick was puzzled for a moment.

"Yes, this tiny little priest, who came into the Coro Baixo."

"I am not quite sure," Hetta replied. "What the Monsignor said was that if we needed him, he would send this Father Martinez instead, because he has no car himself at the convent; the Father has a motor-bicycle, and could come at once."

"Well, I do not see why we need a priest to catch Communist agents," Luzia said airily. "However, no doubt Subercaseaux has some scheme in his head." She got up. "Well, I will go out and do a little gossiping, I think. No, Nick—you do not come too; they will only ask questions about you, and make congratulations. You can take Hetta for a walk!—and she can tell you all about the assassination, which I am sure you are longing to hear."

At dinner that evening the Duke, beaming with satisfaction, announced that he had had a telephone call from Richard, asking if it would be convenient for him and the Ambassador to come on Saturday and stay for a few days? "Of course I told him that we should be delighted. I look forward to meeting Sir Noël very much; from all you both say he sounds a most charming person," he said, looking benevolently at Hetta and his daughter.

"But how can they come? They were preparing to see this important American politician," Luzia exclaimed.

"The visit is postponed, so the Ambassador wished to come now. It suits very well; the vintage will be finished, so I shall be free. We can arrange a drive for Monday." He turned courteously to Hetta. "I am so glad about your husband too —now he will not miss the shooting," he said.

Hetta with difficulty controlled a little shudder at the last words. Really, this was *too* ridiculous—she must not let her nerves get the better of her in this way, she thought, as she expressed her pleasure, and mentioned how much the Ambassador wanted to see Gralheira. She began, nevertheless, to speculate rather anxiously as to whether when Richard came she should tell him about her immediate anxieties. Later she consulted Luzia.

"Let us see what Gil thinks," that young person advised. "He will be here tomorrow by lunch-time."

But before Gil came there was news of yet another arrival. The morning post brought a letter to the Duke from Lord Heriot, acknowledging his invitation, and saying that he and

Lady Heriot would be delighted to come and spend a few days at Gralheira, to meet Nick's future Father-in-law, and see "our dear Luzia" again. He apologised for not writing sooner, but his wife had been a little under the weather; now she was perfectly well, and if it suited, and the notice was not too short, they would like to come next week.

"But this is perfect!" Ericeira said. "Does your Father shoot, Nick?"

"Oh yes, Sir—loves it, especially partridges. He's rather a good shot, as a matter of fact."

"Splendid. We must telegraph at once, and tell him to bring his guns." The old gentleman began counting. "You and I, and Atherley and the Ambassador make four, and with your Father five—we ought really to have one more."

"Perhaps Gil could stay on," Luzia suggested.

"Yes—though he is not exactly a crack shot!" her Father said. "I suppose it is too late to ring him up—he will have started. Never mind—I can lend him a gun." So another telegram was despatched to Pau, and the Duke took Nick off to the *adega;* the wine would be "resting" now, he said, and Nick should be able to see the effect of the gas on a lighted flame. The old and the young man went off together, friendly and easy, Nick rattling a box of matches in his pocket; the two young women watched them go.

"It is *so* nice that Papa and Nick are so happy together," Luzia said. "And I am very glad that his parents come. I think you will like them, Hetta. Now I will go and see about their rooms—you can look after Gil, can you not? Oh, how I wish we had another bathroom! Two is so few, when the house is full—and English people do not always like a sitz-bath in their room!"

She had not been gone long when Hetta heard a car on the drive; she went out into the hall, greeted Gil, and took him into the morning-room.

"Luzia is busy for a little while; she asks you to excuse her. I am sure you would like a drink"—but even as she spoke Elidio and a footman came in with a tray. "No, not for me, thank you; I have not been driving in the heat!"

Gil helped himself, and sat down. "Do *you* know why Luzia is in such a hurry to see me?" he asked.

"Yes. It is my fault, really." Then, as he looked surprised— "It is rather a long story; I think I had better begin at the beginning."

"Do, by all means."

Hetta began with her suspicions of the Parrotts' chauffeur in Madrid, then with what she had overheard at the cigarral, and the accident—"so fortunate, this was"—on the drive back from Toledo. Gil, since he worked in the Ministry of External Affairs, of course instantly realised the Communists' obvious desire to embroil Franco with the Americans by contriving some serious incident in Spain; he asked at once what had been done about the chauffeur, and almost groaned with dismay on hearing that he had been given American papers. He asked such sensible questions that Hetta was rather surprised; she liked Gil, but had looked on him as something of a lightweight. Had the rest of the "ring" been rounded up? Only the Hungarians, she told him.

"Ah, but they will certainly have Spanish accomplices. Were these rounded up?"

"No, and now some strange Spaniards are here"—he frowned as she went on to tell him of the men who had peered at her so intently.

"So this was why you asked me about Communist agents, last week?"

"Yes"—and she recounted Subercaseaux's insistence that he, Gil, should come up, and make some arrangements about having the local police alerted, to keep a watch on the three strangers.

"It is really rather a pity that you did not "come clean", as the Americans themselves would say, when you spoke to me," the young man said. "Of course the Monsignor is right—he usually is! The strictest precautions should be taken, but with very great discretion. This will have to be arranged with the help of the Security Police; if I had known the facts I could have seen them about it while I was down in Lisbon."

"See Colonel Marques?"

He looked at her in surprise.

"Do you know him?"

"No—Luzia spoke of him. He has been here before," she said."

"Yes—and then also in connection with you, Madame Atherley! You have only to come to Gralheira, it seems, to turn the place into a nest of agents!" Hetta thought Gil's smile rather forced as he said this; he looked at his watch. "I begin to think I should go back at once. There is no time to lose, and it might be imprudent to telephone, since the Colonel knows nothing of the background. As you say, it is a long story."

"I am so sorry—" Hetta was beginning, when Luzia came in.

"Well, what do you think of our latest activities on the Communist front?" she asked cheerfully. "Has she told you everything?"

The young man did not respond to his cousin's lively tone.

"Yes—and I do not think it a laughing matter," he replied repressively. "I think I should go back to Lisbon."

"Not *now?*"

At that moment the Atherley baby and her Nannie appeared outside the window; the nurse held Richenda up to tap on the pane with her little fat hand—Hetta, smiling, hastened out to them.

"This is not at all amusing," Gil said then. "It can be exceedingly serious. They will certainly have a full dossier on Madame Atherley, dating back to the part she played in the escape of Dr. Horvath; since that chauffeur was deported they may well think she knows too much, and wish to eliminate her before the next American comes, so that their plans do not miscarry a second time."

"Eliminate her!" Luzia exclaimed, her eyes wide. "You cannot mean kill her?"

"Indeed I do. She is in great danger; these people stick at nothing. Do not alarm her; but until we know more, she should never be outside the house alone."

"Then when Richard comes he should be told all about it?"

"Of course. But he is not coming for some time, is he?"

"Oh yes. He and the Ambassador are coming on Saturday —the American visit has been postponed."

"So. When was this settled?"

"Richard telephoned last night. Papa will arrange a partridge-shoot for them next week."

"Well, I don't suppose this will affect their plans," Gil said thoughtfully—"the Communists', I mean. Richard did not say when he does come?"

"The American personage? No—just that they would come and shoot now, while they had the chance."

"Well, I had better go. Make my excuses to your Father, please."

"But you have had no lunch!"

"I will get some in São Pedro do Sul." Gil was thinking that from the *policia* there he would put through a call to Colonel Marques, ensuring that he could see him at once when he got to Lisbon.

"And your luggage! By now it is all unpacked—I saw Antonio coming out of your room."

"My luggage does not matter—I have things at home. Does your Father know about these men?" he asked suddenly, turning at the door.

"Not that they may be agents—just that there are strangers helping at the vintage."

"Then do not tell him. I shall be back tomorrow. Say that I was telephoned for." He went out; a moment later Luzia heard his car rattling round on the gravel of the wide sweep before the door—the sound faded as it passed up the drive.

The girl sat in great discomfort. Hetta had spoken so

minimisingly of her encounters that somehow her personal danger had bulked less large in Luzia's mind than the congenial idea of once again outwitting Communists; now Gil's words brought it sharply before her. Richard had sent Hetta here to be safe, and she was *not* safe. She sat pondering. What could they do to ensure her safety? She herself had made some vague enquiries about the three strangers yesterday, but had refrained from saying anything to arouse much suspicion; now she realised that she must lose no time in carrying out the Monsignor's suggestion of putting the estate workers on the alert. But exactly how? She was thinking intently when the door opened, and Nick came in.

"Ah, drinks!—good. What are you having?"

"Nothing—I mean not so far. I would like some sherry, please."

"Well, that is a most extraordinary show," the young man said, after also pouring himself out a long glass of soda and lime, and sitting down. "The match really does go out, the moment it gets to within about six inches of the *manta*."

"Oh, does it?" She spoke abstractedly.

"But of course it does! Surely you must have seen it yourself? Only what I don't understand is why, when they start treading again and disturb it, it doesn't affect the men. Your Father says it's because it isn't sufficiently concentrated."

"Oh, does he?"

Nick looked at her, then went over and gave her shoulder a little shake.

"Wake up, darling! What's the matter with you?"

"I was thinking—I am sorry."

"Where's Gil?" he asked suddenly, looking round. "Hasn't he come?"

"Yes—but he has gone again. He comes back tomorrow."

"Where on earth has he gone?"

"Back to Lisbon, to see Colonel Marques."

"Who's he?"

"The Head of the Security Police—we spoke of him yesterday."

"Oh, he wants to consult him about Mrs. Atherley's Spaniards, I suppose."

"Yes. Such matters must be arranged through him."

"Well they'd better hurry—the wine will be run off tomorrow, your Father thinks, and then the ranchos will have their famous dinner of roast *peru*, and all clear off. So if Gil and the police want to catch these types, tomorrow is about their last chance."

"I wish I had known this!" the girl exclaimed, looking worried. "Gil should know it."

"Can't you ring him up? I wonder he didn't ring up this Colonel person, instead of dashing back to Lisbon. No, I suppose he was afraid of the line being bugged."

"What is this, bugged? Do you mean tapped?"

"Yes—it's the Yank word for it."

"Well, I shall telephone him tonight. But now, listen, Nick. Gil thinks Hetta is really in danger; he says she is never to be outside the house alone. You can help with this."

"Does she know?"

"I do not think she fully realises, and it is better that she should not, because of the baby—another is coming. This afternoon, if she wants to walk, you go with her."

"What shall you do?"

"I put our people on the alert. Yesterday I was only making enquiries, in a general sort of way; now I must tell them to keep an eye on *all* strangers, all the time."

"Who shall you tell?" Nick was interested in this.

"That is what I was thinking about, when you came in. The keepers, of course; they are everywhere—and the gardeners, and the men who mend the roads, and who work in the fields."

"What about Senhor Oliveira?"

"I think *not;* he would probably speak of it to Papa, and Gil does wish this."

"Why on earth not? I should have thought the Duke was almost the first person to be told."

"I imagine for fear he should take some action at once. If

agents are left at large, and unsuspecting, one may learn more."

"That seems rather rough on Hetta, if what Gil thinks is true."

"Hetta understands," the girl said; "You heard her yesterday." All the same she looked troubled.

"Well, I'll keep an eye on her, darling. Give me a kiss—I haven't had one since yesterday!"

The Duke was rather surprised, at lunch, by Gil de Castelo Branco's absence, but accepted Luzia's explanation that he had been telephoned for. In fact he was so absorbed in his wine-making during these last crucial hours, that he had little attention to spare for anything else; he did however ask Luzia if she had told Gil to bring his gun with him when he came back?"

"Oh no, I forgot—I am sorry."

"Telephone to him, then."

Luzia promised, glad of the excuse for making the call. But she failed to get hold of Gil, either at the office or at his home; and though she left messages that he was to ring her back, he did not do so. (Colonel Marques' special number was of course not listed in the directory.) She went to bed frustrated.

Next morning the Duke dragged Nick down to the *adega* to see the running-off of the wine; a messenger had been sent up by Senhor Oliveira at 8 A.M. to say that in his opinion it was ready in two of the *lagares* at least: temperature, saccharinity —all correct. Neither Hetta nor Luzia accepted his urgent invitations to go too, sent to their rooms by maid-servants; Luzia professed that with guests coming tomorrow she must arrange the flowers; actually she wanted to see Gil at the first possible moment, or at least to be in if he did telephone—Hetta pleaded fatigue. But that young man did not arrive till after lunch was over—he said he had eaten on the way, but accepted coffee. Nick and his host had already gone off again, to Luzia's relief, for Gil was able to explain his delay. Marques had been out all the afternoon and evening, so he had waited in the Bureau of the Security Police; by the time he had had his interview it was too late to telephone. But the Colonel had sent a rather senior officer up to São Pedro do Sul with him, who had alerted the Chief of Police there, with instructions that all the local policemen were to be on the look-out for any strangers, and to report their movements and whereabouts immediately; but not to act without instructions, and if possible to avoid arousing the suspicions of their quarry.

"That will not be easy," Luzia observed. "Where is he now, this official?"

"He stays at São Pedro—at the *policia,* I imagine."

"He should come at once to the *adega,* and see these men for himself," the girl said.

"What good would that do?" Gil objected. "Plenty of people know their faces already—Senhor Oliveira, and Hetta, and these women who cook for the ranchos, and old Fernando; if it is thought wise to arrest them, they can easily be identified. I think we should let the Security Police deal with the matter in their own way; to bring a strange person to the *adega* might merely put them on their guard, or frighten them off."

"Well, now I shall go out and do my part, anyhow," Luzia said—she felt that the morning had been wasted, waiting for Gil and his telephone call. She went upstairs and fetched a hat, and looked in on Hetta, who was in the nursery with Richenda—it was the Swiss Nannie's afternoon out.

"No, I should not take her out," she said firmly to her guest —"It is rather hot. When it gets cooler, after tea, we can take her into the knott-garden together—I shall be back by then." Easy in her mind on this score, she set out on her rounds.

As things turned out, even if the official from Lisbon had been brought to the *adega* it would not have profited him. When Nick and his host came in for tea they reported that the running-off of the wine was practically completed; the famous *perus* were already being roasted, and they were going back to attend the ranchos' feast—dinner was to be half-an-hour later, the Duke told Elidio. "If you will excuse us, for this once we will not dress," he said to Hetta and his daughter. Gil went with them when they returned to the *adega*, hoping to see the supposed agents himself, but in this he was disappointed. The ranchos were paid off before they had their grand meal; after it the Duke always took a formal farewell of them, shaking each one by the hand, thanking them for their help, and expressing the hope of seeing them again next year. But on this occasion there were three empty places at the long table; the Spaniards, Senhor Oliveira said, had taken their money and gone, saying that they had a long journey before them. The Duke was slightly vexed; Gil and Nick exchanged glances at this behaviour, which increased their suspicions. Gil asked Senhor Oliveira where the Spanish ranchos had gone?

"But back to Spain, where they came from, one supposes," the bailiff said.

"I hope to God they have," Nick muttered fervently in Gil's ear.

WITH THE ARRIVAL of Richard Atherley and the Ambassador on the Saturday, the Duke's preoccupation switched from wine to partridges; the former was made to his satisfaction, and with his head-keeper he was constantly out and about, deciding on which part of the estate the birds were most numerous, where the guns should stand—partridges are driven in Portugal—and which of the peasants should be enrolled as beaters. But Sir Noël, fond as he was of shooting, could at first spare little attention from Gralheira itself—the pictures, the polychrome sculptures, the astonishing array of Chippendale furniture.

"Really, this house is quite fantastic, Richard," he said on the Sunday morning, after his Counsellor had shown him the chapel upstairs, which was even fuller of treasures than the rest of the house. "Have you seen the carpet in my bedroom? I must know what it is; I've never seen one like it—all blues and yellows, absolutely exquisite."

"An Arraiolos, I expect," Richard said, following him along a corridor.

"Now which way do I go? Oh ah; there is the cabinet with the *blanc de chine*—that's my landmark," his chief said. "This place is like the maze at Hampton Court!" It having been established that the bedroom carpet was an Arraiolos, old, deep, soft, and beautiful in its faded tones, they went downstairs again. Sir Noël was as delighted with his host as with the house, and said as much as they strolled out into the knott-garden—"He really is a *complete* charmer. No wonder Luzia is so bewitching. I approve of her young man, too—I hope the old gentleman is pleased about it."

"I think he is, and with good reason." The Duke had told Richard the evening before of Nick's enthusiasm about the vintage, his efforts to speak Portuguese, and his own sense that the young man would really, in time, be able to "run" Gralheira; he passed some of this on.

"Yes, that all sounds very good; a place like this must be a fearful responsibility," Sir Noël said. He turned and looked back at the grey baroque front of the house. "It must be prac-tically half the size of Versailles!—keeping up the fabric alone would be ruinous, in any other climate."

At that moment Luzia and Nick emerged from the morning-room; they both looked very happy and animated. Luzia went straight up to the two diplomats.

"Sir Noël, how do you like my engagement-ring?" She held out her hand. "It has just come."

"It's a most beautiful thing," he said, after looking at it at-tentively. "An antique, surely? And an English setting, one would have thought," he observed to Nick. "How clever of you to find it, Heriot."

"He did not! It has only come back from the jeweller in Oporto; it had to be altered, because it was too big." She re-counted the history of the ring.

"No! Well, that is really charming. It makes me more anx-ious than ever to meet your Mother," he added, turning to Nick. "I am glad I shall not have long to wait."

Gil and Hetta now came out through another of the French windows; Luzia called to them. When they came up—"Hetta, do take Sir Noël to see the fountain in the lower garden, and the *azulejo* seat which has the picture of the hunter driven up a tree by the bear," she said. "Once he gets involved with my

Father and his birds, he will have no time left to see anything!"

Hetta, a little surprised, obediently walked off with Sir Noël —Richard made as if to go with them.

"No, Richard—I want you," the girl said, with her pretty little imperious air, and led him back into the house; Gil and Nick followed. It was Richard's turn to be surprised, but he soon learned the reason for this manoeuvre. Luzia, Gil, and Nick, in conclave, had decided that de Castelo Branco was the best person to inform Atherley of the possible menace that hung over his wife, and to persuade him to fall in with the arrangements of the Security Police. "Since Gil is in External Affairs, he will have to pay attention to him," Luzia had explained to Nick; "Richard can be very stubborn, and is apt to think all Hetta's and my ideas foolish or exaggerated." Now, sitting in her morning-room, he listened to the young diplomat's report on the situation; he was uneasy, a little vexed; at the end he asked some rather probing questions.

"So no one has seen these men but my wife?"

"*Yes*, Richard." Luzia spoke impatiently. "The ranchos have seen them, Papa has seen them at the *adega*, the foreman has seen them working, and says they are not used to treading wine."

"I meant, no one had seen them watching Hetta."

"No, because this they only did when she was walking alone, which now she does no more; but old Fernando saw them spying on the house."

"In any case, Colonel Marques has given his orders, which must be carried out," de Castelo Branco said a little stiffly. "Let us hope it is a pure coincidence that three strange Spaniards should turn up just when more men were needed for the vintage; but it is essential to make sure, in view of what has happened in Spain."

"Yes, of course. Though that may not be so simple, if they have left again already. Have the police reported anything?"

"Not so far," Gil said.

"Has my wife been told that she should not go out alone?"

It was Luzia who replied.

"No—we all thought it better not to alarm her, because of the child which is coming. But we arrange that she does not—and now that you are here, this will be still more easy."

"Have the servants been told?"

"Elidio, yes; and the keepers, and the gardeners—that they should come and say at once if any strangers are seen, while others follow them, and tell the police." She turned to de Castelo Branco. "Oh, I have not yet had an opportunity to tell you—the old miller, him they call The Ferreiro, was in São Pedro do Sul yesterday evening, taking back some flour, and he saw three men at one of the very small inns, asking for a room, in bad Portuguese."

"Did he say which inn? When did you learn this?"

"Only this morning—The Ferreiro comes to Mass now in the chapel, because he is lame. But I rang up the *Policia* at once, and told the *Chefe,* and gave the street in which the inn stands. I told them to telephone to you, Gil, if they find out anything—not to leave a message, and on no account to tell Papa."

"Why, does the Duke not know about this?" Richard asked in surprise.

"No—both Subercaseaux and Colonel Marques thought it better not."

"Subercaseaux? How does he come into it?"

Luzia was beginning to explain when Elidio appeared to say that one asked for the Senhor Gil on the telephone; the others waited impatiently for his return.

"Yes, they stayed there, all three of them: one with grey hair, one with moustaches, one rather small—but they had left by the time the police arrived. The inn-keeper thought they were returning to Spain."

"Pretty hopeless," Atherley commented gloomily.

"The frontier-police have been alerted—they will look out for them."

"Yes, but that is only on the roads," Luzia said; "there are miles of open country between where anyone can cross without being seen."

Richard decided that he had better let British Intelligence in Madrid know what was going on at Gralheira, and went and used the telephone outside the pantry. When he got Ainsworth he began by saying that he was now "staying in the same house as my wife".

"Oh yes. Anything more been seen of the three amateur wine-treaders?" Ainsworth enquired breezily, to his astonishment.

"How on earth did you hear about them?"

"Oh, an old ecclesiastic got word to our indigenous colleagues; it seems he'd been in touch with your Missis, and he asked them to let us know, and you too. I expect you know who I mean—I gathered he was a pal of yours."

"Yes, I know him."

"Well, what goes on?"

"Nothing, at the moment; they've cleared off, but no one knows where to. The frontier is being watched."

"That means nothing, in your part of the world. Have the flatties on the spot been notified?"

"Yes."

"Good. They'd better keep a sharp look-out, because three of the people our Spanish friends rather suspected of being mixed up in that car performance, and were trying to keep an eye on, disappeared ten days or a fortnight ago. That just about fits, doesn't it?"

It did—and Richard returned to Luzia's morning-room with the last remains of his normal incredulity uncomfortably shattered. Gil was pleased to learn that the Spanish Security Police were also on the job, and expressed his intention of driving in to São Pedro do Sul the moment after lunch to inform the Chief of Police there, as well as Colonel Marques' emissary, of the fact that three Spanish suspects had disappeared from Madrid at just about the appropriate moment.

Apart from that, they all agreed rather gloomily that there seemed nothing more to be done, except to keep Hetta under constant watch.

"Yes, let her know that we all think she should not go out alone at *all*," Luzia said firmly to Atherley. "But do *not*, Richard, tell her about these men being missing in Spain. There are her nerves and her health to consider."

The arrival of Lord and Lady Heriot in time for a late tea created a diversion from these worrying preoccupations, and induced a more cheerful atmosphere. The Duke was surprised —and pleased—at the degree of intimacy and affection obviously already existing between Luzia and her prospective parents-in-law. He realised that she had stayed with them, and was fond of them, but he was quite unprepared for Lady Heriot's "Well, my dearest child, *how* happy I am!" as she enfolded the girl in a warm embrace—still less to hear Lord Heriot say "Well, Luzia, now I suppose I am entitled to kiss you too!" as he did so. Luzia, blushing a little, thanked Lady Heriot for her engagement-ring, holding it out to be admired; the old lady pushed it about on her finger.

"I was afraid it would be far too big," she remarked.

"Oh, it was; Nick would not let me wear it till it had been altered. This was so very good of you, Bonne-Mama."

"Oh, is that what you're going to call her?" Lord Heriot asked.

"Yes—Nick and I thought it would be nicest."

"I like that—it's pretty. And what am I to be? Bon-papa?" Luzia looked at him with mock archness.

"Would not Beau-père be more flattering? Also it has a nicer sound."

While Lord Heriot laughingly settled for Beau-père, Nick turned to the Duke.

"So long as you don't wish to call me your gender, Sir," he said hopefully.

Then there were more introductions: the Ambassador, the

Atherleys, Gil. After tea the men all repaired to the gun-room, where their weapons were laid out on a huge table—João, the head-keeper, was busily polishing them afresh. A gun was found for Gil, and their host explained the arrangements to Lord Heriot and the Ambassador.

"We do not use loaders here," he said rather apologetically; "our country-people are not very good at it. Of course there will be a young keeper with you, who will carry your gun if you wish."

Both his principal guests politely expressed themselves satisfied. "Do we walk the birds up?" Lord Heriot asked.

"No, they are driven—after a fashion! It is all rather informal; we do not have regular butts, we stand behind walls, or any suitable piece of cover. But I hope we shall see plenty of birds."

The guns set out the following morning after an early breakfast; the women were to join them for lunch. Luzia and Hetta spent the morning showing Lady Heriot the house, Luzia again lamenting the scarcity of bathrooms.

"Personally, I prefer a sitz-bath," Lady Heriot said. "But I see that it might be convenient to have more than two bathrooms. Is there perhaps a shortage of water?" she enquired practically.

"Oh no—it is just that Papa and Tia Francisca never thought of it. But Papa has promised me that when Nick comes to live here he will put in one for him, and an extra one for our guests—who after all are of another generation, and like a real bath! I hope to persuade him also to put in some basins with running water—it would save at least two maids, when the house is full."

"Do you have any difficulty about getting servants?" Lady Heriot was still practical.

"Oh no, none at all at present—but how long this will last, one does not know. Even here, the young men begin to wish to go to work in the towns. That is why I hope that presently

Papa will accept Nick's idea of having one or two small factories on the estate to use up the resin—that would encourage them to live at home."

"Does your Father not like the idea, then?"

"Oh, Nick has not put it to him yet. He wishes first to learn all about the things that are already done here, like the wine-making, before he suggests any plan of his own."

"Very right," Nick's Mother said. "But don't let him be *too* modest, my dear; if Nick has a fault, it is lack of self-confidence."

"A pessimist, as he says himself!" Luzia replied, laughing. "Yes, I will keep an eye on that, Bonne-Mama."

However "informal" the butts at Gralheira might be, there was no lack of birds; and both the Ambassador and Lord Heriot, after a life-time of shooting-lunches, were startled by the one which succeeded an excellent morning's sport, when the women joined them. Their host ushered them all into a large barn-like building, almost the size of the nave of a village church in England, which with its lofty roof and bare walls it rather resembled. At one end was an open hearth at least fifteen feet across, in which the trunks of three or four young trees were burning; down both sides ran wide trestle tables, their wooden tops scrubbed till they were pale and grooved, set with gay country crockery and large china jugs of wine. At the smaller of these the shooting-party sat down, and were promptly served by four or five smiling women in bright head-scarves with a complete hot meal—soup, roast chicken, spiced baked ham with spinach, and open flans of fresh apricots. All this was brought to the table from a series of small charcoal stoves and ovens, built into the wall on both sides of the huge hearth, and kept burning by an ancient crone who went from one to another, fanning the charcoal with a palm-leaf; Lady Heriot was fascinated by this arrangement. When they were about halfway through their repast the keepers and beaters came in, very quietly and politely, and sat down at the other, much larger, table, followed by a number of farm labourers; the brightly-scarved women served them in their turn with exactly the same food.

"Oh yes," Ericeira said, in answer to a question of Sir Noël's, "this room is in use every day except Sundays. The farm-workers always come in for a hot mid-day meal—they start work early, and continue till late; this is the usual arrangement, it saves the men the fatigue of a walk home, and their wives the trouble of cooking for them. There are such places on all parts of the estate."

"How very pleasant," Sir Noël said approvingly. "No, down, boy!" to a large mastiff-like animal which approached him to beg for food—for with the men had come the dogs, and soon the room was fairly awash with them, of all shapes, breeds, and sizes. The estate gun-dogs, rather good spaniels and pointers, were fairly restrained; but those belonging to the farm-hands were extremely persistent—they swarmed round the guests, putting up muddy and insistent paws; also they smelt strongly of dog.

"May one feed them?" Hetta asked.

"Yes, by all means—throw them some bread. It is a mealtime for them too," her host said smiling.

Over coffee, which they drank out of large thick cups, Lord Heriot looked up at the timbered roof, and round him at the spotless white-washed walls, and then asked about the origin of the building.

"I imagine that it was originally a barn, from its size, and that the hearth and stoves were added when it came to be used for its present purpose."

"How long ago was that?"

"I really cannot tell you. My Father said that in his Grandfather's time it was already in use as a dining-hall, but I fancy the main structure is much older than that—and than the farm out at the back."

"Oh, is that where these pretty women live?" Lady Heriot asked.

"Yes—and at another farm close by."

"Well, it was a marvellous lunch," the Ambassador said—
"in a marvellous setting."

They lingered over their coffee while the keepers and
beaters finished their meal; then they set out again. This time
the women walked with them: Lady Heriot with the Duke,
Nick with Luzia—the girl politely offered to accompany his
Father, but he waved her aside—"You go with Nick, and spot
for him. If I feel lonely I may get one of these girls to come
with me!" he said laughing. The Ambassador had firmly
nobbled Hetta, so Gil and Lord Heriot were alone, except for
the keepers who accompanied each member of the party. Luzia
was in fact eager to see how Nick would acquit himself.

"Splendid lot of birds your Father has here," he said as they
walked across the fields to the first stand. "Very strong on the
wing, too."

"Did you get plenty this morning?"

"Only two brace—I'm not on my day. Anyhow I'm never all
that hot. Your Father's a marvellous shot, and so is the
Amb—an absolute nailer. I don't think he missed a single bird
this morning, and some of them were quite difficult."

The Ambassador's conversation with Hetta began on rather
different lines.

"I *am* grateful to you for all this," he said. "I've been longing to see this place for years, but I don't suppose I should
ever have got here, but for you."

"It was not I—it was Luzia who arranged it."

"Yes, and who had Luzia to stay in Madrid? In any case, I
can see for myself the sort of position that you and Richard
have in this house; without your backing I doubt if the child
would have brought it off alone—insisting on having a strange
Ambassador to stay, on her *ipse dixit!* Do you see her doing
it?"

Hetta laughed. "No, I do not, quite. Obviously your being
Richard's chief made it easier."

"Well, anyhow you have my grateful thanks. That wonderful house!—it's a privilege to stay in such a place; and its owner matches it."

"Yes, he is a very splendid person," Hetta said warmly.

"I'm so glad, for his sake, that precious Luzia has got hold of such an excellent young man," Sir Noël went on. "He will really do his duty by the place, I feel sure—and he's such a nice creature. Of course he could hardly fail to be that, seeing the sort of stable he comes out of."

"Stable?" Even after her years of marriage, an English idiom could occasionally defeat Hetta.

"His parents, I mean. Not only the best possible style, but such an *original* quality. What could be more delightful than that business of the ring, betrothing generation after generation of Heriots?"

"Yes, that is really pretty," Hetta assented happily. "I think they are both quite darling."

"As for the shooting, it's even better than I'd been told. The Duke is very lucky to have got that fellow João; he arranges the drives marvellously—always some sort of obstacle out in front. Usually it's almost impossible to make these Frenchmen get up."

"But what Frenchmen? Here are only Portuguese," said Hetta, again quite at sea.

"The birds, my dear. These are French partridges, the worst possible creatures to drive. But that crafty old boy and João between them always so contrive their stands that one gets some excellent shooting. You'll see. Ah, here we are," as they came up with their host—he and their keeper disposed them in their allotted positions, and after a pause the first drive began. Hetta, amused, did see that the French partridges, driven towards a grove of olives well out in front, rose high and strong on the wing; she watched with satisfaction Sir Noël's skill, as bird after bird dropped to his gun. "*Ai Jesush!*" exclaimed the young keeper, unable to contain his enthusiasm, when after re-loading the Ambassador swung round to catch a bird far out behind; the spaniel he held strained at the leash, whining with excitement. There followed fulfilment for the dog when, at last released, he raced off to retrieve the birds.

"Tell that boy, if you can, that there's another further away to the right—I can't make him understand," Sir Noël said; Hetta obligingly called out *"Mais um; Mais a direito."* When the dog and the keeper returned with the birds—*"Minha Senhora,* six! And not one wounded!" the young man exclaimed to Hetta.

The next three drives were equally pleasant. A shooting-brake was always at hand on some convenient track to drive anyone who wished from one stand to the next; but except for the old Heriots most of the company preferred to walk, over the stiff tussocky grass, now pale and dry at summer's end, or the strips of rough broken ground from which the maize had recently been removed. It was rolling open country for the most part, with here and there outcrops of rocky bluff, sometimes bare, sometimes bush-covered, or straggling groves of olives—some young, and pale of foliage, others of ancient trees with hollow trunks and boughs which writhed in all directions like the arms of an octopus. At the fifth stand the Duke put the Ambassador at the extreme right-hand end of the line, not usually considered a very favourable place.

"They come particularly high out here, to clear that small hill behind you," he explained—"Paolo assures me that however wide they fly, you will hit them all the same! And there will be one or two beaters as a stop, in any case. I am putting Lord Heriot next to you, and then Gil—poor boy, I want him to have some easy shots; I shall be next to him, and shall leave him all I decently can!"

"Where will Richard be?" Hetta wanted to know.

"Right out on the left—he is shooting beautifully, so he can have some of the wide birds, this time."

When the Duke had gone down the line to post his other guests Sir Noël took stock of his situation. First he turned round to examine the hillock which was to afford him the high shots. It was some fifty yards behind where they stood, densely covered with a growth of bushes; in front of them was a stone wall, of a comfortable height on which to lean; beyond this the ground sloped away to a straggling grove of young olive-trees. They could see Lord Heriot away to their left, also behind the wall; João, who spoke a little French, had been allotted to him. It was very pleasant there, leaning on the wall; the sun was warm on their backs, the stone warm under their arms.

"How peaceful it is," the Ambassador said; he settled some cartridges conveniently in his pockets, loaded his twelve-bore, and awaited the birds in the peculiar tension that always accompanies a drive, scanning the ground in front of him for the slightest sign of any movement. Presently a distant sound of tapping became audible—the beaters had entered the olive-grove. Nearer and nearer the sounds came; now, through the spindly trees, they could catch a glimpse of moving figures, and then, on their left, a bird came over—Lord Heriot's shot rang out, and down it came. Now the birds came fast, and right over them, high, as promised; Sir Noël got a left and right, the spaniel began to whine, and there was a perfect fusillade of shots from all down the line. Hetta had moved a couple of yards away from her companion, to give him ample room; suddenly, while he was re-loading, she gave a little cry, and put her hand up to her face.

"What is it, my dear?" Sir Noël asked, surprised.

"Something hit me," she said, getting out a handkerchief; blood was beginning to run down her face from a wound near her eyebrow.

"Impossible!" the man exclaimed—the olive-trees in front of them were much too far away for a ricochet to have been possible.

But Paolo, standing a little behind them, had seen enough to guess what had happened, after Luzia's warnings. He shouted something to João, unleashed the spaniel, and began to run towards the bush-covered hillock to their rear; the head-keeper, also loosing his dog, followed him, shouting to the nearest beaters as he ran. As Sir Noël, bewildered, put down his gun and bent over Hetta, who was now sitting on the ground, something hit the wall close to his head with a sharp "ping"—bits of stone flew out close to his face.

"Good God! That was a rifle-shot!" he exclaimed. "Keep down, Hetta."

But Hetta, on the contrary, sat bolt upright, and began to look about her; she saw João and Paolo disappear into the bushes at the foot of the hillock.

"What on earth can be happening?" the man asked in astonishment.

"It will be the Spaniards—they must have stayed here after all," she replied, not enlightening Sir Noël very much.

That was practically the end of the drive, as far as that part of the line was concerned; the nearer beaters, in response to João's shouts, were running towards the small bushy hill, from which came sounds of shouting and barking; the partridges, left to themselves, took to the ground and crept back through the olives. The Duke, looking angry, strode up to Lord Heriot, who had been methodically dropping every bird that came anywhere near him, and asked where João was?

"No idea. What's happened to the beaters?" the old gentleman enquired.

"This I also should like to know," his host said.

"The fellow's taken the dog, too. There are at least three-and-a-half brace out in front."

"They will be got later." He walked quickly on, but stopped short at the sight of Hetta Atherley, bleeding profusely from a wound in her face.

"How can this have happened?" he asked Sir Noël sharply.

"Someone was shooting at us with a rifle from behind, by the look of it," the Ambassador replied. "Here are the marks,"—he pointed to two white patches on the weatherworn stones of the wall. Ericeira in his turn looked back towards the small hill, just in time to see João and some of the beaters emerge from the bushes, holding a struggling man in their grasp; Paolo followed carrying a rifle. The Duke started towards them—then turned back to his wounded guest.

"Excellency, Mrs. Atherley ought to be got back to the house—can you take her? The shooting-brake is just beyond that field, only about one hundred yards away. I ought really to go and see about this. Can she walk?"

"Yes, I can walk; it is nothing," Hetta said briskly—she stood up as she spoke, and also looked towards the group at the foot of the little hill. "Oh, Paolo has the rifle—good. But have they only got one of them?"

While both men stared at her in astonishment at this question, Gil came running up.

"What has happened? Is Madame Atherley hurt?"

"Someone shot at us with a rifle," the Ambassador repeated, rather stiffly.

"No! So they got her after all!" the young man exclaimed.

"Gil, what does this mean?" Ericeira asked his nephew, in angry bewilderment. "Who are 'they', if you please?"

"Those Spaniards," Hetta said. "Gil, you will have to tell your Uncle all about it, now."

"So I should indeed hope!" Ericeira said sternly. "Excellency, will you see that Mrs. Atherley is taken back to the house at once, and the doctor sent for? I apologise profoundly for this episode, about which many people seem to be better informed than myself! Gil, come with me." He walked off towards the keepers and their prisoner.

"Hullo, what goes on here?" Lord Heriot asked, strolling up—since there were no more birds to shoot at, he had left his stance. "I say, that ought to be tied up," he went on, looking at Hetta's face; her small handkerchief was by now so soaked with blood as to be useless—he took a large clean one from an inner pocket, folded it neatly, and tied it round her head. "Now, we'd better get her home," he said to Sir Noël. "Any idea where that shooting-brake is?"

The next arrivals were Luzia, Nick, and Lady Heriot, who when her host suddenly abandoned her had stood calmly watching Nick's shooting, away on her left. But the infection of some excitement spread down among the beaters, who in turns abandoned their proper task and followed their companions; Nick and Luzia, also left with nothing to shoot, and seeing men running, hurried along the wall to learn what all the fuss was about. When Luzia caught sight of the little group round Mrs. Atherley she left Nick to escort his Mother, and ran like the wind, full of foreboding.

"Oh Hetta, no! So after all!" she exclaimed. "Is it much? Let me see."

"It is nothing," and "No, don't touch it," Hetta and Lord Heriot said simultaneously. "Let's get her home, and let a doctor look at it," he went on. "Where's that shooting-brake?"

"Just across that field—on the track. Yes, she should go home." Then she caught sight of João and his captive. "Oh, how many of them have they got?" In the increasing crowd of keepers and beaters it was hard to see clearly what was going on at the foot of the hillock.

"Only one, I think," Hetta said. "But Gil and your Father are there."

"Oh, so they are. Yes, let us go. I will go and get the brake ready"—and off she ran.

"Well, let's get a move on," Lord Heriot said impatiently.

"Someone should find Richard," Richard's wife said, starting across the field on Sir Noël's proffered arm.

"Nick can do that," Lady Heriot observed. "Tell him we're going home, Nick—but don't frighten him," she added, in a lowered voice.

As the Heriots followed Hetta and her companion—"What happened?" Lady Heriot asked her husband, in an undertone. "Did the Ambassador shoot her by mistake?"

"He *said* someone shot at them with a rifle. Anyhow, all the keepers and beaters knocked off, and spoilt one of the best drives I've ever had! That young Gil fellow seemed to have been expecting something of the sort—he said, "So they got her after all!" when he heard about the rifle. Funny sort of party! I suppose we shall hear all about it some time."

When they reached the shooting-brake they saw why Luzia had raced on ahead: the side of the track on which it stood was heaped with the feathered bodies of partridges, which she and the driver had pulled out; the man was now replacing the back seat, which had been folded down to make room for the birds.

"Marvellous bag!" Lord Heriot commented.

"I think Mrs. Atherley had better sit in front," Luzia said—"it smells a little in there. Bonne-Mama, shall you mind? And Beau-père? Sir Noël, do you come with us?"

"Thank you, I think I'll join your Father, and walk home —if you will be all right?" Lord Heriot also opted for this course; in fact he wanted to make sure that his last three-and-a-half brace were picked up, and also to learn the facts about this highly peculiar episode.

"Then I think we should not wait for Richard. Sir Noël, will you tell him that we have taken Hetta home?—and that I shall get the doctor at once?"

"Of course."

"Tell him that it is nothing—I am quite all right," Hetta called as the shooting-brake drove off.

10

BACK AT THE HOUSE, Luzia ran first of all to her Father's study, and telephoned to São Pedro do Sul for the doctor. He was in, and promised to drive over at once; all the girl told him was that there had been "an accident, out shooting"— but he laid it on her urgently that the wound should on no account be touched till he arrived. So still wearing Lord Heriot's handkerchief Hetta was taken up to her room, and persuaded to lie down; tea was brought, and she and Luzia and Lady Heriot all sipped it thankfully, and ate small sand-wiches. Lady Heriot was of course full of curiosity as to what lay behind the incident, but both the young women were too security-minded to tell her much; to her one cautious question Luzia said—"I think perhaps Hetta should not talk too much, Bonne-Mama," which gave the good lady a reluctantly admir-ing respect for her prospective daughter-in-law.

Then the doctor came, and demanded small bowls, boiling water, and all the old-fashioned accessories to an examination; the huge marble wash-stand was cleared of half its cumber-some double set of basins and ewers, maids came flying with a kettle, bowls, towels and napkins—having prepared himself and his instruments, the doctor made Hetta sit in a chair under the window, and began his examination. The bleeding had stopped, but began again when he put a probe into the wound; Lady Heriot knelt beside Hetta and held her hands in a firm, reassuring grasp.

"There is something in it," the man said; he had laid his instruments out on a towel on a small table, and now took up a pair of forceps.

"Condesa, tell the Senhora that this may hurt a little," he said; Lady Heriot guessed his meaning, and tightened her grasp of Hetta's hands. But Hetta sat unflinching while he felt in the wound, and drew out a small object about half the size of a pea, which he dropped into a bowl of water; then he bathed the place, and put on an antiseptic dressing.

"It should really have two stitches," he murmured to Luzia, as he washed his hands.

"For this the Senhora must have a local anaesthetic; she is expecting a child," Luzia replied firmly—all this in Portuguese, in low tones.

"How soon?"

"In about five months."

"So—then she had better have one." He hunted in his bag. "No, perdition!—I have not brought the stuff. I shall have to go back and fetch it."

"Could the chauffeur bring it, if you told him where to find it?"

"No, for I cannot tell him! It should have been with me," he said, vexed. "I go." But first he turned to the bowl in which he had dropped the thing which he had taken out of the wound. "I must see what this is," he said; poking about in the pink-tinged water, he drew out the small object with his forceps, laid it on the towel, and examined it carefully. "It is not a shot!" he exclaimed in surprise. "It looks more like a piece of stone, or mortar."

"It *is* stone," Hetta put in. "I was standing near a wall, and the shot struck the stone, and the piece must have flown out."

"But this is most extraordinary! One would not have thought the pellet from a shot-gun would have had the power—and to cause so deep a wound."

· 149 ·

Luzia of course had not yet had many details as to what had happened; she had arrived on the scene too late to hear the Ambassador's reiterated remarks about the rifle. But she realised that Hetta's assailant would certainly have had a more powerful weapon than a shot-gun, and moreover scented danger in any undue curiosity on the local doctor's part.

"Dr. Mendes, should you not fetch the anaesthetic at once, so that the Senhora can have the stitches put in, and then be free to rest undisturbed?"

"Yes, Condesa; you are right. I will leave all this till I return—and I will also bring a sedative with me." But he turned back once more to the fragment of stone on the white linen. "I do not understand it," he said, in a dissatisfied tone, as he left the room.

A moment or so later Richard hurried in.

"Darling, are you all right?" Then he caught sight of all the medical litter strewn about the room—"Goodness, what has been going on?" he asked in dismay.

"The doctor has dressed the place—he will be back soon, to do a little more." As she spoke Luzia took up the morsel of stone, wrapped it in cotton-wool, and put it in an envelope off the rack on the writing-table.

"Are the others back?" Lady Heriot asked.

"They will be in a minute—the Duke sent for the Land-rover. I cut across the fields, to save time."

"Then I think I will go down and wait for them." Tactfully, she removed herself.

"Where is the man?" Hetta asked.

"Coming back in the shooting-brake, with the rest of the bag!" Richard said, with a wry grin.

"Did they get only the one?"

"It seems so. They beat all through the cover on that little hill, but there was no trace of anyone else. He might have got away too, but for the couple of beaters that João had put as stops for the birds—they turned him back, and then the dogs found him." He turned to look at the bandage on his wife's head. "Darling, does it hurt much? Will it leave a scar? I wish I could see it."

"It is only a tiny place," Luzia replied for Hetta. "You will see it when Dr. Mendes comes back. Richard, can you help me with something?"

"Yes—what?" He spoke a little impatiently.

"I want this big basin carried out into the corridor; it is in the way on the floor. I will take the jug." She opened the door as she spoke.

"I should have thought the maids could do that," he said, still impatient, nevertheless doing as he was told. "Gosh, it is a weight!"

Out in the corridor—"She must have two stitches put in," the girl said. "The doctor had not brought the local anaesthetic, so he has gone to fetch it—she must have this, because of the child; it can be very painful, without. But I have not told her—I did not wish her to wait, expecting it."

"Quite right," he said—"Good girl!"

Back in the bedroom, Richard looked at his watch.

"I hope this doctor won't be too long," he said. "Your father will want to see you when he gets in, Luzia."

"Is Papa very angry?" she asked, calmly.

"Well, he isn't best pleased at having been kept in the dark—I don't think I should be, in his place. Anyhow he means to hold a regular inquest into it all!" Atherley said, grinning again.

"Oh well, we only did what Colonel Marques wished—perhaps a little in advance! And the Monsignor was of that opinion from the start," Luzia said, quite untroubled.

The doctor returned fairly promptly, gave the local anaesthetic, and put in two stitches; Richard was relieved to see that the wound was indeed quite small, just outside the eye, below the eyebrow. "That will hardly show at all," he said. "But what a God's mercy it missed the eye!"

"Yes indeed, Senhor; the Senhora was very fortunate. But I

am puzzled about this piece of stone in the wound"—he went to look for it. "It is gone!" he said.

"Yes—did you want it?" Luzia asked. "I threw it away."

"That is a pity." He turned to Hetta. "Senhora, were there cattle in the field where you stood? Or horses?"

"No," Hetta replied, puzzled. Luzia however guessed what he was thinking of—like many continentals, she was thoroughly tetanus-minded.

"There have been no cattle in that field for at least seven years," she pronounced. "Maize is grown there, and lucerne, in some seasons." She asked him then if he wished to sterilise his instruments before he left? But he said he would do them at home, bundled them together in a polythene bag, gave Hetta some sedative tablets, and took his departure. "I will look in tomorrow," he remarked, as he left. Luzia rang for a maid, had all the bowls and towels put on an empty shelf in one of the twin cupboards under that vast Victorian wash-stand, and having settled her friend comfortably on the sofa—Mrs. Atherley refused to go to bed—went off to her own room to wash her hands and tidy her hair before she went down to face her Father. "Be sure to send for me if he wants me," Hetta called after her as she left the room.

The Duke held his "inquest" in his study, over whisky for his guests; as Luzia went downstairs she encountered Elidio, who told her that the Senhor Duque required her presence. In the hall was also João, sitting on a marquetry chair; he rose as she came down.

"Where is *esto homem* now?" the girl asked him.

"In an empty shed in the back court-yard, *Minha Condesa* —locked in! We searched him, but found nothing but some spare cartridges in his pocket—no papers."

"*Pena* that we did not get the others," Luzia said. "Is he one of those who trod the wine?"

"The Senhor Oliveira will know that," the man replied. "He has been sent for; he is gone to the Romaria at São Zefirimo."

"Ah yes—his wife comes from there," Luzia said, as usual familiar with the affairs of all the employees about the place. She went on into the study; the five men rose as she entered— her Father from the upright chair behind his desk, Gil, Richard Atherley, Nick, and the Ambassador from deep leather ones disposed about the room.

"How is Mrs. Atherley?" the Duke asked at once, waving her to a seat.

"Tired, a little—she is resting. But she is not in pain; she said I was to tell you that if you wish to see her she is perfectly able to come down."

"That is very good of her, but I hope it will not be necessary. I gather that you, and Gil here, know as much as anyone about what lies behind this deplorable incident, which was, it seems, not unexpected by either of you; so perhaps you will both now explain why I was not informed in advance, so that proper precautions could have been taken." He bent his bushy grey eyebrows, over the deep-set grey eyes, sternly on her and her cousin as he spoke; Gil looked uncomfortable, as well he might.

"I hope we can satisfy you, Papa," the girl said, respectfully, but cheerfully—"though we do not yet know as much as we ourselves could wish. By the way, Gil, have you told this officer from the Security Police what has happened?—and that we have the man here?"

De Castelo Branco, looking more uncomfortable than ever, said that he hadn't.

"But surely this ought to be done at once. If you ring up the *policia* they will inform him. Papa, could you excuse Gil while he does this?"

"What man from the Security Police? How do they come into it?" Ericeira asked in surprise.

"Colonel Marques sent him up to São Pedro do Sul to keep an eye on these men who were watching Hetta, and try to find out if they were agents from Spain; he did not wish them to be alarmed, or arrested, till he had learned more."

"But how did Colonel Marques know about them?—he has not been here himself."

"Gil went back to Lisbon on purpose to tell him, when he had heard Hetta's account of the odd way they were behaving; it was too long and too confidential to be explained on the telephone—but especially after the episode at Toledo, it seemed to the Colonel possibly very important."

"What episode at Toledo? Is this something else of which I have not been told?"

To Luzia's relief, the Ambassador here took a hand.

"Duke, I am partly responsible for Mrs. Atherley's and your daughter's silence about that," he said. "Might I explain?"

"I should be infinitely obliged if you would," the Duke said, looking surprised and also slightly relieved. "I seem in need of all the explanations I can get."

"Thank you. But Luzia is right—your nephew should telephone to the police at once, if there is any possible connection between the man you hold here, and that incident."

"There seems every reason to believe that there is the closest possible connection," Atherley put in. His host swung round on him in surprise; the Ambassador too looked startled.

"Not really?" he said.

"Yes; I was speaking to Ainsworth yesterday, and three of the Spanish suspects disappeared from Madrid about twelve days ago, just when those men first showed up here." He turned to Ericeira. "Excuse me for butting in, Duke. But the police should really be informed immediately."

"Then go and telephone, Gil," the Duke said resignedly. As the young man, thankfully, escaped, he turned to Sir Noël. "Now, Exellency, I am all attention."

Diplomats do not spend much of their lives drafting memoranda for nothing; they are rigidly trained in the discipline of brief and lucid exposition. Richard Atherley listened with professional relish while his chief recounted to their host what had happened at Toledo—skilfully outlining the political importance of Admiral Luxworthy's Spanish visit—before he went on to Hetta's suspicions of the Hungarian chauffeur, and the attempt at assassination which she had, half-accidentally, foiled; the Duke listened too, in fascinated horror. At the end —"But though the chauffeur had been deported, and his Hungarian associates rounded up, both the Spanish Security Police, and our own Intelligence in Madrid, were anxious to have the whole thing kept as quiet as possible, since obviously the Hungarian agents were not working *in vacuo,* but must have been part of a Spanish Communist cell, or ring. So both your daughter, and Mrs. Atherley, were urged to say nothing about what happened at Toledo, except that Mrs. Atherley had broken her wrist in a car accident—which was strictly true. This was an official decision, since it was hoped to learn more."

"*Suppressio veri,* with only a hint of *suggestio falsi!*" the Duke said, smiling a very little. "Thank you, Excellency; I am most grateful to you. I see a little more light—of a rather lurid sort!" He was not completely mollified, however. He turned to his daughter. "But when suspicious characters appeared *here,* on my own estate—surely there could be no embargo on your mentioning at least that fact to me? Menacing one of my own guests! I still wish to know why you did not."

"Well, to begin with, they did not actually menace Hetta; they merely behaved oddly, peering at her, and hiding afterwards. She herself did not wish anything said, for fear she might be mistaken, and cause innocent people to be falsely accused; indeed she did not mention it even to me, until the Monsignor said that she must, and Gil should be sent for at once."

"The Monsignor?—Subercaseaux?"

"Yes, she consulted him that day when we went over to Sta Maria da Trapa."

"Still, he can hardly have hold her that I was not to be informed," Ericeira said rather stiffly. Luzia blushed.

"Oh darling Papa, he did say precisely that!" she exclaimed, with the strangest mixture of mirth and apology in her voice.

"He was actually emphatic that only Gil and Colonel Marques should be told, while the men were still here, treading the wine."

"*These* men trod the wine? Communists?" He looked horrified.

"Yes, these three Spanish-speakers, whom Senhor Oliveira took on when the vintage was so huge, and he had not enough ranchos; Hetta recognised them at the *adega,* the night we all went down."

The Ambassador could hardly refrain from smiling at his host's expression of dismay and disgust at this revelation—his good wine trodden by Communist feet!

"I am surprised that Subercaseaux should have given such advice," he said at length. "Treading the wine!" he repeated. "And no warning given; no precautions taken—it seems to me strangely irresponsible behaviour on the Monsignor's part."

"No, Papa, he was not irresponsible—one must be fair to him, even if he is such an old fox! He insisted that Gil should come at once, and inform Colonel Marques and the P.I.D.E.; and he also said that all our people must be told to keep a watch on these persons, and report if they behaved suspiciously."

"And who was to give these instructions, may I ask?"

"*I* was—and I did," the girl said firmly. Then, at something in her Father's expression, her own face altered. "Oh, Papa, *darling,* do not look so!"

It was perhaps as well that at that precise moment Gil reappeared, with the tidings that the official from the Security Police was out, but would come to Gralheira as soon as he could be found. The Duke looked at his watch, then asked the Ambassador if he would have any objection to dining a little earlier?—"Then, with good fortune, we may get our meal undisturbed." Sir Noël of course agreed; Elidio was rung for, and told to advance dinner, and to see that João was given a meal in the kitchen. "And you, my child, see to it that the

Heriots are told at once, so that they are not too much hurried."

"Yes, Papa." She gave him an eager penitent kiss before she sped away.

Hetta insisted on coming down to dinner, and Richard, having satisfied himself that she was really equal to it, was rather glad that she should—company, he thought innocently, would be better for her than solitary brooding on what had happened. "And you may be able to pacify the Duke a bit," he said. "He's pretty vexed with Gil and Luzia for keeping it all so dark. H.E. was splendid—he told the old boy that it was 'an official decision' that nothing should be said about the performance at Toledo. But he wasn't best pleased that the Monsignor should be in on it, when he was left out, and should actually have advised against Luzia's telling her own Father."

"*Poor* Duque! She didn't tell him that?"

"Yes—really she had to. She did frightfully well, but it was all a little awkward."

Dinner was just over when the official from the Security Police arrived, accompanied by the local *Chefe* and poor Senhor Oliveira, dragged away from his village festivities—they had overtaken him on the road, and recognising the police car, he had stopped them and begged a lift. When Elidio came to the drawing-room and announced their presence the Duke, after asking Lady Heriot and Hetta to excuse him, went to the hall, taking Gil along with him; João had been summoned from the kitchen, and they all went out to the shed where the would-be assassin had been shut up. Now the Duke had a mania for electricity everywhere, even in out-buildings; considering, rightly, that the risk of fire was less than if paraffin lamps were carried about. So when João had pulled out a large key and unlocked the door, he switched on the light—the six men stood aghast at what it revealed. The wooden table in the middle was covered with blood, so was part of the stone-flagged floor; on it, beside the chair from which he had fallen, lay their prisoner, unconscious, with blood oozing from his left wrist.

"Perdition!" the Security man exclaimed. "Now we may lose everything!" He knelt down and felt the right pulse. "A doctor, immediately!—he is not dead," he said, without getting up—"And some cloths; we must put on a tourniquet." As he spoke he rolled up the man's sleeve, and put his thumb, expertly, on the wrist above the cut; when he pressed on the artery the blood ceased to well from the wound.

There ensued some minutes of feverish activity. Elidio, who had been lurking in the yard, ran unbidden to the kitchen and despatched Antonio, his underling, to the scene of action with cloths, towels, and a wooden spoon; then he hastened to the telephone and summoned Dr. Mendes—"It is most urgent."

"Is the lady worse?" the doctor asked, alarmed.

"No, it is not she—another. The Senhor Duque desires the doctor to come without losing an instant."

"I come," said Dr. Mendes, as Elidio rang off.

In the shed the Security official, still pressing on the artery, caused the local Chief of Police to tie one cloth into a thick knot, and wrapped it in another; then, with his left hand, he placed the knot in the crook of the elbow, and bade Gil tie the cloth firmly; now he inserted the handle of the wooden spoon, and with both hands twisted it round.

"Wipe the place," he said briefly to Gil, who took up a towel and did so. "Yes, that has stopped it. Hold this steady" —he took one hand off the spoon-handle; while Gil held it he tore another cloth in half, and bound the spoon in position along the man's arm with the two pieces.

"There—that will do for the moment. Now, let us get him onto the table—and we shall need blankets." With João's help he lifted the unconscious man and laid him on the table, putting a folded towel under his head; Antonio, who had overheard the demand for blankets, hurried off in search of them.

The official wiped his hands on yet another towel, and turned to the Duke.

"This is extremely unfortunate," he said. "Who put him here?"

"My keepers." Ericeira indicated João, who was also wiping the blood off his hands and the knees of his trousers.

"Did you not search him for a weapon before you left him?" the Security man asked sharply.

"*Minho Senhor,* yes—all over, even in his shoes! Also we bound his hands," the head-keeper replied wretchedly.

"Then the cord should be here, and the weapon also. It was probably a razor-blade. Ah, here are the blankets—let us wrap him up. Lift him!" he said brusquely to the keeper and Gil; when they did so he took one blanket from Antonio and put it, folded double, on the table; the man was laid on it, and three more blankets wrapped round him. Antonio had also brought a pillow in a tartan cover, like those provided for the ranchos in their sleeping-quarters; this the official slid under the head. "He must be kept warm," he said to the Duke. "Are there any hot-water bottles available?"

"Yes, certainly." Antonio was despatched for these. "Should he be given brandy?" Ericeira asked.

"Not till the doctor comes, I think."

"Or be taken indoors?"

"No—we will move him as little as possible till the doctor has seen him."

João meanwhile had found some straw in a corner, and with a wisp was wiping away the blood on the floor. "Senhor Duque, here is the weapon!" he exclaimed, as he picked up a safety razor-blade. "And here is the cord," he went on after a moment, holding out a blood-soaked length of the loose hairy brown twine which is used on farms to tie up straw or faggots. The officer examined it; the knot was still tied.

"But this is absurd!—he had bitten through it!" he exclaimed. "Did you not tie his hands behind him?"

"No, my Senhor; in front." João's distress was pitiable to see —his master intervened.

"I regret that this should have occurred," he said, with rather stiff politeness. "Here, at Gralheira, we have little experience in dealing with criminals; also we did not expect quite so long a time to elapse before the appropriate authorities took charge of the affair. Now, is there any way in which we can help the Senhores in their enquiries?"

Yes, there was—the P.I.D.E. official wished to know if the man could be identified as having been seen before? Oliveira stepped forward—the prisoner was certainly one of the three strangers who had taken part in treading the wine; yes, he spoke Spanish, not Portuguese; he had given his name as Fernando Molineiro, and had said, like the other two, that he came from near Pamplona; with them, he had presented himself at the *adega* and asked for work; as they were short-handed for the treading, all three had been taken on.

And was the Senhor certain that he was one of the men who had followed the Senhora from the Castelo, and aroused her suspicions, the Security man next enquired—the bailiff gaped at him in utter bewilderment. "A Senhora from the Castelo? —I know nothing of this."

Gil spoke up.

"No one was with the Senhora Atherley when she saw these men watching her; they did this only when she was alone. But when she went down to the *adega* she recognised them, and established that they were Spaniards—which increased her suspicions regarding them, in view of what had happened in Spain."

The official, well briefed by Colonel Marques, knew all about what had happened in Spain; he now said that the English Senhora herself ought to come and identify the man. The Duke was not over-pleased at this idea; but he hardly felt in a position to refuse. He did however insist on going himself to ascertain if Mrs. Atherley felt equal to coming to look at the man—"She has been shot at today, and has had a shock; moreover she is not in very robust health." He told João and Antonio to clear away the blood-stained chair and towels—"And get sand to cover over the stains on the floor; and bring a clean chair or two." Then he went through into the drawing-room.

The party there was waiting anxiously for news of what went on; when her host asked Hetta, rather tentatively, if she would be willing to go and look at the captive, to say whether he was in fact one of the men who had followed her, they all listened intently. "It is only to look at him, and tell the Security Police yes or no—he cannot speak."

"Why not? They have not gagged him?" Hetta asked, horrified.

"Oh no—he is unconscious." The Duke explained about the man's attempted suicide. "We expect Dr. Mendes at any moment, and this Security officer has put on a tourniquet. But he is greatly upset; if the man dies without speaking, they will learn nothing."

Hetta suddenly looked very alert.

"Yes, I will come at once," she said, getting up.

"You're sure you are up to it?" Richard asked, with concern.

"Perfectly sure." As she spoke she looked in her small evening bag, and took out a tiny pocket diary.

"I should like to come with her, Duke," Richard said.

"Do, by all means—I am sorry that Mrs. Atherley should be put to this trouble, but the P.I.D.E. individual is very insistent."

"He is quite right," Hetta said. But out in the hall she turned to her host.

"Please, before I go to see this man, I must use the telephone," she said. "May I do it from your study?"

"Of course, if you wish. But will it not do later?"

"No. If the man is possibly dying I must lose no time." She spoke with a quiet firmness that there was no gainsaying; the

Duke obediently led the way into his study, and indicated one of several telephones on his desk. "Do sit down. Can I get you the number?"

"Yes, please," she said, sitting down in the desk chair; opening the diary she read out "Vale da Cambra 346."

Ericeira put the call through; as they waited—"For whom shall I ask?" he said.

"For Monsignor Subercaseaux, I think—if he is not available for Father Martinez. And please give my name—then one of them will certainly answer."

Greatly intrigued by this, the Duke nevertheless did as he was bidden, and in a few moments heard that rich ecclesiastical voice—he handed the receiver to his guest.

"Monsignor Subercaseaux? Here Hetta Atherley. Can you send Father Martinez over to Gralheira at once? We need a priest, and one who speaks Spanish; it is exceedingly urgent."

A long comprehending "Aah" came down the line. "So you have them?"

"One. But the Father should hurry."

"He is with me—he will come immediately."

"Good—thank you." She rang off, cutting short the Monsignor's voice in mid-flood, and got up.

"Thank you very much," she said. "Now, where do we go?"

Richard, after his talk on the telephone with Ainsworth, was less surprised than his host at his development; but both men recognised the necessity for bringing a priest to a dying man, and the great desirability, in the circumstances, of securing a Spanish-speaking one. As they walked through into the back regions Hetta explained briefly that the Monsignor had suggested sending Father Martinez if any emergency should arise—"though how he could have foreseen this I do not know."

"Do you know this other priest by sight?" Richard asked.

"Oh yes—I asked to meet him while I was at la Trapa, so that there could be no mistake."

"Good."

In the shed João and the footman had put clean chairs, and were still strewing sand on the floor. The Duke presented the P.I.D.E. official to Hetta, adding—"I am afraid I do not know your name."

"Major Belmonte"—bowing.

"Ah, thank you."

"Now, Sehnora, can you tell me if you have ever seen this man before?"

Hetta went up to the blanket-covered figure; it was the man with the black moustaches.

"Yes—three times."

"Where?"

"First, out in the country; he hid in some reeds, and peeped at me through them. When I tried to speak to him, I saw him running away. Then, quite close to the house, here, in the woods."

"Did you speak to him then?"

"No—he ducked down among some bushes, and I came away, because his behaviour was so peculiar—not at all like the people here, who are always friendly."

"Quite so. And the third time?"

"We went down to the *adega,* to see the dancing at the wine-treading; he was there, with the other two, and I asked the Senhor Duque about them, and learned that they were strangers, and spoke Spanish, not Portuguese."

"You had not seen them before, when you were in Spain?"

"No."

"But you did not at once report their behaviour to His Excellency, since it struck you as so peculiar?"

Hetta treated the official to a cold stare.

"No, Senhor Comandante, I did not." She turned to her host, and said in English—"Dear Duke, if you desire to preserve this man's life, should he not be put somewhere more suitable?" She looked round the windowless shed—it was at once chilly and stuffy, and seemed full of people. "It is not very warm here, and he gets no air."

"It was thought better not to move him till the doctor comes," Ericeira replied.

"And where is the doctor to put his things, when he does come? Here is nothing but the floor," she replied vigorously. "Surely at least a room should be prepared, and something to carry him on?"

Major Belmonte understood English, it seemed.

"Excellency, the Senhora is right," he said. "A bed should be got ready, and a stretcher, if you have such a thing."

Gralheira did not run to a stretcher, but Elidio murmured in his master's ear that a light door could be taken off its hinges instead; he was told to see to this, and a room, and hurried away.

"Now, if the Senhor Comandante has heard all he wishes from the Senhora, we will leave you," Richard said, a little stiffly.

"Certainly, Senhor. I regret the necessity for disturbing the Senhora; my best thanks," Major Belmonte said, with another bow to Hetta.

"And I will return to my guests," the Duke added. —"I shall be available later." And he and the Atherleys made to leave the shed. As they went out, Dr. Mendes walked in.

11

DR. MENDES, like Hetta, took a dim view of the shed as a place in which to treat his new patient. He felt the pulse, listened to the heart, and loosened the tourniquet—the hand was turning blue; then he demanded that the man should be taken to a proper bed immediately. By Elidio's orders this had been prepared with surprising speed; the man was laid, not on the door, but on a blanket, and so carried to a small decent room, with a table on which the doctor could place his effects—there Mendes said that the foot of the bed must be propped up, so that what blood was left in the body should flow back towards the heart and head. This was done; then, and only then, the doctor re-tied the tourniquet, examined the wrist, and asked a few questions. Was it known at what time the man had slashed himself? No—he had been searched, bound, and left in the shed at some time between 6.30 and a quarter-to-seven, João said; he very sensibly produced the cord which had bound the wrists and explained that the man must have bitten through it; but that, he thought, could only have taken a quarter of an hour, at the most. Major Belmonte, all this time, looked on and listened in acute anxiety; at last he asked the doctor what the prisoner's chances of survival were?

Poor—nothing but a blood-transfusion could safe his life, Mendes opined; and he was in no condition to stand the journey to the hospital, the only place where it could be given. "If he had known better where to cut himself, he would have been dead by now—but he tried too near the hand, where the tendons are in the way, and missed the main artery." As he spoke he began to strap up the wound with plaster.

Major Belmonte was aghast at this. Could nothing be done, he asked urgently, to bring him back to consciousness. "It is vitally important that he should speak."

Dr. Mendes gave him a queer look at that.

"For his own sake, in any case, he should be given a warm drink," he said rather sardonically. "Warm, and very sweet— milky coffee, with much sugar," he added to Elidio, who hastened off to supply this fresh need. He finished strapping up the wrist, removed the tourniquet, and tied the arm loosely up in a sling. "We might try bandaging his legs, to get more blood up to his head," he said to the Major. "Take his trousers off." While João and the Major did this he hunted in his bag for bandages; as he bandaged one leg—"Why do you so greatly wish him to speak?" he asked.

"He made an attempt on someone's life, only this afternoon; we have reason to suppose that he is a Communist agent," Belmonte replied—so much he had to say.

"With what weapon?"

"A rifle," João replied. "We have it in the house."

"Ah—a rifle! I thought a shot-gun could not have done it," the doctor observed, puzzling the Security man, who had not been told the precise nature of Mrs. Atherley's wound. At that moment Elidio returned with a jug of milky coffee; the brilliant servant had also brought a feeding-cup. "That is well," Mendes said approvingly; he held the jug against his cheek. "No, it is not too hot—excellent. Raise him a little," he pursued, pouring some coffee into the cup; then, while Elidio held the man up he put a hand behind the head, and gently inserted the spout between the pallid lips. Elidio snatched up one of the cloths which had tied the tourniquet and placed it under the chin—wisely, for at first the man merely gulped, and the fluid ran down. Then he began to swallow.

· 166 ·

"That is right—gently, by little and little," Mendes said, refilling the cup. They persevered, with frequent pauses; Major Belmonte watched in painful anxiety. At last the eyes opened, but in a moment they closed again. "Can he speak now?" the Security man asked.

"*Pazienza!*—not yet." He filled the cup again, and continued to hold it to the mouth, giving the coffee in little sips.

"Senhor Doctor, he is getting warmer," Elidio observed presently.

"Yes, I also think so."

In the distance a bell rang—Elidio looked anxiously at Mendes.

"Senhor Doctor, that is the front door. Could João here hold him up?—I should go and answer it."

"Yes, I suppose so." João came and took the servant's place, with one arm round the injured man; Elidio hurried away. Presently the patient with his free hand tried feebly to push the cup aside, and muttered something; Major Belmonte came near and strained his ears to catch it—so did Oliveira. "He is speaking Spanish," he said. "None of them speak any Portuguese."

"Do you speak Spanish?" Belmonte asked him.

"No, Senhor Comandante—three words, that is all!"

"And you?" the Security man asked, turning to João.

"*Minho Senhor,* no; a little French only."

The local Chief of Police, and Dr. Mendes, equally denied any knowledge of Spanish; meanwhile the man opened his eyes again, and made an attempt to speak.

"Well, I must try myself—I used to speak it," Belmonte said. "Can I begin now?" he asked the doctor.

"You can try," Mendes said, putting down the cup; he placed a pillow under the head, and told João to lay the man down on it; he again opened his eyes, at that, and stared vaguely at the faces around him—"Where am I?" he asked faintly, in Spanish.

Before anyone could answer, the door was opened by Elidio,

who ushered in Mrs. Atherley, followed by a small priest. "How is he?" she asked Mendes.

"Just alive," he replied in a low tone.

"Ah, that is well—*gracias a Deus!* Here is the priest—Father Martinez, Dr. Mendes." The two men bowed to one another; the small Father, calm and businesslike, drew a chair up beside the bed, and sat down.

"Senhora, *I* am about to question this man," Belmonte said, with emphasis.

"That must wait, Senhor Comandante," Hetta replied, quietly, but with authority. "All should leave, now. Father, have you everything that you require?"

"I should like the table near me," the priest said; Dr. Mendes bundled his effects back into his bag, and João brought the table over and set it down by the bed.

"Senhora, my business is official," Belmonte protested.

"The soul comes first—this way, if you please," she returned implacably—fuming, he followed her and the rest out of the room. In the passage she drew him aside, and spoke in French, very low.

"The Father knows precisely what is at stake, Monsieur le Commandant, and he speaks fluent Spanish; if he is able to help you, he will, I am confident."

"A confession cannot help us," the Security man replied gloomily.

"Naturally not."

"Then why is Madame so confident? Do you know this priest? How does he come to be here, in any event?"

"I sent for him—it was arranged in advance, with Monsignor Subercaseaux, that he should be sent for if—if anything untoward happened."

At the mention of the Monsignor's name Major Belmonte looked slightly less gloomy. "Ah, so he is concerned in this? How, I wonder."

"I asked his advice. But do come downstairs; I believe some supper has been arranged for you," she said, and led him through into the front part of the house. There Elidio was waiting in the hall with Dr. Mendes, and took the two men into the dining-room, where a supper had been prepared for three; however the local Chief of Police, Elidio explained, had driven back to São Pedro—"but when the Senhor Comandante desires to return, a car will take him."

Hetta went into the drawing-room. When Elidio had come up to her and in an undertone announced the priest's arrival, she had excused herself to her host and slipped out; he, and Luzia and Richard, at once realised what was happening; the others remained mystified. Now questions began.

"Yes, it was Father Martinez; he is with the poor man now," she said to the Duke.

"Is he conscious?"

"I think so—this Major said he was about to question him; but I said that the priest must see him first."

"How did Belmonte take that?" Richard asked.

"He was displeased. But I told him it had to be so, and really he could not help himself."

"Of course not," Ericeira said firmly. "The man must make his confession, if he can—which please God may be the case. Though a confession will not help the police much."

"That is what Major Belmonte said," Hetta remarked.

Lord Heriot was slightly shocked by this attitude.

"But really, Duke, since this man is a known criminal, can it be right to prevent the police doing their duty, and learning all they can?"

Luzia put in her oar.

"Dear Beau-père, just *because* he is a criminal, is it not essential that he should make his peace with God?" The old peer grunted disgustedly—he could not bring himself to attempt an answer. His wife tried to console him.

"As he is a Communist, perhaps he won't make a confession at all," she said cheerfully; Richard and Luzia laughed; the master of the house frowned on them, and turned the conversation.

"Are the police having some supper?—and the doctor?" he asked Hetta.

"The doctor and the P.I.D.E. man, yes—the *Chefe* has gone back," she told him.

They continued to wait, talking disjointedly. Presently Elidio ushered in Major Belmonte, and asked his master, in an undertone, if he should perhaps bring drinks to the salon? Luzia overheard.

"Oh yes, Papa, *please*—just this once. I am sure Hetta ought to have some whisky, after all this."

"*I* think Mrs. Atherley should go to bed," Lady Heriot observed, with motherly concern. But the idea was not welcomed.

"*After* she has had some whisky, Bonne-Mama," Luzia said brightly; Hetta gave her a grateful glance. The trays were brought in, and glasses filled; all, in their rather dampened and shaken state, were glad of this restorative. The Duke made laborious conversation with Lord Heriot and the Ambassador; no one spoke of the subject which was uppermost in all their minds till Major Belmonte, after a furtive glance at his watch, suggested that it might be as well to go and see how the sick man was? Ericeira glanced questioningly at Hetta.

"I think not," she said. "Father Martinez will come as soon as he is ready, and this person is in no condition to escape."

In fact quite soon after that Elidio showed the priest in; everyone in the great room gazed with deep interest—and some astonishment—at the minute figure in the black soutane. But with the urbanity and smoothness which so many sons of the Church acquire quite early on, he dealt with the situation in a way that somehow brought ease into it at once. Tactfully, Hetta Atherley introduced him to their host in French, to Lord Heriot's manifest relief—he was able to listen eagerly to their conversation, with a hand cupped round his ear. Yes, the man was now comforted, and had made his peace with God, the priest said—at which Major Belmonte's face fell, to the

Ambassador's secret amusement. But Father Martinez had something for him too. After telling the Duke that the man was still alive, and that an elderly maid-servant, produced by Elidio, was sitting with him, he turned to the Security officer.

"Being in theory, at least, a Communist, he did not wish to make a confession," he said. "Therefore I am at liberty to pass on certain information which I managed to obtain. His two companions are, he thinks, still in Portugal; they were to remain in case his attempt failed. But he could not say where—I think he was genuinely in ignorance of their precise whereabouts; he said something about their all having been instructed to "separate" before the actual shooting today."

"Who gave him these instructions?" Belmonte wanted to know.

"His "superiors" in Spain; he is a Spaniard, and the organisation is there."

"Well, you can pass that much on to the Spanish police," the Duke said to Belmonte. "And I hope pursue your enquiries here—I shall be more at ease when those other two have been accounted for."

"This we shall certainly do," the Security man said rather stiffly. He again glanced at his watch, "I wonder if I had better see him myself."

"You speak Spanish?" the priest asked.

"Very little."

"Then I wonder if that will serve you much. He is an ignorant youth, and at present very weak—he mutters, and rambles; it is hard to hear what he says. But of course that is as you and His Excellency wish."

His Excellency did not wish it in the least. "If you feel it essential, of course you shall see him," he said to Belmonte. "But he, at least, can do no further harm; I am more concerned about his companions, who are still at large." At this rather broad hint the Security man decided to leave it for the present, and asked if the car could be sent for? "And the weapon—I must take that with me." The rifle was fetched from the study; the car, it seemed, was waiting—the Duke asked Father Martinez if he would like a lift as well?

"I thank your Excellency, but I have my little machine, which seldom fails me! And the night air is good for clearing the mind before the evening devotions," he said blandly. As Ericeira politely led the Major out into the hall, Father Martinez went over to Mrs. Atherley.

"The Monsignor sent you his warmest good wishes, and asked me to tell you that he so much regrets that he probably will not see you again, as he goes into retreat tomorrow until he leaves La Trapa. But he bade me give you this, and express his desire that you should study it at once." As he spoke he drew out of his soutane a little book in an exquisitely-tooled eighteenth-century binding, and handed it to her. "It is a work of devotion; the Monsignor is confident that it will assist your progress."

"Well really, Hetta, I'd no idea that you and old Subercaseaux had got onto *those* terms," Richard said, when the small priest had made his farewells, and hummed away on his Vespa. "Let's see this famous work of devotion."

"I will show it to you upstairs—Lady Heriot, if you will excuse me, I think I will go to bed."

"My dear, you ought to have been there long ago," the good lady said. "Really, this *tedious* policeman wanting you to go and identify your own assassin, at this time of night! Have you got something to make you sleep?"

"Yes thank you—Dr. Mendes left me some tablets."

"Well, go and take them. Goodnight, my dear, and sleep as well as you can."

But up in their room Hetta did not take her tablets at once.

"I will just get into bed; then we will look at it," she said, putting the small volume on the bedside table, and beginning to throw off her clothes.

"I shouldn't bother with it tonight at all, if you're tired," Richard said. Hetta made no reply, but continued her undressing, slipped into her nightdress and a soft white liseuse, got into bed and lay back on the pillows with a long sigh of relief. Then—"Yes, we must look at it at once; there is something in it," she said, and took it up.

"What do you mean?" But he soon saw what she meant. Tucked into the pages were some sheets of thin paper, covered with fine writing; she smoothed these out on the sheet, and began to look at what was written on them—Richard pulled a stool up beside her, and they studied the priest's message together.

It was, as they presently saw, of considerable importance; even though at first—as Father Martinez had told Major Belmonte—the Spaniard's mutterings had been rambling and disjointed. He had definitely refused to make a confession, but had asked if a message could be sent to his Mother—the Father, from then on, had jotted down his words as they came, however confused and disconnected. There were constant references to "El Lobo" (the Wolf). "El Lobo said we were to come—I was never abroad before. . . . El Lobo said if I did not take the rifle, and shoot the lady, he would menace *mia Madre*. . . . El Lobo gave me the rifle and the bullets—and the blade; it was he who said I was to cut my wrist if I was taken. . . . Yes, I know it was a sin. . . ." He had asked the priest, weeping a little, to look after his Mother, a widow—"La Viuda Elizondo", and had given the name of her village near Pamplona; his Father had been an *albanil*, a mason.

"Well, that will be easy enough to verify," Richard Atherley said with satisfaction. "What's on this next sheet?"

On the next sheet the Father mentioned that he had asked for, and been given some indications about El Lobo—which Richard at once realised would be a code name. "We met in that *tasca* (wineshop) behind the old *mercado* (market). . . . Yes, in Madrid. . . . Yes, El Lobo sent us in a car to near the frontier."

"Then," Father Martinez' fine small script reported, "he became much distressed, and wept; I questioned him no further, but attended to the needs of his soul. I was able to shrive him, in the end; he should have Christian burial, if he does not live. I hope this little that I have learned may be of some help to you. J. Martinez."

"Clever little creature!" Richard exclaimed. "Belmonte would never have got half as much. Old Subercaseaux knew what he was about when he sent him."

"I think he always does know what he is about," Hetta said, smiling a little. "Give me my tablets, please, Richard; they are on the wash-stand—and a glass of water." After she had swallowed them—"How craftily he arranged for the information to be passed to me, too, without others seeing," she went on, taking up the beautiful little volume.

"Yes, it has assisted your progress quite a bit!" Richard agreed, grinning. "What is the book?"

It was in fact that rather famous work *Caractères de la vraie dévotion* by Père Nicholas Grou, S.J.—the title-page bore the date 1788.

"Oh, Father Antal had this, in his study on the Alfold, only in German," Hetta said. "He said once that it was a wonderful book. I expect it will assist my progress in other things also! Now hurry and get undressed, dear one—I want to go to sleep."

"Does your head hurt?" he asked rather anxiously.

"Not so much; but I am a little tired."

"Yes, it's been a gruelling day for you all round. I hope to goodness it hasn't done the child any harm. Sure you feel all right otherwise?"

"Perfectly sure."

The first thing Richard did next morning was to seek out the Ambassador in his room, and take counsel with him as to the next step; unwisely he took the little book as well as what had been enclosed in it.

"Very skilful," Sir Noël commented. "Let's see the book." He fairly jumped at the sight of the title-page. "But this is a first edition! What a treasure!—it's beyond all price. The old Monsignor must think the world of your wife to give her that, as a cover-up!" He turned the book over and over, fingering the pages reverently. "Contemporary binding, I should say—and in mint condition. I wonder how on earth he came by it?"

Richard, too late, regretted heartily having brought Père Grou's devotional work along; he had forgotten what a bibliophile his chief was.

"Yes, but look here, H.E., what are we to do about this information? Do look at it. Ought we to pass it on to that P.I.D.E. man, or what?"

Reluctantly, the Ambassador turned his attention to the Father's written sheets. "Beautiful script the fellow has," he commented—"clear as print." He read them through carefully, however. "H'mm," he said at length. "No, I don't think we need let the gallant Major in on these items at this stage—this is something for the Spanish Intelligence people. Wherever else El Lobo is, he isn't in Portugal." He looked at the middle sheet again. "Wonder which old market he means?" he speculated. "Even I know at least three in Madrid! However, that's up to them. The key thing is to have El Lobo's trade name—that can be most useful."

"But how are we to get the stuff to them?" Richard asked.

"Oh ah, yes. Someone will have to take it—that's the only safe way."

Richard looked gloomy. "I suppose it is," he said, rather glumly. "And that I'm someone."

Sir Noël laughed.

"I have an idea," he said. "Ring up Ainsworth and tell him to come and meet you at the frontier at Shaves, or whatever the place is called; you can get there and back in the day. Then you'll only miss one day's shooting."

"If the old Duke goes on shooting at all—I have a feeling that he may not want to, till the other two types are rounded up," Richard observed.

"Then you'll miss nothing except your Missis's delightful company! How is she this morning, by the way?"

"Very fit; she slept splendidly. She's tremendously tough."

"That's good. Well, ring up Ainsworth at once; if he starts quickly he could meet you tomorrow. Oh, and I shouldn't say anything to that nice Gil boy—he may have official feelings about the Major! No good asking for trouble."

"What about Luzia?"

"Oh, tell *her*—she'd find out, anyhow! I saw her watching that little priest last night like a lynx. She's probably cross-examining Hetta at this moment!—but she is perfectly capable of keeping her mouth shut. Look at her with her Father last night!"

Not for the first time, Richard Atherley was slightly irritated by the fact that there were only two telephones connected with the national system in the whole huge house at Gralheira; the one in the Duke's study, and that other so public one outside the pantry; he also wished that his host were not such an early riser. However, to the pantry he betook himself, put in his trunk call to Madrid, and sat down, also not for the first time, on a case of wine to wait. Here he was found by Luzia; she came up to him, her face sparkling with mischievous amusement.

"So! You are ringing up Madrid, I suppose," she said in English. "I am glad Hetta is so well this morning."

"The Ambassador was right," Richard grunted.

"Plait-il?"

But at that moment Richard got his connexion, and asked for Ainsworth's extension.

"May I listen?" the girl asked.

"Yes, provided you don't tell Gil! Oh, good morning," he said, hearing the voice he wanted. "We've got some news for you—rather handy, we think. . . . No, I can't tell you—you'll have to come over and get it. . . . No, not here, only to the frontier. Got a pencil? All right, just jot down the names. *Not* to the Fountains of Honour, but the road to the Keys." Here Luzia giggled audibly; he ignored her. "Got that? Right; look them out on the map, with a dictionary—you can't miss the place. I'll be there tomorrow about noon, and stroll across and see you. . . . Yes, there is one other thing—you might tell your so co-operative indigenous pals to be looking out for someone in sheep's clothing. . . . Don't be dumb—I said 'in sheep's clothing'. . . . Yes, translate it into Spanish. Right. See you tomorrow." He rang off.

"I so like the way you talk to him," Luzia observed as they went back to the hall; "it is most clever, and amusing. Few would guess that you meant Fuentes de Onoro and Chaves. But what is this, in sheep's clothing? I could not follow. What wears sheep's clothing, but a sheep?"

"It's an old phrase—a wolf in sheep's clothing. He'll get that all right."

"Ah, so!" She did not repeat the Spanish word. "What a convenient proverb! But why I am not to tell Gil?"

"Because he may feel he ought to pass it on to the Major, and this is really a matter for the Madrilenos."

"Oh, this Belmonte! Already he has telephoned Papa, to say he is coming over early, to interview that man."

"Oh well, it's his job, after all," Richard said charitably. "But not this part of it." As he made for the staircase Elidio appeared from the direction of the back regions.

"Senhora Condesa, *esto homem* is dead," he said.

The girl crossed herself, murmuring "May his soul rest in peace." Then she turned briskly to Atherley. "That settles the Major!" she said, in a satisfied tone.

12

RICHARD ATHERLEY, after consultation with Hetta, went in to see his host, and explained that Father Martinez had in fact furnished his wife with "some further information" about the Spaniard, and had expressed the opinion that the poor youth's Communism was only skin-deep, and that he should be given Christian burial—he had admitted that his attempt at suicide was a sin, committed under orders. The Duke was relieved; and the fact that he had been out of the room, seeing the Major off, when the priest left made this rather selective version of Father Martinez' information quite easy to put across. As Richard had foreseen, there was no question of further shooting that day or the next; the Duke set about making arrangements for the funeral, and when Major Belmonte arrived he dealt calmly with his frustration at finding that death had robbed him of his quarry—"At least now, Senhor Commandante, there is nothing to deflect you from your pursuit of this unhappy creature's two companions."

Then, while the Major started to scour the countryside, Luzia and the two Atherleys concerted their plans for Richard's drive to Chaves the following day.

"No, I do not see any point in telling Papa *why* you are going," the girl said. "It will only make him more curious—and perhaps vexed again. Chaves is a pretty place, with things to see—can you not look at the Roman Bridge? You could take the Ambassador—oh no, better not; he does not know."

"Well, he does know, as a matter of fact—but I don't think he's the ideal passenger."

"Why not take Nick?" Hetta suggested. "He hasn't seen Chaves—he came by the other road." She was secretly determined that Richard should not go on this errand alone.

"Then he also will have to be told," Luzia observed.

"He knows all the rest, anyhow—so I don't see why not," Richard said. "Yes, bring him along, Luzia, and we'll explain it all."

Nick was delighted with the scheme. "Meet Our Man in Madrid—I'm all for it," was his reaction. But Hetta had a further idea.

"Richard, should you not write to the Mother of this young man, and let her know that he is dead, but made a good end, with a priest? Then Ainsworth could post the letter in Spain. We know her name, and that of her village."

Richard was not sure about writing. "Ainsworth could tell her—I expect he will want to check on her, anyhow. The Spaniards certainly will."

"Yes, and *how* will they tell her? Perhaps brutally. No, Richard; she should have something written, that she can keep always."

"Provided she can read," Richard said.

"The priest will be able to read it to her," Luzia put in. "Hetta is right. I know!—Hetta, do, you write it, in Spanish; and Nick can copy it out on my typewriter. And we will put in a piece of his hair—I will get it at once." She darted away.

"Don't tell my Father all this," Nick said, with a half-rueful grin. "He wouldn't get the idea at all."

"Your Mother would—but we shall not tell her," Hetta replied.

The two young men set off early next morning, Nick in tearing spirits at the prospect of seeing fresh country. The drive was in fact not without interest: beyond São Pedro do

Sul the road drops to cross the **Douro** at **Regua**, on the southern edge of the Pais do Vinho, the Wine Country, and the young man gazed eagerly at the golden-buff terraced hillsides stretching away up the great valley whence, alone, port comes. "My Father simply must come and see this," he remarked. Then up and on, over the great rolling uplands of Traz os Montes, never more beautiful than in autumn, when the pale golden stubble stretches for miles on all sides—to drop again to a lesser river, spanned by the Roman bridge which still carries all northbound traffic into Chaves. They paused to have a look at this; they were in good time, and the frontier was only a few kilometres beyond the pleasant watering-place—then they drove on. Richard had purposely come in his own car, with the C.D. number-plates, rather than Nick's; he pulled up short of the wire barrier which closes the road, turned, parked, and then, on foot, went up and spoke to the frontier officials. No, he did not desire to drive into Spain; he and this young Senhor just wished to walk across and take a stroll on the further side. Yes, of course they had passports; if the Senhor wished to put on exit visas for a matter of half a kilometre, let him by all means do so!—he said laughing. The frontier-guard consulted with his colleagues on this knotty point, but at length, encouraged by the C.D. on the car, and the *laisser-passer* which Richard produced from his passport, he rolled back the barrier and let them through. They walked on, Richard wishing aloud that there was a bend; however presently the road did curve very slightly round a low piece of hill, and looking back they could see that the hut at the frontier post was no longer visible.

"Good—this will do," Atherley said; they sat down on a rock by the roadside and waited. After a few more minutes a cloud of dust in the distance proclaimed the advent of a car; Richard went and stood in the road, and when he saw the number-plate he held out his arms to stop it—the car slowed down and Ainsworth leaned out.

"Pull into the side, here," the diplomat said; Ainsworth did so, and got out, followed by a younger man—he too had brought a companion. "This is Johnnie Miller—he's just been sent out to join me," he said.

"Then our seconds had better meet—this is Nick Heriot," Atherley replied. As the two others shook hands—"Mr. Heriot has been at Gralheira since the start of this affair," he added, "he's been in on it all along."

They re-seated themselves on the rocks and got down to business. Richard recounted, briefly, the shooting episode, the assassin's attempt at suicide, and Father Martinez' arrival; then he handed over the priest's notes. Ainsworth studied them carefully.

"Yes, that should give the Hispanos all they need," he said, in a satisfied tone. "In fact they were thrilled to pieces when I passed on what you told me on the telephone; it seems they've had their suspicions of The Wolf for some time. Now haven't you had a P.I.D.E. man up there too? What is he doing?"

"Chasing the other two!—he hasn't been shown these papers. H.E. thought it better not; quite unusually, this P.I.D.E. man is rather a hamfisted type, and speaks no Spanish. We should have got next to nothing if my wife hadn't got the little priest over."

Ainsworth asked after Mrs. Atherley—"A horrid thing to happen—I hope she's not too much upset?"

"No, thank you—she takes these things in her stride! She wouldn't even go to bed till she had got hold of the Father, and coerced the wretched Major Belmonte into letting him shrive the assassin at once. Oh, and look, Ainsworth—here is something else she insists on." He took an envelope from his pocket. "This is a letter, typed, to the boy's mother, to tell her that he is dead, but that a priest was with him, and that he is being given a Christian burial."

"Who signed it?" Ainsworth asked at once.

"Luzia Ericeira—we thought that best. And the only address we've given is "São Pedro do Sul, Portugal." But my wife is very anxious that you should give it to the woman yourself, and tell her about it, *kindly*—from Martinez' notes you'll be able to explain what happened. Oh, I'm not sure if the letter says that he had the doctor, but he did—doctor *and* priest."

The Intelligence man looked again at the notes in Father Martinez' fine clear script.

"Yes, I think I can do it from that," he said. "Someone will have to go to this village anyhow, to check—we'd better do that ourselves," With well-trained thoroughness, he felt the envelope all over. "There's something in it," he said. "What's that?"

"A bit of the man's hair—the Condesa cut that off and put it in," Nick Heriot said.

"Very nice—very thoughtful. Well, we'd better get going. Johnnie, turn her, will you?"

While Miller was turning the car Ainsworth took Atherley aside. "If these clues about the wineshop and the old *mercado* enable our Spanish colleagues to round up El Lobo and his little lot, it ought to be all right for this other American," he said. "Time's getting on. When do you and the Ambassador think of coming back?"

"Well, nothing's settled yet. I think H.E. hoped for a bit more shooting—of course the Duke isn't too keen on that until he knows that there are no more Spaniards with rifles hanging about! I'll let you know when anything is decided. Give me a ring when you've seen la Viuda, and tell me how she took it. My wife will want to know."

"I'll do that thing." He also got into the car, and drove off with his companion.

Richard and Nick did not go back to the frontier by the road; they struck up the hillside behind them for a couple of hundred feet, and then strolled along. The withered yellowish grass was full of small, pale-pink autumn crocuses, with strap-shaped petals; Nick gathered a bunch for Luzia. "We have these in the Pyrenees too," he said, "but I don't think she went high enough to see them there."

"Good idea," Atherley commented; he too sought for flowers to pick, but found little except some dull purplish thistle-y plants, and a sort of whortleberry in fruit—however he took all he could.

"*Varias qualidades de floras!*" the Portuguese frontier-official commented when they dropped down onto the road quite near the barrier—and Richard agreed that, yes, they were *botanistas,* but that it was getting late in the season for flowers. The man asked if they had seen a car coming from Spain? —"It must have turned back, for it did not reach the frontier." Richard said blandly that they had paid no attention; they were seeking flowers, not *automoveis!*—at which the man laughed. He saluted politely as they drove away.

They ate a late lunch in Chaves, and got back in time for tea, to find their host calmly satisfied, and Major Belmonte jubilant—the other two Spanish agents had both been captured. The local police, by his latest orders no longer inhibited from doing anything to alarm the intruders, had pursued their search with the utmost vigour; the country-people, indignant that "an outrage had been perpetrated," and on a lady from the Castelo, had co-operated with all their might, and the wretched men, lost and hungry, had been found trying to make their way to the frontier in the desolate stretches of the Terras de Barroso, not far from Chaves. They would be handed over to the Spanish authorities after further interrogation, but Belmonte was fairly satisfied that they had received no co-operation locally. "Except from us!" Luzia put in irrepressibly.

"How so?" her Father asked.

"We employed them, and housed and fed them, Papa."

"Nonsense, my child. So tomorrow we shoot again," he concluded cheerfully.

After tea Richard and the Ambassador took a stroll in the garden, and Richard reported his meeting with Ainsworth, and the latter's confident expectation that Father Martinez' information would enable the Spanish Security Police to clear up the "cell" completely.

"Well, that will be a mercy," Sir Noël said. "We don't want any more near misses! I'm thinking more about Hetta than any American V.I.P.s; it always seems to be she who gets it—just as it's always she who produces the crucial information. How is she standing up to it all?"

"Pretty well, I think," Richard said slowly. "But I've been thinking, H.E.—I have a feeling that it might not be a bad idea to get her out of the Iberian Peninsula altogether till this next baby is safely over. It can't do an unborn child much good to be shot at or tipped out of cars all the time, however quietly the mother takes it."

"I agree. Where should you send her? To her Mother in the States?"

"Definitely not that! Dorothée isn't much good with people," Richard said temperately. "I haven't thought it out yet—my own people are dead, except for one old Aunt who's nearly as tyrannous as Countess Páloczy! But I expect we could arrange something."

"What about the Heriots? I should have thought they would be ideal—they both seem to like her immensely."

"I must think it out, and talk to her," Richard said. "I'm glad you approve, anyhow. I may lay you on to help to persuade her! She hasn't many friends in England, except old Mrs. Hathaway—and I hardly think her flat would run to taking in a nurse and baby, as well as an expectant Mother! But she'd be sure to have good ideas."

Hetta did not take very kindly to the notion of a five months' separation from her husband when he first put it up to her.

"Where should I go?" she asked. "Our house is let for another year—and I do not want to be away from *you*. I see no necessity." However she agreed that he might write to Mrs. Hathaway, and ask her advice—and Luzia presently coming in, she put the matter to her. "You do not mind, Richard? Luzia also has good ideas."

· 184 ·

Luzia was rather startled at the scheme—she considered it gravely.

"Do you know, I think it might be a good plan," she said at last. "These people are very tenacious—and even here, where you came for safety, you have not been safe!" This fact had bitten deeply into the girl's mind; she could not get over it. Then she produced her good idea. "But as well as Mrs. Hathaway, why do you not write to Miss Probyn? She has a young baby herself, and her husband also is abroad. You might live together."

Hetta was much better pleased with the plan under this aspect; she remembered Julia Probyn, as a wise confidante and a tower of strength, at the time of her first visit to Gralheira —and Richard too approved strongly when he recollected that "Miss Probyn" was now Mrs. Philip Jamieson, and that her husband was pretty high up in British Intelligence. That they should live together seemed too much to hope for, but if Hetta could even be settled somewhere near her, it would be an excellent thing. He wrote, guardedly, to Mrs. Hathaway, explaining that for "a variety of reasons" he thought his wife would be better in England until her second child was born, and invoking her good offices to find a suitable place, since their own house was not available. As before, the two young women both wrote to Julia, but in Luzia's case a good deal less guardedly. "It is really important that she should go away as soon as possible. In Spain, when that American was there, she was involved in a nasty car accident, which was not purely accidental, and broke her wrist; it was due to the same people who menaced her before, when you were with us. And only three days ago she had another narrow escape—*here*, at Gralheira! Now it is thought that these people will be caught, and dealt with, and that all will be safe for her—but how does one know? She ought to be in England, at least till this second child is born; all these incidents cannot be good for it. Do please try to arrange something, *quickly*."

Of course Richard Atherley wanted to know what they had

written—his wife showed him her letter; Luzia's was already stamped and sealed.

"I was very careful," she protested. "I only said that she had broken her wrist in an accident that was not an accident, in Spain, and that there had just been another incident, here—and that it was caused by the people Miss Probyn knows about, from when she was here before."

"Well, that doesn't sound too bad, but they'd better go by bag, anyhow," Richard said firmly. Gil was due to return to Lisbon next day; Richard put both letters in one envelope, with English stamps, and asked the young man to hand it in to the Chancery messenger at the British Embassy. On Luzia's instructions he addressed it to Gray's Inn, the Jamiesons' London home—"By now Miss Probyn must be returned from Scotland, I think;" Richard of course sent his to Mrs. Hathaway's Mayfair flat. Then they sat back to await results.

Ainsworth telephoned a couple of evenings later. He had plenty to report. He and Johnnie Miller had gone to the village near Pamplona, and sought out la Viuda Elizondo; as Richard had surmised, she could not read, but she had wept over the lock of her son's hair, and clung to the letter after it had been read to her. They had gone on to visit the village priest, where Ainsworth had first, tactfully, arranged for a Mass to be said for the repose of the boy's soul; then he had made some enquiries. Molineiro, the sur-name he had given to João, was of course a false one, but his Christian name was Francisco all right; he was not a bad lad, *el Cura* said, until the Communists got hold of him—then he became full of wild and silly ideas, went to meetings instead of sticking to his work, and ceased attending to his religious duties; eventually he left home and went, it was believed, to Madrid. The priest had burst out in anger against the Communists, coming from the cities into peaceable God-fearing villages, deluding the young men, corrupting their minds, and often, as in Francisco's case, luring them away—at least five had gone from his own parish. And not only from the cities—from abroad, these contaminators came, he heard; from Moscow, probably.

Ainsworth, not a particularly religious man, had been touched by the evident relief of the middle-aged priest on hearing that the boy had "made a good end", and was to be given Christian burial. "That is right, isn't it?" Ainsworth asked, interrupting his narrative.

"Yes, he was buried yesterday—Dom Pedro, the chaplain, gave him the full treatment; Nick, the boy you met with me, went, and so did the keeper and some of the servants. And the ladies made a couple of wreaths."

"Oh, good." This point cleared up, Ainsworth went on, more guardedly, with his account. Armed with the information he had brought them, which filled out their own suspicions, the Spanish Security Police had pounced on "that pub he mentioned", and had secured "the person in the fleece", and the whole gang. "It was quite a big organisation, run on orders and cash from the late lamented Dr. Beans' capital"— Richard realised that this meant Prague—"and our local colleagues are tickled pink. So are the Yanks—after that earlier show of your wife's they had really begun to get the wind up about this next visit; not before it was time! But now it's 'safer than safe', as the ad.s say, again thanks to her. Day is making a signal to that effect to the Capitol City! By the way, I hope she's none the worse?"

Richard duly reported this to his chief.

"Yes, well that all sounds very good. But I hope you will stick to your plan; we shall both be easier in our minds if you do."

"I intend to—as soon as we can get a place arranged in England. It's awkward that our own house is let, but I'm sure that Mrs. Hathaway and Mrs. Jamieson between them will be able to fix something. She'll have to come back to Madrid, of course, to do some packing, winter clothes and so on—but I don't think we need worry for that short time."

"No. Back to Madrid!—I don't like the sound of it. This is an idyllic place; one could be happy here for ever! However, I suppose next week we shall have to make a move—we mustn't shoot all the dear old Duke's birds! But I must say I rather envy young Heriot, settling down here to make it his life's work, with that lovely creature."

"Yes—and I think he'll make a go of it," Richard agreed. "He's full of frightfully sensible ideas about modernising without spoiling, and making use of the local products."

In fact, now that the vintage was over, and he had learned all he could about that, Nick's thoughts, in the intervals of partridge-shooting, were beginning to turn again to the utilisation of that major product of the forests, the resin. He had happened one day to pass the railway siding on the estate, and seen the huge piles of metal barrels being loaded onto trucks and chugging off to the coast, to be exported at a needlessly low price, and it bothered him. He decided to raise the subject with his Father, and get his reaction—after all, he was more or less in their host's age-bracket. Being Nick, he began diffidently; but the result was almost startlingly encouraging.

"Oh, ah; I was thinking about that myself," Lord Heriot said, stuffing tobacco into the bowl of his pipe—they were in the smoking-room. "I was down by the railway t'other morning before breakfast, and saw all those tons of stuff waiting to be shipped off. The Duke tells me he gets a wretched price for it. Much better to do something with it on the spot, and get a higher-priced product to sell."

"What would you do with it?" Nick asked.

"Well *not* make linoleum!—that's one of the great outlets for resin, but it stinks appallingly; smell it for miles! Varnish isn't quite so bad, but it's quite bad enough."

"Plastics?" Nick asked.

"Don't know a thing about them; I got the idea that they only used this modern synthetic stuff for them—do they call it phenolic resin? Cheek to call it resin at all! No, I should set up one or two small distillation plants, like they do in the

Landes, and make turpentine; that's a nice light, clean smell, doesn't travel like linoleum—and there's an endless market for turps."

"*Do* they distil turps in the Landes?" Nick put the question eagerly.

"Oh yes. That old Count Thingummy—your Mother would remember his name—that died last year, went in for it in a big way as part of his forestry; he showed me all over his place once, when we were staying there. He was very scientific about it all, and a good man of business into the bargain. When his plantations were twenty years old, and about forty feet high, he used to plan his thinnings, and bleed them to death—they actually call it *gemmage à mort*—before he felled and sold them for pit-props, so he got a double profit there; the rest he left standing, about eighty to a hundred to the acre; they were bled twice a year, what they call *gemmage à vie,* and they'll stand that for another sixty or seventy years. Then clear-fell and sell as pulpwood, replant, and begin all over again." He puffed at his pipe. "Very sound business," he said appreciatively. "Slow, but sound."

"What sort of pines are they in the Landes?" Nick asked.

"Same as here, maritima—believe they call it something else, now."

"Pinaster?" Nick queried.

"I daresay."

"Well, I wish the Duke would start some distillation plants," the young man said. "It would give more employment, and keep the young men at home; it worries Luzia, the way they're starting to drift off to Oporto. And it would obviously pay him to."

"Don't suppose he's ever thought of it. He has no need to worry about money, and he's a bit set in his ways. Look at those wash-stands!"

Nick laughed. "I know. And I'm a bit shy of suggesting things, especially till we're married. Even then I don't know how he'd take it."

The old peer looked very benevolently at his modest elder son.

"Like me to throw a fly over him?"

"Very much so! Especially as you've seen all this in France yourself. It would come better from you."

The fly-throwing took place that very evening, in the drawing-room. Lord Heriot was never one to beat about the bush; his fly fell with a loud plop.

"I wonder you don't do something with all that resin of yours here on the place, Duke, instead of selling it in its natural state, for next to nothing."

"It is not quite as bad as that," his host said smiling. And like Nick, he asked Lord Heriot what he would suggest? "In Oporto, I know one firm buys it for soap-making, but I should not care to make soap at Gralheira—it smells!"

"Ah, and linoleum smells even worse! No, I wasn't thinking of that—what I had in mind was small distillation-plants for making turpentine, on the spot; get a much better price for that, and halve your freight-charges, if not more." He repeated what he had told Nick about the defunct French Count's enterprises in the Landes. Ericeira showed some slight interest, and enquired about the size of the plants?

"Oh, quite inconspicuous," Lord Heriot reassured him. "Tuck them away anywhere in the woods, so long as there's a track that's carrossable for lorries, to bring the barrels in and take the turps out."

Luzia became eager. "Papa, this could be marvellous! It would give work to the young men, and keep them at home." She turned to Lord Heriot. "What is this turpentine used for?"

"Making paint," said three people at once; the conversation had now become general. Someone asked if resin was not used in the manufacture of varnish?—the word caught the Duke's attention.

"Yes, certainly," he said. "From the time of the Egyptians."

"Not really?" Sir Noël enquired, startled.

"But yes. Certainly the ancient Egyptians used some natural gums for varnishing their mummy-cases, to make them air-tight, and as a preservative. Do you know the origin of the word *vernis*, the French form?"

The Ambassador didn't. "Do tell us."

"It is derived from the Queen of Cyrene, Berenice, who became the wife of Ptolemy III. She had long golden hair, which she cut off and sacrificed on the altar of Venus to ensure her husband's safety in some battle. So the ancient Greeks called amber 'the hair of Berenice', and thus the Latin word 'Verenice' came into use for resins. Originally, indeed for many centuries, this only applied to the resin itself—when mixed with oil to make varnish it was called 'Verenice liquida'. But hence, later, the French word *vernis* and the Spanish *bernis,* for varnish as we know it."

"This is pretty, this story," Hetta remarked.

"Yes, and of course the English would have to mispronounce the word," Richard said—"Changing the vowel and adding the H."

"*Quite* fascinating," Sir Noël observed. In fact he was if anything less fascinated by the story itself than by his host's remarkable familiarity with this ancient lore, and apparent ignorance of the modern potentialities of Berenice's Hair, of which, he soon learned, Gralheira produced hundreds of tons annually. This seemed to the diplomat so wholly in character as to afford him intense secret pleasure.

But the Duke, once alive to the possibilities of his bulky product, showed a thoroughly practical interest in them. Later, in his study, when the men repaired there for whisky last thing, he asked Lord Heriot some very penetrating questions about the type of machinery required for the distillation plants, the amount of labour necessary, the degree of skill, and what sort of fuel was employed. "Petrol? Oil? I imagine that these substances are fairly inflammable. Could electricity be used?" Indeed Lord Heriot was soon rather out of his depth. He had seen the plants, and knew that they were not unduly large; he had a rough idea of the reduction in bulk by the process of distillation, and was firm on the increased profitability—but as to quantities of labour, and the precise motive power, he could not give exact answers. "Someone would have to go there, and look into it all on the spot," he said. "Pity the old Count's dead, but he has a very good estate manager, who'd know as much as he did himself, or more. Anyhow, I'm sure you'd find it worth going into, Duke." The Duke thought so too; he discussed it further, principally with Atherley and the Ambassador, and before the house-party at Gralheira broke up it had been settled that Nick, on his return to France, should pay a visit to the estate in the Landes, and prepare a full report. Nick was impressed by the list of questions given him by his future Father-in-law—"I hope to goodness that I can find out all he wants," he said to Luzia. "He is a marvellous old boy."

"You will—and it is marvellous that he sends you. You see he relies on you already!" She gave him a happy kiss.

13

"WHERE'S JULIA?" Philip Reeder asked, coming with the post into the library at Glentoran. "Letter for you, Mrs. H."

"Oh, thank you, Philip. She went out with Edina—to do the messages in the village, I think."

"Two for her," Reeder said. "One from her Philip, and a very fat one, sent on from London; come by bag, by the look of it—it's in an Embassy envelope." People in the isolation of the West Highlands are apt to take this close interest in everybody's mail, one of their main links with the outside world.

"Then it may be from Hetta Atherley," Mrs. Hathaway said. "She sometimes writes by bag. Will you excuse me, Philip?"

"Of course." As she opened her letter he stooped and put some wood on the fire, pushing the half-burned logs expertly together with his foot before doing so. "If that's a Portuguese stamp, could I have it?" he added. "I keep them for little Tony Menteith."

Mrs. Hathaway, half-absently, held out the envelope; she was reading her letter with close attention. When she came to the end she turned the sheets and began to read it through again, with a slightly worried air.

"No bad news, I hope?" Philip asked, noticing her expression.

"I don't think so," the old lady replied—"At least he doesn't actually say so. It's from Richard Atherley."

"What does he say?" Reeder asked; he was rather surprised by this apparent uncertainty.

"He asks if I can suggest somewhere for Hetta to stay in England till the next child is born—their own house is let, it seems—with her baby and its nurse; he seems to want her to come as soon as possible."

"Well, that's fair enough. Is he coming too?"

"No—that is what puzzles me. I gathered that they have a *very* nice flat in Madrid, with excellent servants—so why send her back to England, if he can't come himself? They weren't in London long enough for her to make many friends before he went to Paris to work for Nato. So it seems rather strange, to me."

"H'm—yes, I see." Reeder's mind was running back to an earlier letter from Mrs. Atherley. "We never heard what was really worrying her before about that American Admiral, did we? When she wrote and asked Julia whether Torrens could go out?"

"*I* never did, certainly."

"Julia would have been sure to tell you if she'd heard any more. Anyhow nothing happened on that visit; the Admiral —what's this his name was?—yes, Luxworthy, that's it—went to Spain, and went down to that big naval base of theirs, Rota, and flew home to the States, all serene-oh. It was all in the papers; no "untoward incidents" of any sort. So I suppose it was all a mare's nest—she just got into a fuss for nothing. Women in that state often do."

"Richard isn't in that state," Mrs. Hathaway remarked, rather repressively. "He must have some reason for wanting her to come home."

"I s'pose so," Philip said meekly—"And something he doesn't want to tell us—on paper, anyhow. Have some sherry, Mrs. H.—it is twelve."

In a few minutes Julia and Edina came in, the latter in a state of jubilation.

"*Look* what Madame Bonnecourt has done for me!" she exclaimed to Mrs. Hathaway, holding out a small bundle of handkerchiefs. "The most exquisite monograms on my hankies! She twitched them away when she was doing the washing, and cut off the name-tapes, and put these lovely letters on instead."

"It's beautiful work," Mrs. Hathaway said, putting on her spectacles to examine the fruits of the embroidery frame which she had procured at the Frenchwoman's request. "How nice, Edina."

"Two letters for you, Julia," Reeder said. "Can I have that Arabic-looking stamp?"

Julia pinched the stamp out of the thin airmail envelope, and became absorbed in her husband's letter; it was a long one, and took her some time to read—Mrs. Hathaway waited with admirable patience. At last the younger woman opened the other letter, forwarded from Gray's Inn—she gave a slight exclamation of surprise as she began to read.

"*Is* it from Mrs. Atherley?" Philip asked.

"Yes, one is, Mr. Parker!—and one from Luzia. But why should you expect that?" Julia enquired coolly.

"Because Mrs. Hathaway has had a rather odd one from the husband, and we jaloosed that she might have written as well, as it's in an Embassy envelope."

"Well, she has. She says she wants to come home till the next baby arrives, Mrs. H." Julia said, turning to that lady. "Is that what he said to you?"

"Yes—does she say why?" the old lady asked, earnestly.

"No, only asks if I can find somewhere for her to stay, with Richenda and her nurse, because their house is let. He isn't coming."

Edina, who was opening her own mail at her desk, swung round in her chair.

· 195 ·

"Don't tell me they're splitting up already," she said.

"No, I shouldn't think it was that for a moment. Much more likely the same dose as before; some worry about Communist thuggery."

"Nothing came of that last time," Philip put in.

"Not that we heard of. But we might not have heard—Richard is so desperately cagey and official, and I think he tends to infect Hetta. Could I see his letter, Mrs. H.?"

"Of course. But what does Luzia say?"

"Oh yes—I was forgetting Luzia's." She opened the other enclosure from the official envelope. "Here are some Portuguese stamps, Philip, if they're any good to you not postmarked," she added.

"Thanks. Why stamp a letter and not put it in the post?" Philip enquired, stowing the stamps in his wallet.

"More of Richard's fuss, I expect." She read, and then gave another exclamation.

"What is it?" Mrs. Hathaway asked, anxiously.

"Just what I said—those thugs again! Broke her wrist in a car accident that wasn't an accident when that American was in Spain, and has just had another "narrow escape" at Gralheira!"

"Do they know definitely that it was Communists?" Reeder enquired, with the usual masculine tendency to incredulity.

"*Yes*, chum! Luzia spells it out: 'The same people who menaced her before, when you were with us,' is what she says."

"Merciful Heavens!" Mrs. Hathaway exclaimed, horrified.

"How exactly did they 'menace' her before? I don't know that I ever heard," Reeder said.

"Kidnapped her, drugged her, and gagged her!—if that's enough. Mrs. H. found her unconscious in a car after another smash, and saved her life. 'Menaced' is a bit of an understatement," Julia replied crisply.

"And she broke her wrist in Spain, while the American was there?" Mrs. Hathaway asked.

· 196 ·

"That's what Luzia says—in a bogus car accident."

"Then you see it wasn't a mare's nest, Philip, when she wrote before," the old lady said, rather severely.

"No, I give you that, Mrs. Hathaway. I wish we knew what *had* happened. Anyhow from the point of view of international relations it's just as well that it was her wrist that got broken, and not the good Admiral's."

"Oh, really, Philip," his wife protested. "With the wretched girl expecting a baby, and all! You are a callous creature."

"Sorry, Edina. But Nato is pretty important, you know; and now that this second American is going to Spain as well, it is rather vital that nothing should go wrong there."

"What second American?" Julia asked. But before Philip Reeder could answer, his wife broke in.

"Honestly, Julia, if yet *another* official Yank is going to Spain, I think Hetta would be better out of the country. You don't want her acting as a sort of lightning-conductor to American V.I.P.s! Was there anyone high up at Gralheira, that they might have been after, when she had this second narrow escape?"

"Luzia doesn't say so. I daresay they were after Hetta herself—they always keep tabs on anyone they've once got tangled up with, or who has thwarted them in any way," Julia replied gloomily. "Of course we've no means of knowing what happened in Spain, but we do know that she was afraid that something might happen to the Admiral, and that nothing did, only to her—so she might have frustrated some attempt, for all we know."

"And she and Luzia between them were responsible for that man—'the Principal' as the Portuguese police called him—being arrested at Gralheira, when I was in Portugal," Mrs. Hathaway said, thoughtfully.

"While you helped them to mop up the others!" Julia said briskly. "They may or may not have a dossier on you, Mrs. H., but they will certainly have one on her. Yes, she ought to come home."

"Well, have you any plans for where she can stay?" Edina asked.

"I am trying to think," Mrs. Hathaway replied, looking worried. "If it weren't for Richenda and the nurse, I could have her in my flat, but I don't know—" she paused, doubtfully.

"Oh, I don't think that would work very well—your old trouts would hate having a nursery on their hands!" Julia said. Mrs. Hathaway laughed, rather unwillingly, at this description of her elderly maids. "And there just *isn't* quite enough room in Gray's Inn, even if we turned Buchan out." (Buchan was the Jamiesons' cook and man-servant, and general factotum.)

"Oh, you couldn't do that!" Mrs. Hathaway exclaimed. "Whatever would your Philip say?"

"Quite—I couldn't really, very well." She reflected.

"Aren't there hotels?" Philip Reeder asked.

"Yes, of course—only *they're* so tiresome about children now! One would really have to go and get several, and be sure of a place where she would be properly looked after." She frowned. "It looks as though I shall have to bottle the Philipino, and go and do a recce," she said still frowning.

"My dear, I shouldn't do that," Mrs. Hathaway said. "I can go—I can get the maids back quite quickly, with a couple of telegrams. In fact, once one is *in* London, I expect it would be fairly easy to find a place in a private house; so many people are thankful to have p.g.'s today, when servants, and heat and everything, are so expensive. That would be nicer for her than an hotel, if she weren't feeling too well. She ought to have someone to look after her, these last months."

Edina Reeder had continued, intermittently, to open her mail while this conversation went on; now she got up, left her desk, and came over to the fire, getting herself a glass of sherry on the way.

"I think that's a thoroughly *bad* idea, Mrs. H.," she said.

"What, Hetta's p.g.-ing?" Julia asked.

"No; Mrs. H. going South, and wearing herself out finding a place—or you bottling the brat, either. If Mrs. Atherley and her private crêche are going to p.g. anywhere, why shouldn't they come here, for a start, anyway? There's oceans of room, and we can get in any extra help that's needed. Then she'll be among friends. What do you say?" she enquired of her husband.

"Yes, by all means—on one condition."

"What's that?" his wife asked suspiciously.

"That she tells us *all!* I really can't wait to hear what's at the back of all this—it's too tantalising to be on the fringe of history in the making, and only get these hints and scraps."

Edina laughed; Julia frowned slightly.

"If you're going to pester her, Philip, she'd better not come here. I'm sure she'll tell us anything she thinks proper, but she oughtn't to have to fence, or be careful."

"Oh, nonsense, Julia," Mrs. Reeder exclaimed. "You know he wouldn't really bother her."

"Sorry," Julia said at once. "I take that back, Philip. It's just that I'm worried about her; I feel she must have had pretty well all that she can take."

"I'm sure she has," Mrs. Hathaway said. "But really, Julia, I think it's a most excellent idea. As Edina says, she will be with people she knows and trusts—and Dr. Macfarlane is very clever at confinements, isn't he, Edina?"

"He's done me all right, *twice*—and unless she wants a gamp of her own, Nurse Campbell is an exceptionally good midwife," Mrs. Reeder replied.

"I'm sure it would be a great relief to Richard's mind if she came here," Mrs. Hathaway pursued.

"Yes, so do I, really," Julia said. "Thank you, Edina—and you too, Philip. I'll write this afternoon, and run down and catch the bus with it." She looked across at her hostess. "I'm sure you'll like her," she said—"And she'll love Glentoran. She's a very countrified creature."

"Good. And you can tell her wretched Richard that if any

Communists *should* turn up in Tarbertshire, we've got a professional thug-hunter on the spot!" Edina said gaily. "Good for Bonnecourt to keep his hand in."

"Don't suggest anything so horrible, Edina!" Mrs. Hathaway protested.

"Sorry, Mrs. H.—I was only funning."

"Why not telegraph?" Reeder said to Julia.

"No, I think I'll write. Letters are quite quick to Portugal. Edina, you'll have to think up a figure per week, so that I can tell them."

"Is that really necessary?" Philip enquired. "There's no need for them to come as p.g.'s."

"Oh, I'm sure they'll insist on that, and they're not in the least poor. Make it a rational sum, Edina, that they'll believe in."

"Right-oh." Mrs. Reeder returned to her desk, and began jotting on a block. "Heat, light, board, extra milk for the child, an extra maid for the cleaning—I can make it sound quite a lot."

"You needn't itemise it!" her husband said, looking shocked.

"Of course I shan't—that's only for myself." She scribbled away. "There! Fifteen pounds a week," she exclaimed triumphantly.

"Make it guineas—sounds more realistic," Philip said.

"Oh, I am so glad about this," Mrs. Hathaway said fervently. "Do start your letter, Julia. You won't have much time after luncheon."

"Use my desk," said her hostess. "I've done." Mrs. Reeder always bestowed her correspondence immediately in large wire trays; her INs and OUTs were as methodical as any civil servant's—so the large area of green blotting-paper in the centre remained uncluttered. Mrs. Jamieson sat down at the desk, pulled a sheet of paper out of the rack, and began to write rapidly. Her handwriting was large; she was already on a second sheet when she swung round in her chair.

"How's she to get here?" she demanded of the room at large. "From London, I mean? They'll have too much luggage to fly to Renfrew. Won't someone have to go down to London to meet her, and bring her up?"

"Can't the good Atherley do that much?" Edina enquired.

"If he can get away, with this second American coming— that's the question," her husband said.

"Why on earth shouldn't he? Surely this visit must be the American Embassy's funeral?" Edina persisted.

"In theory, yes; but the whole thing is a Nato set-up, and he was fairly high up in Nato in Paris till quite recently, so he might be a useful person to have on hand."

"Well, if he can't come, someone will have to cope. They'll want sleepers, for one thing, and then there's that awful journey down to Gourock, and getting onto the boat—and she won't be able to understand a word that's said to her in Glaswegian, I don't suppose," Julia said.

"I should leave all that for this letter," Mrs. Hathaway advised. "You can go into details nearer the time. I can perfectly go down and meet her, if it is necessary—I have done the journey often enough! Which are you writing to?"

"Her—Hetta, I mean. I can write to Luzia tomorrow."

"I think I will send a line to Richard," the old lady said, getting up. "No, don't move, Julia; I have all my writing-things in my room. If you will post my letter with yours, that will be very kind."

"Of course, Mrs. H." Julia went back to her writing. When she had finished—"Well, I think that's everything," she remarked, folding the sheets. "I've said any time, and the terms, and Dr. Macfarlane being a good *accoucheur;* and I *did* put in that Mrs. H. would go down and meet her if required. And Edina, I ventured to say that if my Philip doesn't come dashing home, I should still be here. That O.K.?"

"Perfectly O.K. by me," said her hostess.

"And by me," said her host. "Yes, all that ought to satisfy them."

14

IT MIGHT REALLY have been better if Julia Jamieson had accepted Philip Reeder's suggestion of sending a telegram, however non-committal, to say that a place was arranged for Hetta; it would have set several minds at Gralheira at rest. As it was, the delay in getting a reply to their respective appeals began to worry both Richard and Hetta, well before the letters came.

"I cannot *think* why Julia, at least, does not answer," Hetta repeated, unhappily; Richard began to wonder if the letters could have been sent to Madrid, and went so far as to ring up the Chancery—but everything with an English postmark had been forwarded at once—and nothing had come in the last forty-eight hours.

The Ambassador was beginning to fret, too; it was time for him to return, and he would have preferred to have his Counsellor with him when he did so—on the other hand he quite understood Richard's desire to accompany his wife on her journey to Madrid, and did not wish to thwart this. Uneasily, they all waited.

Nick and Luzia were the least troubled; they had plenty to occupy their minds. Lord Heriot had undertaken to arrange for Nick's visit to the Landes as soon as he returned to Pau—"I can do it all in no time when I'm there; get that factor fellow on the telephone"—for the Heriots too were contemplating their departure. The date of the wedding was settled: for the spring, shortly after Easter; in the meantime, Luzia was firm with her Father over settling precisely where the new bathrooms and fitted basins were to go, so that the work could be put in hand during the winter.

Over this, Nick gained fresh kudos with his prospective Father-in-law. The old gentleman was considerably bothered over the problem of getting hot water to such a distance from the boiler-house; he feared that the present boiler might be inadequate to the task, for the water was by no means always very hot even in the existing bathroom. Nick looked, and measured, and made some neat diagrams; then he unfolded quite a different scheme. Cold water already ran up to the bathroom and lavatory; from there *cold*-water pipes could be inserted inconspicuously behind the skirting-boards and run along to his and Luzia's suite and their personal guest-rooms; so could power-wires—then instal really large immersion-heaters in the bathrooms, he said, and the only hot-water piping required would be that to connect these with the fitted basins. The Duke was first startled, then delighted, at these wonders of modern science; he actually insisted on driving to Oporto to see an immersion-heater for himself, and returned greatly impressed. Luzia laughed gleefully—"You will see, Papa will soon have a fitted basin with hot water in that little cloak-room next to his study!" she told her fiancé. "He does not like washing his hands in cold water in the winter, and it will save him walking upstairs." By immemorial custom hot water, in brightly-polished copper jars, appeared before every meal on the wash-stands of all occupied bedrooms, as well as night and morning; but it had never occurred to the Duke to have this luxury downstairs, though there was a small basin in an antique fitted mahogany stand in his little cloak-room, with a tiny ewer of cold water.

But what pleased Ericeira most over all this was the anxiety displayed by his future son-in-law to do nothing to injure or disturb the beauty and character of the house. This required considerable ingenuity, but Nick seemed equal to it. He demonstrated, by means of his neatly-drawn plans, that by cutting a strip off the end of one spare-room, putting up partitions and making new doors, two extra bathrooms could be provided for the guest-suites. "Personally, I should move the panelling; then the Blue Room will all be in harmony—people who haven't seen it will not notice that it has been touched," he said earnestly. "And there will be quite enough panelling on the end of the piece cut off to make into two new doors, for the Blue Room *and* the Gold Room. But of course you will want to consult your architect," he added modestly. The Duke, practical over matters of which he had some knowledge, wanted to know where the waste-pipes would go?

"Well, that is rather a worry. Of course a single pipe will do both baths, and another both W.C.'s; but it is right on the East Front, I know. It would cost a fearful lot, but it would be *possible* to run the pipes down in the thickness of the wall, so that nothing would show outside at all; and the outdoor drains could go along the edge of the drive and be pushed under the wall of the back yard, and join up with those from the kitchen and pantry. I made a sketch"—he showed it.

The Duke really minded less what it cost than that the exterior of Gralheira should not be spoiled in any way. However he made some calculations, and it was finally decided that the waste-pipes should be hidden in the great thickness of the walls; as for the expense—"From the additional profits which we shall make from the turpentine, once we get those distillation plants going, it will easily be covered," he said gaily. And later on he spoke, almost shyly, to Lord Heriot in praise of his son. "He has such *understanding*, as well as all his practical knowledge," he ended. "I"—he hesitated—"I should wish you to know how fortunate I count myself." To which Lord Heriot could only grunt out that he was glad, and that the boy wasn't a bad boy at all.

Mrs. Jamieson's letter, when it finally did arrive, fully satisfied the Atherleys, after it had been digested and discussed. "I *am* to stay with Julia!" Hetta announced triumphantly—"At least in the same house. But not in London; at Glentoran, where we wrote before," she said to Luzia. "This is in Scotland, no?"

"Yes—it is Colin Monro's home," Luzia replied.

"So? We are to pay the fees to some people called Reeder," Hetta pursued.

"Yes—Mrs. Reeder is Colin's sister." During her prolonged stay with Julia Jamieson in the Pyrenees, before the latter's baby was born, Luzia had not only seen much of Colin, but had become quite *au fait* with the family connections; indeed she had met most of them, briefly, the year before when she went to London to be the single bridesmaid at Julia's wedding. "Colin's sister, and Miss Probyn's cousin," she added, to make everything clear. "They look after the estate for Colin, since he is constantly away."

"What fees are you to pay to these Reeders?" Richard asked, a little doubtfully.

"Fifteen guineas a week, for us all—me and a maid, if I want to take one, and Richenda and *la Suissesse*. Julia says that as we shall be there for some time, she thought you would wish it to be a business arrangement," Hetta replied, turning the page. "Oh, Mrs. Hattaway will be there also," she exclaimed, delighted.

"That is *very* nice, I must say," Richard said.

"Yes—and she will come down to meet us in London, and take us up," Hetta pursued; "Mrs. Hattaway, I mean. It seems it is a rather complicated journey: two trains, and a ship, and then cars."

"Sounds rather out-of-the-way. I wonder if there's a decent doctor?" Richard speculated. Hetta was reading on; after a few moments—"Yes, there is! He has delivered both Mrs. Reeder's babies; there is also a good midwife in the village, she says."

"Well done Miss Probyn! She seems to have thought of everything." Richard was at last quite appeased. "Fifteen guineas is dirt cheap, anyhow," he said. "It would be that for one person in an hotel, these days. And I shall feel much easier in my mind to know you're among friends."

"There is another very nice person there also," Luzia put in. "To Miss Probyn he was a *good* friend."

"Who is that?" Hetta asked. "Oh, she says there is central heating, and that the house is always very warm, so that we shall not feel the cold."

"Perfect," from Richard.

"Now, who is this other friend?" Hetta asked, folding up the letter.

"Bonnecourt, from Larège. He is a splendid person!" the girl said with enthusiasm.

"Who and what is Bonnecourt?" Richard asked, without much interest.

"Well he *was* a smuggler!" the girl replied, giggling a little. "And also an *isard*-hunter, and a guide to *alpinistes*. But now he works as game-keeper to Mr. Reeder."

"Funny idea to have an ex-smuggler as one's game-keeper," Richard observed. "How does that come about?"

"Oh, he had to leave France, because he had been connected, a little, with the O.A.S., so the police wanted him. But he had also worked for British Intelligence before, so Colin and Colonel Jamieson arranged to get him out; a friend of Nick's flew him into Spain, and Colin drove him to Gibraltar. He is a *splendid* person," she repeated. "Nick will tell you all about him—he used to take Nick and Dick out after *isard*."

Richard was not particulary interested in Bonnecourt. He asked to see Mrs. Jamieson's letter, and read it through. "Well, that all sounds excellent," he said. "Of course writing to London will have delayed things. But I wonder that I haven't heard from Mrs. Hathaway."

"There is a letter for you in the hall," Luzia told him. The inhabitants of Gralheira did not subject their guests' mail to such a close scrutiny as habitually took place at Glentoran.

Richard went and fetched the letter—it was from Mrs. Hathaway, and confirmed the relief and satisfaction which he already felt.

"I think you are so wise to send her away—I am horrified at what she has been through," the old lady wrote. "But this place will be ideal for them all, until you can arrange something more permanent—there are three young children in the house already, so there will be a nice *big* nursery party; Hetta's Nannie will have plenty of company on walks. And on her days out she will be a godsend to Madame Bonnecourt, if she will visit her sometimes and talk French to her; the poor woman doesn't get on very fast with her English. Edina is quite thankful that they are coming, if only for that reason— but it was her idea, originally; I did not even have to suggest it. And she and Philip only agreed to let them pay anything because Julia said you would prefer it."

So grateful letters to Glentoran were written, but again not sent by post; Richard said he would send them by bag from Madrid. By an ironical turn of fate he, who had so often accused his wife of imagining things, had now become far the more nervous of the two. A couple of days later they all set off for Spain—Hetta and Luzia in the big Rolls with the Ambassador, while Richard drove Richenda and Élise, her Swiss Nannie, plus Luzia's maid. Luzia had volunteered to come and give Hetta any help she could with her packing and other arrangements, and this was gratefully accepted—the Heriot party, in any case, was leaving the following day. But before this—

"Well, darling, I'm much happier today than I was the day I arrived, I can tell you," Nick said to Luzia as they took a last walk in the lower garden beside the fountain, "although we shan't be seeing one another for a bit. You always said I should like your Father, but I hadn't expected him to be such a *complete* darling; nor that he would be so good to me. I do think it has gone all right, don't you?"

"Yes—I could not have wished it to go better. I am so happy that he has taken to your ideas about the resin; that will give you more to do."

"Do you want me to have more to do?" he asked, taking her arm and peering inquisitively into her face.

"Oh yes. Then you will not be *désoeuvré,* and bored. It is very isolated here, you know—though of course we shall sometimes be in Lisbon; and people come to stay. I hope your parents and Dick will often come. But *en principe,* men cannot have too much to do," she said, smiling at him.

"Can women?"

"Nature generally sees to it that they have at least enough!" she said, and then blushed a little.

"Oh my darling!" He took her in his arms and kissed her.

"Easter isn't all that far away," he said then. "But I dare say I shall see you before that; I'd like to bring this famous report myself, really."

"Oh, shall you? That would be *so* nice. Also, it is especially nice that your parents and Papa are so happy together," she added. "I wish they had not to leave just now, when I go to Madrid—but I think I ought to."

"Yes, I'm sure you ought. Take care of Mrs. Atherley; she needs it. And take care of yourself too, my dearest one—and write often. Promise?"

Back in the flat in Madrid, Hetta at first gazed about her with a curious sense of surprise. It was almost as if she had never left it; all the events of the past few weeks might have been a dream.

"What is it?" Richard asked, noticing her expression.

"The last time I was in this room was on the morning when we started so early, to drive to Toledo," she said slowly. "That is odd, no?"

"*Haven't* you been here since? Oh no, of course you went

straight to Gralheira from the Isabella. Well, I am very thankful that you're here now," he said, giving her a kiss. "Not too tired?"

"Not, not really." She put up a hand and touched the strapping on her forehead.

"Headache?" he asked anxiously,

"No. I just make sure that it all really happened."

"Like Hell it happened! But it's all over and done with now." He watched her a little nervously, puzzled by her mood.

The telephone rang—Hetta automatically lifted the receiver.

"*Diga-me?*" (The Spanish "Tell me" always seems so much more rational than our "Hullo?")

"La Señora Atherley, please."

"It is me, Nell," Hetta said. "How are you?"

"Oh darling, you *are* back. Well thank Heaven for that, anyhow! When can I come and see you?"

"Tomorrow—not too early," Hetta said; Richard was frowning and shaking his head at her.

"What time? Half after eleven? I simply have to see you."

"No—half-past twelve. I have things to do before that. How are you?" Hetta repeated.

"Oh, everything's terrible! I must tell you."

"Tell me tomorrow, Nell," Hetta said firmly. "I have only just got in. Goodbye." She rang off.

"Now look here, Hetta, you simply must make that little creature understand that you can't be at her beck and call the whole time, as you were before," Richard expostulated. "You've got too much to do, and you aren't up to it. If you won't be tough with her, I shall speak to Walter—otherwise she'll fag you to death."

"I shall see to it—I think you need not worry Walter."

"Well mind you *are* firm. She's really almost as much of a menace as the Commies!" he grumbled. Hetta laughed, and went to her room. This was definitely the old Madrid, just as it had been before the drive to Toledo; except that then Richard had not worried unduly about how much she did—and that she did, undoubtedly, tire more easily now. When Luzia came in to suggest that she should have her dinner in bed she agreed gratefully, and asked that the cook should be told that she would see her tomorrow.

Mrs. Parrott duly arrived, after Hetta had seen her household, paid some bills, given orders about meals, and visited Richenda in her sunny nursery.

"Well, darling, it's wonderful that you're back at last—it has seemed an *age*. But what have you done to your head?" Nell asked, looking curiously at the strapping on her friend's forehead.

Hetta was disconcerted—she had forgotten to think up a story for Nell, or indeed for anyone else, to account for her injury.

"Oh, it is nothing," she said. "I tripped and fell against something sharp," she added lamely. "Now tell me everything."

Nell burst into a flood of her own affairs. "And Mr. Hardiman Everitt is coming himself!" she presently announced, round-eyed.

"When?"

"The week after next. I shall have to give a party for him, like I did for the Luxworthys, and a luncheon too—and I may have to help act as hostess at the Embassy reception, because Mrs. Packer has gone home."

"Goodness, why has she done that, just now?"

"Oh, her kidneys have gone wrong after the scarlet fever—it seems they often do. Anyway she's gone—it's most trying."

"Very trying for the Ambassador," Hetta agreed.

"Well, it's trying for everyone! So I thought you could help me make a list of people for the luncheon, and for the cocktail-party."

"For the cocktail it is easy—use the old list."

"That's what Walter said. But I threw it away."

"Oh Nell, that was foolish. You should always keep your lists." She reflected. "Never mind—ring up Commander Mansfield; he is sure to remember who came. And he will be able to advise you as to whom you should ask to the luncheon."

"Why yes—that's a good idea. But I thought maybe you and I could do it all, jus: the two of us together."

"Commander Mansfield will know far better than I do who ought to be invited to the luncheon," Hetta said.

"I s'pose so," Nell said doubtfully. "And then I don't know whether we hadn't better have that at the Castellana-Hilton."

"Why not at home?"

"Oh, it's all so difficult now! Luis used to fix everything, and make suggestions about dishes and wine and flowers, but this new chauffeur is no manner of use!—he can't even speak English. And he doesn't seem to care to help in the house." She was almost tearful.

"I am sorry," Hetta said.

"It was so *funny* of him, going off like that, without saying a word! I thought he was so fond of us," Nell went on. "I know I was of him; he was such a help. And Walter won't even *try* to get him back!—he just shuts up when I talk about it, and says he believes he's left the country, and that it's no good asking about him." She did now sniff, and dab at her eyes. *"You* don't know why he cleared off, do you?" she asked suddenly, peering intently at her friend.

Oh, Nell and her questions! Poor Hetta groaned inwardly.

"But Nell, how could I? I was in the clinic when he left—don't you remember?" she said.

"Yes, I know—but you were there when the car crashed. I thought maybe you might know something."

"No, I cannot help you about that," Hetta said firmly. She got up. "I haven't given you a drink," she said—"How careless of me? Sherry, or a Martini?"

"A Martini, please." As her hostess mixed the cocktails— "Luis made such marvellous Martinis!" Mrs. Parrott lamented.

"There!" Hetta said, handing her a glass. "Now, would you like to ring up Commander Mansfield, and see if he can come to see you this afternoon? For the luncheon, at least, the invitations ought to go out as soon as possible."

Nell agreed to do this, and secured the Commander for five o'clock. "But you'll come along too, won't you, so we can all plan it together?"

"No, Nell, I shall not be able to come today—I am sorry."

"Oh darling! Whyever not?"

"I shall have to rest—yesterday was a long drive, and in any case I often try to rest now in the afternoons, for the sake of the baby."

"But you'll come to the luncheon? And the cocktail-party?"

"If Richard is free, and Commander Mansfield thinks we ought to be included in the luncheon, I am sure we shall be delighted to come—for the cocktail, yes, for my part." She almost said "If I am here," but remembered in time not to refer to leaving Madrid. For *that*, at least, she and Richard must agree on a suitable story.

"I'm sure Mansfield will think you ought to come to the luncheon," Nell said—"Anyway *I* want you! How will I manage alone?" She was rather upset by Hetta's formal tone.

"You might ask Luzia Ericeira to come and help you—she is with us again."

"Well, she's nice, and she knows lots of people—but it's not the same thing as having you. I know who *will* be pleased to see her," Nell said, perking up a little, and looking arch.

"Who is that?"

"Ellington—he's coming with Mr. Everitt; well a few days before, I believe. He'll be here for the whole visit."

"Oh, I am glad—I like him so much," Hetta said. "He, also, will be a great help to you. By the way, Luzia is now engaged to be married," she added to check the archness in good time.

"Is she? Who to?"

"A young Englishman—Lord Heriot's son."

"Poor Ellington!" Nell said, with a little laugh. "He liked her a lot." And presently she took her departure, rather to Hetta's relief.

Richard came home to luncheon. In spite of a busy morning, catching up with his backlog of work, he had found time to get on to the travel agents, and secure passages for his party on a Highland Line boat, sailing from Vigo for Tilbury in a little over a fortnight.

"Yes, it's a good line," he said. "Very comfortable boats. I've taken a berth for Speranza too—I can always cancel that when I send tomorrow to collect the tickets, if you don't want her."

Hetta pondered.

"I wonder if I shall need her," she said at last. "I am accustomed to doing things for myself—at least I used to be! And in Scotland, in the country, I suppose there will not be much going out; here, it is useful to have a maid, because one's clothes must be pressed so often. And she might be homesick, in a strange country. What do you think?" she asked Luzia.

"I should take her," that young person said, unhesitatingly. "I do not see why she should be lonely; she and Élise are great friends, and if Élise should get influenza or something, Speranza could look after the child. Richenda adores her!"

"There is something in that," Richard said. "Yes, I should take her, Hetta."

"Also one hears that there are not so many servants in England today," Luzia pursued "Mrs. Reeder may be very glad of an extra maid. Would she like to go?"

"I did not ask her yet—but I expect so. Half the maids in Spain seem to want to go to England now!"

"Very well, that's settled."

"Yes, but now we must settle something else, Richard. When I tell Speranza that we go to England, in ten minutes the whole household will know it—and in two hours more, half Madrid! We must give some reason."

"I know—H.E. and I were talking about that this morning. Crafty old boy, he'd got it all worked out!"

"What?" both girls asked.

"Physio-therapy for your wrist! Particularly good in England, and needs prolonged treatment, two or three times a week, for ages."

"But my wrist is nearly all right."

"Yes, only people here needn't know that. Back you go into your sling, my girl!—everyone knows you broke your wrist, in a car-crash that can be talked about as much as you like. And it hasn't got quite right, and a renowned Portuguese doctor has urged this course. No need to go into details; just stick to your story, and everyone will believe it."

Luzia began to laugh; Hetta frowned a little.

"But Nell saw me this morning, without the sling."

"Well, when she sees you with one, you can just tell her you took it off for half an hour. How did you get on with her, by the way?"

Hetta related what had passed.

"Quite right to turn her over to Mansfield—he's the proper person to deal with her invitations, of course."

"But I said that perhaps Luzia would help her with the cocktail-party. Do you mind?" she asked her guest.

"Oh, this I can easily do—and for *you*, willingly."

"Thank you. But Richard, besides my wrist, she asked about my head."

"Bother the woman! What did you say?"

"That I stumbled, and fell against something with a sharp edge, and cut it. It was all I could think of, to a sudden question."

"Well, that will do all right—I'll tell H.E.. We four are the only ones who know otherwise, except Ainsworth; and I'm seeing him this afternoon, so I'll alert him. I ought to have thought of that before. Had she anything else to say, besides these moans about Luis?"

"Only that Ellington comes back for this American's visit."

"Good. That's a nice boy—he'll be a help to poor Nell, and to Mansfield too."

Hetta thought that Luzia looked a little disconcerted at the mention of Lieutenant Ellington's name. When Richard had gone the girl said to her—"This is certain, that Ellington comes?"

"Yes. And Luzia, I told Nell of your engagement—I

· 214 ·

thought it might be wise to do this. I hope you do not mind?"

"No. I am glad that you did." She gave a brief laugh. "It will save putting the announcement in the newspapers!"

"Everyone will see your ring, and ask questions, in any case."

"Yes. You are perfectly right."

When Richard saw Ainsworth later that afternoon he began by telling him at once about the plan for Scotland.

"Well, I don't imagine it's necessary now, but I understand how you feel," the Intelligence man said. "It has been very tough for her. By the way, I passed on to Day everything you told me about what she'd done in Portugal—getting that priest over, who produced all the dope about El Lobo, *and* doing it with a hole in her head! He's tremendously impressed, and so are his people in Washington—and grateful too. They'd have been on tenterhooks all through Everitt's visit if that cell hadn't been cleared up. Major Day would like to come and call on her one day, and thank her personally."

"That's very nice of him, but I don't think it's necessary. I'd really rather she wasn't reminded of any of it," Richard said. "That's one reason why I want to get her away. Can you stand him off? She has got her hands rather full, actually, with her packing, and settling which servants to get rid of, and farewell calls, and so on."

"I'll try," Ainsworth said, rather doubtfully. "I think it's more than just Day—I gather Washington would like some official recognition of what she's done to be expressed."

"Oh well then, let them give her the Purple Heart, and have done with it!" Atherley exploded. "She's got a perfectly good wound! Oh, by the way," he went on, as Ainsworth laughed, "the cover-story for her head is that she tripped and fell against something, and cut her forehead open—not very convincing, but Mrs. Parrott put her on the spot before we'd thought anything up, so that's what she said; and now we must stick to it."

"I should think that's good enough."

"And as for her going home, a big Portuguese shot has said that to get her wrist really put right she must have physiotherapy for it for several months, and that's better done in England than here."

"Oh, I *am* sorry," Ainsworth said, with genuine concern. Richard laughed.

"Nonsense! Her wrist's practically cured already; she never saw any high-powered Portuguese at all, just a rather good man in Oporto. That's merely the "Authorised Version", Ainsworth."

"Oh, I get you. Right, I'll remember." He paused. "Do you think I could see her, just for a few minutes? It's only to tell her about that poor woman near Pamplona," he added hastily.

"Yes—I'm sure she'd like that very much. Could you look in for a drink before lunch tomorrow? You can? Fine."

15

WHEN AINSWORTH ARRIVED at the Atherley's flat next day he found Hetta alone; Richard had not yet got back. He looked, rather furtively, at the strapping on her forehead, but made no reference to it.

"I am so glad to see you," Mrs. Atherley said. "It is kind of you to come." After giving him a drink—"Now, tell me about this poor woman. I was most thankful when I heard that you had been to see her."

"I was glad I did, myself, when I got there," Ainsworth said simply. "She'd been terribly anxious about the boy, hearing nothing for so long; in a way I think she almost expected it—well, some bad news, anyhow." He paused. "These Spanish peasants have such a frightening dignity," he went on. "I turn up, a total stranger, to tell her that her only son is dead, and she *thanks* me for coming!"

"Poor creature!"

"Yes. It was an inspired idea, sending the lock of hair," Ainsworth pursued. "She only broke down when I opened the letter, and gave her that—she kissed it, and then she kissed my hand! I was so very glad you'd thought of it."

"I did not—it was the Condesa Ericeira."

"Well, it was absolutely the right thing. She asked me to thank "The Lady", anyhow."

"I will tell her—I am sorry that she is out just now. But Mr.

Ainsworth, did you tell her *how* her son came to die? I mean, that he killed himself?"

"Well no—I rather slid over that. I said that he had attacked someone, and been arrested, and got wounded, and died later. I concentrated more on his having had a priest, and one who spoke his own language. She didn't seem surprised, or even very curious—as I said, I think she expected it. Spaniards do expect Communists who attack people to die," Ainsworth added flatly.

"Has she anything to live on?" Hetta enquired.

"I asked the priest about that. Precious little, I gathered—a couple of goats and a few fowls, and a small plot of land; the *Cura* said the boy used to send her something occasionally after he left. In fact—I don't know if I did right—but I had seen in Father Martinez' notes that her son had asked particularly that his Mother should be "looked after", so I left some money with the priest, for him to give her a little once a week."

"Will that be all right? Will he really give it to her, I mean?"

"Oh, I'm sure he will—he struck me as being an excellent man. I had to be a bit careful about it; it wouldn't do for the idea to get round that anyone official subvented the families of Communist assassins!" Ainsworth said, with a wry grin—"and the priest, at least, must have tumbled to the fact that I was connected with officialdom, or I shouldn't have been in possession of the facts. So I told him that the money came from the Portuguese lady who signed the letter and sent the hair."

"Very right—excellent." She asked how much Ainsworth had given, opened her purse, and repaid him at once. "Now 'officialdom' is guiltless," she said, with a smile.

"Thank you very much, Mrs. Atherley. You needn't really have bothered, but that does put me in the clear."

"How long will that last her?" Hetta wanted to know.

"The *Cura* thought two or three months."

"Could we send her some more, through him?"

"Oh, easily, I should imagine, provided your husband can find some go-between. It might not be advisable to send it too directly."

"I know who will see to it," Hetta said.

"Who is that?"

"A Portuguese Monsignor—Subercaseaux."

"Oh, him! Yes, he'll fix it like a shot."

"You know him?" Hetta asked, surprised.

"*Of* him, yes. He's in close touch with Spanish Intelligence; he tipped off the Special Police about all this recent business in Portugal at one point. Oh by the way," Ainsworth said—"Talking of the Special Police, I managed to arrange that they should not go and see the poor woman. I explained that I had been myself, and made all the necessary enquiries; and as it was we who had put them onto El Lobo and his pals they were willing to leave it at that—they more or less had to be."

"What has happened to El Lobo and those who worked with him? Are they in prison?"

"Yes."

"And the Hungarians from the earlier time, what about them? I know that Luis, the chauffeur, was deported."

"Yes, because he had American papers; it was easy to arrange that with the authorities in the States. But I think the others are in jug here; the ones who were to have carried out the actual ambush, I mean." He checked himself. Atherley had said he did not want his wife to see Major Day for fear she should be reminded of "any of it", and here he was talking about the Toledo ambush itself!

But Hetta went on with her questions. Her conscience was at work again; she was in a way responsible, and she wanted to know exactly what she was responsible *for*. At last she had got a member of British Intelligence to herself, and she was determined to make the most of the opportunity. How long would the Hungarians be kept in prison? And those two—the dead boy's companions—who had been caught in Portugal?

Ainsworth was thoroughly embarrassed.

"Well, the ones in Portugal were quite small beer," he began, "and not very efficient. . . ." Again he checked himself.

"No—they were sent to liquidate me, and failed to do it!" Hetta said, brightly. "But how long will they be kept in prison?"

Ainsworth thought only of getting off the hook, at that moment.

"Well really, Mrs. Atherley, I can't tell you exactly. Major Day knows much more about this than I do; the whole business has been handled by the Spanish Security Police, and naturally they show up to the Americans, because it's an American whose safety has been at stake, both times—here in Spain, I mean," he added hastily.

Hetta managed not to smile.

"Major Day is in American Intelligence?" she asked.

"Yes, he's their man here."

"Oh, I *wish* I could see him! I do so much want to know more about this."

"Well, in fact he wanted to see you," Ainsworth began. "Only—" oh damn, this was getting worse and worse!

"Only what?"

"I think your husband thought you would be too busy," he said lamely.

"For this I am certainly not too busy. Will you tell him that I should very much like to see him?"

Ainsworth tried to stall.

"Perhaps your husband could let him know," he suggested.

Ah, and perhaps he wouldn't, Hetta thought to herself. Obviously Richard, for some reason, was trying to prevent her from seeing Major Day—and she was not going to be prevented, if she could help it.

"Oh, I am sure he could," she said easily. "I will ask him to ring him up, if you will just give me his telephone number—it will not be in the directory, of course," she added smiling, "but you, I am sure, know it; you need to."

"I'm not sure that the Major would care to have it written

down," the wretched Ainsworth said, wriggling desperately on his tormentor's hook.

"But naturally not! I shall do nothing of the sort. I have an excellent memory," the pretty tormentor said, still smiling.

Ainsworth had to give way, of course; and in the course of this conversation he had come to the conclusion that any fears Atherley might entertain for his wife's health or nerves, as a result of recalling her recent experiences, were completely unfounded. She was as cool and determined a customer as he had ever come across! He gave her the number, and left as soon as he could. If she did see the Major, and Atherley was vexed, it would be just too bad, he said to himself as he drove back to his office.

Hetta telephoned the moment he had left the room, and caught Day just as he was going out to lunch; he was obviously surprised, but also pleased, at being invited to come and have tea with the British Counsellor's wife. "Then at 5.30? That suits you? For me it is a good time. Au revoir." She rang off abruptly as Richard walked in.

"Who was that?" he asked. "Not that wretched Nell?"

"No—someone else. How *nice* your Mr. Ainsworth is!" she exclaimed, and embarked immediately on a flowing account of his kindness towards la Viuda Elizondo; before it was ended Luzia had come in, and they went to lunch—Atherley forgot about the telephone call. Quite casually and normally, over coffee, Hetta extracted from him what his movements were to be that afternoon, and learned that, as she had expected, he would be in the Chancery from five till half-past six or later—"Then I shall try to get in a game of squash with Marchant." This would allow her plenty of time with the American, if he was punctual; she must just hope that he would be.

He was.

"Well, Mrs. Atherley, this is very good of you," he began. "I'm *so* glad to meet you at last. I suppose Ainsworth let you know how badly I wanted to see you?"

"He just mentioned that you had wished to—but I wanted

to see *you*. That is why I telephoned; I made him give me your number."

Day looked a little startled at this announcement.

"He didn't tell you why I wanted us to meet?"

"No."

"Well, may I get my part over with first?" he asked, very nicely.

"Of course—but do let me give you some tea. Cream and sugar?" She poured out for them both with her right hand; her left arm was in a sling. "Now, what is your 'part'?" she said, sitting back.

Major Day proceeded to make her a little speech. His "bosses" in Washington, he said, had asked him to seek an opportunity to thank her formally on their behalf for all the information she had produced in matters vital to their security arrangements for two visits of major political importance, and to express how greatly they regretted that this information should have been obtained at so much risk and cost to herself; also how earnestly they hoped that she would suffer no permanent ill-effects. He was obviously speaking from a prepared text, and it all sounded a little pompous and heavy-footed— Hetta was rather taken aback.

"But this is quite unnecessary!" she exclaimed when he had finished. "What else could I have done, once I knew what they planned? In fact I was not very efficient—I ought to have spoken before we left the cigarral, so that the Admiral would not have been in that car at all."

"Well, I don't know about that—what I do know, and what they know at home, is that but for your information that chauffeur would still have been driving our Naval Attaché around!" Major Day said with some warmth; he too was slightly taken aback by this reception of his little complimentary address. "*And* that something would have been fixed for the Secretary of State, but for the way you handled things in Portugal, getting a Spanish-speaker to that dying man. They're grateful, that's all—and I don't know since when gratitude has become unnecessary. Anyway, that's not the way they feel in Washington!"

Hetta saw that he was hurt, and apologised at once.

"I am so sorry—do forgive me. It is just that I was taken so by surprise! It is very kind of those people in Washington; and of you too, to come and tell me. Please thank them very much for me. It is only that I really did not *do* very much myself; and for my hand and my head, they were things that just happened."

"That's quite all right, Mrs. Atherley. I see how modest you are—only you mustn't expect other folks to take you at your own valuation!" the American said pleasantly. "Now, what was it that you wanted to see me about?—for I realise you hadn't an idea of why I had to see you."

Hetta began her questions. The Hungarians who were to have carried out the ambush—had they been sent away, or were they in prison here in Spain? The latter, he told her; Spain had no diplomatic relations with Hungary. And how long for? Well, probably fifteen to twenty years—"You couldn't expect them to be released all that soon; after all, they were planning a cold-blooded murder."

And the ones from Portugal? Much the same, or maybe life sentences. "Was this what you wanted to see me for, to ask about these men?" Day enquired, studying her dismayed face, with the strapping across the left eyebrow.

"Yes. Ainsworth said you would know, since the Spanish Police were dealing directly with you."

He continued to look at her. "Would you like to tell me why you want so much to know about them?" he asked at last.

Rather haltingly, Hetta tried to explain her private worry; she did not do it very well, and ended rather desperately— "You see, in a way it is through *me* that they are shut up, maybe for all their lives; and if they have wives and children, or old parents who will not see them again! I wish it had not been through me."

Major Day looked at her very benevolently.

"I guess I understand," he said, when she stopped speaking. "But I think maybe you're getting a little mixed up over this, through being too tender-hearted. Look here—you said yourself just now that there was no need to thank you over that Toledo business, because once you knew that the Admiral was to be ambushed, and about that chauffeur, you had no option but to report it. Isn't that so?"

"Yes—it is true that I could not help it."

"And these men in Portugal—well, you say you did tell that young Portuguese, and had the P.I.D.E put on the alert, don't you suppose that if they went loosing off rifles at you or anyone else, the old Duke's people would have caught them anyway, and handed them over to the police?"

"Yes—yes, I suppose so."

"Of *course* so! It was what they did, or tried to do, that landed them in trouble; not what you did."

"But all these others, the ones here; about this I *did* do something, when I sent for that Spanish-speaking priest—it was he who learned about El Lobo, and was it not through him that they were found, and caught?"

"Yes, Mrs. Atherley, it was, and it was God's mercy that they were," he said, now very gravely. "Some of El Lobo's gang told the truth, and so the Spanish Security Police learned the details of the whole fresh plot. Would you like to know what they were? Maybe you'd better. There are traffic lights in a place that our Secretary of State has to pass through, quite close to Rota—they were to be tampered with, and while they were stuck at red, and the cars held up, plastic bombs were to finish off him, and our Ambassador, and Walter Parrott, and any innocent Spanish police and by-standers who happened to be around! The bombs were *found*. Wasn't that nice? Parrott and our Ambassador have wives too, you know! But there's almost *no* defence against *plastiqueurs,* which is about the dirtiest form of murder going."

"This is horrible," Hetta said, looking shocked.

"Yes it is—and are you going to get all upset, and *stay* upset, because some action of yours prevented it? Anyway, was it your own idea, sending for the priest who spoke Spanish?"

"No. A—a friend suggested it."

"The old Monsignor, eh?"

"Yes, it was he. Why, do you know him?"

"Yeah—he came on here from that convent where you spoke to him."

"But he was to be in retreat!" Hetta exclaimed, startled.

"Well, I wouldn't know about that; anyhow he came over to see the Spanish Intelligence people, and I met him. A character, if ever there was one!" the Major said, looking amusedly appreciative. "But now look here, Mrs. Atherley—he's a priest, and on balance I would say a *good* man; do you think he told you to call up for that young priest simply so the murderer could be confessed, or whatever they call it, in his own language?" He looked keenly at her as he spoke, with such a quizzical expression that she almost laughed.

"No. I am sure he would have wished that, but he probably had a second motive," she admitted.

"I'll say he had! And I should have thought that as a diplomat's wife you would have had a fair idea of what that motive was—to uncover enough facts to forestall any attempt on Mr. Everitt's life, here in Spain. Well, that is precisely what happened—but do you mean to tell me, young lady, that you *really* don't realise how much harm it would have done if the Secretary of State had been blown up while he was in this country?"

"I had not thought much of that aspect of it," she said slowly.

"Well, you should. Think about that pretty hard; don't just go indulging your private feelings about your personal responsibility. These people left you no option—you have to make up your mind whether you want the free world to stay free— in which case our relations with Spain have to be good enough for us to go on using Rota as a base—or you don't." He was silent, and looked rather sternly at her; Hetta too sat silent for some moments, looking in front of her.

"Yes, I see," she said at last, in rather a small voice.

"Well, if you do see, couldn't you stop worrying so much? This is quite a big thing—don't you think that the security of the free half of the world is more important than the freedom of a few perverted individuals? Freedom they'd use primarily to go on blowing innocent people up?"

Hetta was silenced; she was also three-parts convinced. "Well?" Day asked, as she did not speak.

"Yes. Yes, I believe you are right," she said. "Thank you very much for explaining it all to me."

He looked rather ruefully at her subdued expression.

"I'm glad you feel that way at last." Then he grinned a little.

"I wouldn't make much of a diplomatist!" he said. "I came here to thank you—officially—and I seem just to have given you a regular scolding. Will you pardon me for that?"

"No—I shall thank you!" Hetta said. "You have helped me to see this affair differently—I think more in proportion."

"Yes—in proportion is the word. So now maybe you'll let me say again what a big service you've done us, and assure you that we appreciate it." He wrung her hand and went away.

A few minutes later Richard came in.

"Hullo, darling—you all right? I'm just going to change. Is that tea?"

"It is cold and horrible—I will get some more."

"Not to worry! It's *wet*—I'll have it with lemon." He poured himself out a weak cup, and stood drinking it. "I thought I saw Day driving down the Avenida," he said. "He didn't come here, did he?"

"Yes, he did."

"Damn Ainsworth! I told him I didn't want you to be bothered with seeing him. This is pretty cool, I must say," he fumed.

"I sent for him," Hetta said calmly.

"Sent for him? How do you mean?"

"I telephoned and asked him to come. It is not poor Mr. Ainsworth's fault; he told me you did not wish me to see him. But I *did* wish it, so I rang him up."

"What on earth did you want to see him for?"

"To ask him some questions. And I am very glad that I did, for the things he told me have made me much less unhappy."

Richard Atherley put down his cup and stared long and earnestly at his wife. What could she have wished to ask Major Day so much that she had deliberately gone against his own known wishes? And what could the American have said that had made her "much less unhappy"? Not for the first time, he realised that Hetta had a life of her own into which he did not always and automatically penetrate; he had often been strongly aware of this in the early days of their marriage, but latterly the occasions had been fewer. Or had they only seemed fewer? Almost timidly, he said—"I should like to know about this, if I might?"

"Yes indeed—I will tell you everything. But not now," she said, with a glance at the clock, "or you will keep Colonel Marchant waiting. Give me a kiss."

As he stooped and kissed her—"Did Day say anything about his people being grateful for all the dope you produced?" he asked.

"Oh yes—he made me such a speech!" she replied, laughing. "You shall hear all about that also later on. And do not be cross with Ainsworth—to get Major Day's number from him was like pulling teeth!"

"Wretched Ainsworth! I expect he was like putty in your hands," Richard said, laughing too, and gave her another kiss.

Soon after he had gone off for his game of squash the telephone rang; Hetta was hardly surprised to hear Commander Mansfield's voice, asking if he might come round and see her?—"Right away, if I might." She said Yes, rang, and had the tea cleared away, and drinks brought in.

"I'm sorry to see that your wrist hasn't mended yet," the Commander said as soon as he arrived.

"No; it is being rather slow, and troublesome," Mrs. Atherley replied.

"And what have you done to your head?"

Hetta gave the pre-arranged reply.

"That's too bad, on top of the other injury—I am very sorry." He paused. "Are you up to going out at all?"

"I have not tried yet—we are only just returned," she answered smiling. "Why?—does Mrs. Parrott want something?"

He laughed out. "There's no fooling you, Mrs. Atherley! Yes, she does; she very much hopes that you and your husband will come to her luncheon for Mr. Everitt. And I personally shall be very thankful if you can make it."

"When is it?"

"On the twenty-fifth—at the Castellana-Hilton."

Hetta took out her little diary, and turned the pages; the twenty-fifth was the day on which their ship sailed from Vigo.

"Oh no—I am so sorry, but I shall not be here."

"You're going away again?" He sounded surprised.

"Yes. I am going to England to get treatment for my wrist. It seems there are wonderful places there for such things." She had decided that no one was better suited to receive, and to spread these tidings than the Commander.

"Shall you be away long?" he asked.

"For some months, I expect. It seems the trouble is worse than they thought at first—and I do not want to be one-handed for the rest of my life," she said, with a little smile.

He was greatly concerned. "That is terribly bad news, Mrs. Atherley. I'm more sorry than I can say. That wretched Luis!" he exclaimed, striking his hand on the arm of his chair. "*And our people at Camp Kilmer!*—I don't find it at all easy to forgive them for being so inadequate. If they had done their job properly he would never have gotten a post with the Peabodys, and none of this would have happened."

Hetta had forgotten about Camp Kilmer, and asked; Mansfield explained that that was where the Hungarian refugees had been kept till they were screened. But the mention of the chauffeur's name sent her thoughts off on another tack.

"Commander Mansfield, do you not think it would be better, now, to tell Mrs. Parrott part of the truth about Luis? It seems she is still hoping that her husband will get him back, and is vexed that he doesn't; this must be rather tiresome for him."

"Poor Walter! I'll say it's tiresome—and a good deal more! Only it isn't a thing one wants talked about, and—well, you know Nell."

Hetta did know Nell. "Nevertheless, she speaks too much about him, and indiscreetly; to anyone who knows the facts, it makes her look foolish. If she were told, she could perhaps be got to keep quiet."

"I'm afraid you're rather too optimistic, Mrs. Atherley," he said grimly. "And she isn't the only person who's made to look foolish! But there are the Spanish Security people to consider —they wouldn't like it a bit if she went talking about his having been deported. I'll think about it, and talk to Day and Walter—but I'm pretty sure it had better stay the way it is till this visit is over." He paused. "I'm beginning to wish Rota was at the bottom of the sea!" he said.

"Like its Polaris submarines!" Hetta responded merrily. Mansfield laughed, and took his departure.

16

SOME THREE WEEKS later Julia Jamieson and Edina Reeder were standing on a damp quay-side in Scotland, watching the red-funneled steamer ploughing its way towards them across the water. It was one of those rare, fine late-autumn days which are so lovely in the West Highlands when they do come; the soft pale sunshine brought out the lingering purple of the heather on the hills behind the rather ugly little town, and caught the last scraps of gold in the almost leafless birchwoods on their lower slopes; the air was mild and sweet.

"Well, at least it isn't raining for her," Edina said. "I do *hope* she'll be all right here."

"Don't fuss, Edina—of course she will. I've told you she was brought up in the country."

"Ah, and so was Madame Bonnecourt—but she hates this climate! I wonder if I'd have time to go and see if she's got her thick shoes all right?"

"No, the boat will be in in two minutes. I told Mrs. McKerrow to see to her herself, and they were getting on fine when I left. As for Hetta Atherley, I should think she'd be so glad merely to feel *safe* that she wouldn't give a blow for any climate."

The boat came in, and manoeuvred up against the quay; Julia waved vigorously at a small group standing by the rail—

Mrs. Hathaway, tall and erect in a grey Inverness cape, a short fair woman carrying a baby, and an even shorter dark one holding a morocco dressing-case; a strikingly pretty girl in a fur coat and wearing a head-scarf stood by them, and presently, catching sight of Julia, waved back.

"Is that her, in the mink?" Edina asked, now waving too.

"Yes."

"Well, at least she has the wits not to travel in a hat, like most foreigners," Mrs. Reeder said hopefully.

The gangway was let down and the passengers came ashore, while luggage was humped down a second gangway; after the locals the Madrid party, with Mrs. Hathaway in the lead, stepped ashore.

"There you are, safe and sound," Julia exclaimed, giving Hetta Atherley a warm hug. "Lovely to see you. Now this is Mrs. Reeder."

Edina turned from kissing Mrs. Hathaway to greet her new guest. "How do you do? Welcome to Scotland," she said.

"How do you do? It is so kind of you to have us," Hetta said, in her pretty plummy English. "Oh, Julia, all our luggage has *red* labels. There is a terrible quantity, I'm afraid."

"That's all right—Bonnecourt has brought the Land-Rover. Ah, there he is. Bonnecourt, all the bagages of Madame have red labels." She turned to greet the nurse and baby. *"Bonjour, Élise. So this is Richenda—oh, she's *exactly* like her Father!"*

"N'est-pas, Madame?" the Swiss said, beaming. Then Julia addressed Speranza in Spanish, to the latter's manifest satisfaction—especially when she added that Madame Reeder's cook, Olimpia, was a Spaniard too. "And Monsieur and Madame Bonnecourt will talk French to you, Élise," she went on. "We are quite a little U.N.O., here."

Bonnecourt and a blue-jerseyed porter were rapidly stowing the luggage—pram, carry-cot and all—in the Land-Rover, and presently the party walked out to the road, where the two cars waited. "Now, how shall we go?" Edina asked.

"Why don't you take Hetta and Speranza, and **Mrs.** Hathaway and Élise can come with me. Madame Bonnecourt can go in the Land-Rover," Julia said. This lady at that moment came hurrying up, and proudly displayed her feet; she was wearing the *souliers forts* which she had just acquired at Mc-Kerrow's.

"Yes, those are much more the style, Madame; now your feet won't get wet," Mrs. Reeder told her. And at last everyone was bestowed in some vehicle, and they drove off.

Julia had her own reasons for suggesting that Mrs. Atherley should drive with her hostess. She had been a little disturbed by her cousin's unwonted display of what she called "fuss" on the quay, and thought that the sooner she and Hetta had a chance to come to terms, the better; a tête-à-tête drive immediately seemed to her a good idea—once they got back to the house Edina was liable to be engulfed in all manner of domestic and farm affairs.

Her scheme worked better than such plans often do. Almost immediately after leaving the town the road ran down to a long narrow arm of the sea enclosed by hills—the nearer end was covered with swans, at least two hundred of them, and Hetta exclaimed at the sight.

"Oh, how beautiful! So many! This is a lake?"

"No, it's a sea-loch."

"So?—I thought swans lived in fresh water."

"Oh, they don't mind the sea. Anyhow this end of the loch is almost fresh, so many burns run into it."

"What are burns?"

"It's the Scottish word for small streams."

"Oh yes, I see." She scanned the hills, down which indeed several burns came tumbling, creamy and foaming from last night's rain; now she noticed their colour. "But how extraordinary!—these hills are almost purple!" she said.

"Yes, that is the heather. It's going over now; a month ago it was much brighter."

"It is most strange!" She continued to stare at the mauve-tinged slopes in silence; Edina, amused, realised that her visitor, though too polite to say so, obviously shared the opinion of the young English officer in General Wade's army, who wrote from Scotland in the eighteenth century that the Scottish hills were "most of all disgusting when the heath is in bloom."

Presently the road left the loch, and climbed gently through pastures and cultivated land, now mostly stubble and plough; Hetta at once asked what the crop had been—wheat?

"No, it's too wet for that here; oats is our main crop—and of course roots for the cows."

"Oh, do you keep cows? How nice. Many?"

"About three hundred." She pulled in to the side of the road to let a large tanker pass; the driver waved his hand at her. "That's some of our milk going in to Glasgow," Edina said.

"Milk? In that? But does it not get too much shaken?"

"No worse than in churns—and of course it's chilled and pasteurised first."

"Pasteurised? You like this? But with pasteurised milk surely one cannot make butter?" Hetta said earnestly, surprising her hostess.

"No, but the people in Glasgow don't want to make butter, only to drink the milk. Of course we don't pasteurise it for the house, where we do make butter," Edina said, smiling a little; she was relieved at the newcomer's practical interest.

"Oh, I am glad of this. Of course in Madrid and in Paris we had to use pasteurised milk; but for children especially, I do not think it is so good as natural milk."

"How right you are."

Just then the car topped a rise, and the immense view of the Sound opened in front of them—endless miles of sunlit water, out of which rose the great shapes, blue and rounded, of mountainous islands; Hetta caught her breath.

"But this is *so* beautiful! How fortunate you are to live here!"

"Wait till it rains!" Edina laughed; "then you won't see a thing."

"But to see this even sometimes is worth many wet days!"

The road ran down almost to sea-level, and then along the coast through fields; Hetta was startled by the intense greenness of the grass, which she obviously preferred to the unnatural colour of the heather. They came to cows; she had never seen Ayrshires before, and commented on their long and pointed horns. "But they are chiefly for milk, yes?" Then a man with a tractor, scattering mangolds across a field, caught her attention—"Is this sugar-beet that you feed to them?"

"No, swedes."

"But is it not early in the year to begin feeding? There seems to be so much grass still."

"Yes, it is, rather; but that lot are pedigree cows, and extra heavy milkers; we are working up their butter-fat record," Edina said, increasingly pleased with her paying guest, who did not conform in the least to her preconceived ideas of a foreign-born diplomat's wife. Of course Hetta wanted to know how butter-fat records were kept, and was told. Then they swung into the drive, where the saw-mill was plainly visible on their right, and audible too—the whine of the circular saw came loudly to their ears.

"To whom does this belong?" Hetta enquired.

"To us." At that moment a lorry loaded with sawn timber came up a by-road from the mill, and paused to let the car pass.

"Where is that going? To Glasgow, like the milk?"

"No, down the road to Kilmartin; the County Council is putting up a new housing estate, and we are supplying most of the timber."

"Does this pay well?"

"Oh yes, very well; it's only a few miles away, so the freight costs are negligible. And of course we use a lot on the place too, for gates and fencing-stobs."

"Where are your forests?" Hetta asked, looking about her

—near at hand no trees were to be seen but groups of sycamores and limes, with a few exotic conifers.

"Up the hill behind the house—I'll show you tomorrow, if you'd care to see the woods."

"I should like to very much. What sort of trees? *Pinus maritima?*"

"No—here it's mostly spruce, or larch on the wetter ground. What is *Pinus maritima?*"

"In Portugal it is the principal tree. Do you extract the resin?"

"Goodness no! Do they in Portugal?"

"Indeed yes—thousands of tons of it." They were still happily talking about resin extraction when the car drew up to the front door.

Hetta got out and looked with eager interest at the house where she was to make her home for the moment—with interest, and with a certain dismay. Anything more unlike Gralheira, with its formal baroque elegance, it was impossible to conceive. The architectural style of Glentoran was "Scotch baronial" at its worst: round towers, sham battlements, pepper-pot turrets were stuck irrelevantly all about the main structure; the outline of the house seemed to bristle like a giant porcupine. Edina saw her astonished face, and laughed.

"Isn't it ghastly?" she said. "And it's almost as bad inside. Wait till you see the stained glass in the hall!"

"It is—curious," Hetta said. "Is it really old, or built to look so?"

"Oh, sham as can be—nineteenth century. The old castle was down there, where the kitchen-garden is now. But come in—at least it's *warm* inside."

The business of settling in such a large party inevitably took time, but Julia and Edina did not allow Hetta to weary herself with it; they led her into the library, gave her a whisky, and left her there in Mrs. Hathaway's care while they dealt with the luggage, the allocation of rooms, and the introductions to their own Nannies—helped by both the Bonnecourts and by Olimpia, who abandoned her kitchen to come and welcome Speranza, and carry suitcases upstairs. Only when everyone had been installed where they belonged, with their correct possessions, did they allow Mrs. Atherley to go upstairs to her room.

"Here you are," Edina said.

"Oh, I have this view! How lovely," Hetta said, running to the window.

"Yes. I'm afraid you have to share a bathroom with Élise, but I thought you'd like to be near Richenda."

"Oh yes, please. Where are they?"

"Through here." She opened another door and led the way into a bathroom as large as a fair-sized bedroom—which it had in fact been originally; this, beside the usual fittings contained not only a bidet, but a proper sink, two heated towel-rails, and a large old-fashioned wooden clothes-horse.

"Oh, how convenient! Everything can be washed here," Hetta exclaimed, delighted.

"Yes." She opened a door on the further side into a bedroom where a log fire burned brightly behind a brass-topped wire fender, flanked by two arm-chairs covered in bright chintz; a vast wardrobe occupied the whole of one side of the room, and there was a proper dressing-table and two or three ancient Victorian chests of drawers, ugly but ample.

"But this is perfect!—so much space," Hetta said.

"Glad you like it. And here's the day nursery," Edina pursued, opening yet another door. Hetta fairly gaped—again a fire, with more arm-chairs beside it; a large round table in the middle of the room, and several smaller ones, on one of which stood an electric kettle; there was even a play-pen, and bright cups and saucers occupied a row of shelves on the wall. "So Élise can be quite independent if she wants to," Mrs. Reeder explained.

Hetta turned and threw her arms round her hostess's neck.

"You are *too* kind! You have thought of everything. It is absolutely perfect," she said, and kissed her warmly. "But where are they?"

"Along with the others, I expect," Edina said, a little embarrassed by the kiss, but not altogether displeased. They went out into the corridor and followed the sound of voices to the main nursery, where a perfect babel of French, Spanish, and soft Highland English mingled with the shrill voices of the children; Edina, with cheerful firmness, thanked Madame Bonnecourt and Olimpia for their help—they took the hint and departed. Then she introduced her guest—"Nannie Campbell, this is Mrs. Atherley, Richenda's Mother; John, Duncan, come and say How do you do to Mrs. Atherley. And this is Nannie Mackenzie, who looks after Julia's Philipino. How is he today, Nannie Mack? Are the motions a better colour? Oh, good."

"What has she done to her face?" John Reeder asked, staring at the plaster on Hetta's forehead. He was a sturdy upstanding creature of about five, with his Father's brown hair and blue eyes.

"John! Who is "she"? The cat's Mother?" Nannie Campbell asked sharply.

"Sorry, Nannie. But what *did* the lady do to her face?"

"Mrs. Atherley hurt herself," Edina said. "It makes her head ache, so you mustn't shout when she is there."

Hetta stood, a little bewildered by the number of strange faces, but also amused and pleased. A stout fresh-faced girl was laying a table at one end of the room; big wholemeal loaves, great round shapes of butter, jugs of milk, and platters of oatcakes already stood on it, and she was taking plates and cutlery out of a square opening in the wall—when she had finished she pulled a cord, and shut the doors.

"That's the food-lift from the kitchen," Mrs. Reeder said, noting Hetta's glance of enquiry. "One couldn't possibly have everything carried up and down. Now John, you'd better sit up to the table, and you too, Duncan. There's the other highchair for Richenda, Élise."

"Merci bien, Madame." "Mais comme tout est bien organisé dans cette maison," the Swiss murmured in an aside to her mistress. *"On sera très bien ici."*

While the children were being installed in their chairs, and bibs tied on Edina said—"I thought Speranza had better eat up here, today; she'll want to be doing your unpacking afterwards. Tomorrow we can settle whether she feeds up or down. Olimpia has shown her her room—it's up on the top floor."

"Oh yes; thank you. Whatever you say," Hetta replied, rather abstractedly. She was thinking how intensely she agreed with Élise—everything in the house was so well organised that there would be no need for any special thought or effort on her part; and the sight of those small happy faces round the laden table was somehow immensely reassuring. It would indeed be well with one here! Glentoran might be ugly externally, but within it had almost every advantage over Gralheira. Back in her pretty bedroom she took off her head-scarf, ran a comb through her hair, and washed her hands in that astonishingly well-equipped bathroom; then she went to the window, threw it up, and leaned out, gazing up the Sound at those blue island shapes. How sweet and soft the air was!—she had never tasted air so soft; the colours of sea and shore were soft too, quite unlike the sharp glittering brilliance of Portugal and Spain. And how tranquil those cows looked, lying in a field below the house, chewing the cud. An extraordinary sense of peace and safety flooded over her; she dropped to her knees; her whole body felt relaxed almost to the point of weakness. (This, though Hetta did not know it, was partly the normal effect of the West Highland climate.) Presently, with an effort, she got up and went downstairs.

Philip Reeder had come in; he welcomed her with bluff but genuine warmth. "Very nice indeed to have you here. I hope you'll be comfortable, and be able to relax a bit—you must need it," he said. Then they went in to lunch; Hetta noticed a side-board laden with cold joints as she sat down to a perfect *risotto*—like all other new-comers to Glentoran she could not resist an exclamation over Olimpia's food: "But this is *too* delicious!"

"Yes, the old girl does pretty well," Philip said, pleased; then they talked about the journey. They waited on themselves; Julia and Philip whisked away the empty plates, while Edina took a dish with a silver cover from a hot-plate and set it down before her husband. As he re-seated himself he lifted the lid and examined it.

"Oh, good—here they are at last," he said—"and done on cabbage. Will you have a partridge, Mrs. Atherley?"

Hetta stared at the small birds lying on their *couche* of cabbage and gravy; the sight brought back such a sudden spate of memories as to give her an actual sense of revulsion. She glanced at the side-board.

"Might I perhaps have something cold?"

"Yes, of course—come and choose," Edina said pleasantly, though some of her old disquiets returned at this. What was wrong with partridges? "Venison pasty? Or cold beef?"

"Oh, the venison pasty, please. I have not eaten that since I was a child."

When she and Edina had sat down again—"I'm sorry you don't care for partidges," Philip Reeder said, conversationally. "We look on them as rather a treat up here; we don't often get them."

"In Portugal I had rather too much of them," Hetta said lightly, and praised the venison pasty; Mrs. Hathaway gave her an approving glance. After lunch the old lady suggested that Julia should take her up to lie down till tea-time; Hetta agreed gratefully. When they had gone—"I wonder what on earth she has against partridges?" Edina speculated.

"She made a great mistake; they were absolutely perfect," Philip said. "You were quite right to keep them that extra day, Edina."

"She got that wound in her forehead during a partridge-shoot," Mrs. Hathaway observed quietly.

"No! Did she really?"

"Yes. The Communists thought it a good opportunity, with people standing still during a drive, and shots going on to mask the sound of the rifle. But it is understandable, I think, that she might not care very much about partridges at the moment," Mrs. Hathaway said, dispassionately.

"Good God no—I should think not! Did they get the man who shot her?"

"I think so—I am not quite sure. She didn't seem to want to talk much about it, and of course I didn't ask her."

"Good God!" Philip said again. "Poor girl. Did she tell you about the car smash too, Mrs. H.?"

"No. I expect she will tell Julia."

"Well, I don't suppose she'll mind grouse—they don't have them in Portugal," Philip said, getting up. "I'm glad she's here —I hope she'll rest now, and get over it! Any letters, Edina? I'm going down to the village."

Up in her room Hetta obediently took off her skirt and lay down on the bed, while Julia folded back the counterpane and made up the fire. Speranza had unpacked her case, and everything was tidily set out on the dressing-table; she was making a start on one of the trunks, but ran to fill a hot-water bottle when she saw her mistress lie down.

"Does she know where to get hot water?" Julia asked.

"I expect so—there is an electric kettle in the nursery. It is all *so* well-arranged, here; your cousin has thought of everything. She must be a wonderful person," Hetta said.

"She is uncommonly practical," Julia admitted.

"Oh, but so kind, too; Mrs. Hathaway said that it was she, Mrs. Reeder herself, who suggested that we should all come, though she has never seen us."

"Yes, she did—I think she guessed that you'd had a pretty rough time, and wanted you to be able to take it easy for a bit."

"Well, that I can do better here than anywhere, I think— there is nothing left to me to think of, or arrange, Ah, *muchas gracias,* Speranza," as the Spanish girl put the bottle under the eiderdown near her feet.

"I should tell her to leave the unpacking for now, and let you get a nap," Julia suggested.

"Yes, I will." She spoke to the maid, who nodded and vanished. "But do not you go just yet, Julia. Oh, I am so glad that you are here—that makes it *quite* perfect. We shall be able to talk and talk!" She leaned back on the pillows, and spread her arms out luxuriously. "Such a wonderful bed!" Then she glanced a little anxiously at her friend. "I hope Mrs. Reeder will not have been vexed that I did not want to eat partridge. You see *this,*" she touched her forehead—"happened at a partridge-shoot."

"Was that what Luzia called your 'narrow escape' at Gralheira in her letter?"

"Yes. The man had a rifle, and how he missed me I cannot think, for he was hidden in a small wood not at all far away, and I was standing with the Ambassador, watching him shoot."

"Goodness! But he did hit you, didn't he?"

"No, the bullet hit the wall, and a piece of stone flew out, and went into my head. And then they took me back to the house in the game-van, and to make room they threw out the birds—dozens and dozens of them, onto the track, all feathers; somehow they looked a little horrible, lying in a heap like that! And the sun was hot, so the van still smelt of them, *strongly.* But I am sorry I did not eat them—another time I am sure I can. I hope Mrs. Reeder will not mind," she repeated.

"I'm sure she won't, especially if I may tell her the reason?"

"Oh do. I thought it would be embarrassing if I spoke of it."

"Quite right. Anyhow I don't suppose there'll be another time; we haven't any partridges at Glentoran. These came from a shoot at the Menteiths, down the coast. But what Ambassador?—the one from Lisbon?"

"No, ours from Madrid."

"And were the thugs shooting at him or at you?"

"Oh, at me! You see when we were spending a day at Toledo with an American Admiral—Luxworthy, such a dear man!—I overheard some Hungarians planning an ambush to kill him; I suppose they spoke foolishly loud thinking that no one would understand. But I *did* understand. . . ." She went on to pour out the whole story of Luis and her suspicions of him; of the curious way in which her prayer in the car was answered by the crash, and the man's face when she cried out in Hungarian; then of his deportation. Mrs. Jamieson listened with fascinated horror; the very baldness and unemphatic flatness of Hetta's account somehow added tension to what was in itself a sufficiently dramatic recital.

"So then Richard took me to Gralheira, thinking that I should be safe there, but they came after me."

"Yes, Luzia wrote about that; she was terribly upset that they should have pursued you even there," Julia interjected. "But Hetta dear, don't you think you had better have a nap now, and tell me the rest later on? We've got all the time in the world."

"Yes, perhaps that might be best. The journey was quite comfortable, but somehow there seemed to be a lot of walking, and standing."

"Oh, don't I know it! Right; you have a shut-eye. Want your curtains drawn? I'll tell Speranza not too come till you send for her, shall I? And I'll come later and see if you'd like tea up here."

"Oh yes, do come back! It is such a luxury—more than you can imagine!—to be able to talk *quite* freely to someone, after being careful for so long."

Julia was struck by those last words. Surely, she thought as she went along to the nurseries, Hetta must have been able to talk freely to her Richard? Well no, perhaps not—she had probably had scruples about his worrying. She looked in on Élise and told her that Madame was going to sleep for a bit;

Speranza was there, and was instructed not to disturb her mistress. Then she went and visited her Philipino, who was on the point of going out in his pram with Nannie Mackenzie—"I'll come to give him his feed at a quarter-past four, Nannie."

"Very well, Mistress Jamieson. I hope Mistress Atherley is going to get a rest? That Swiss nurse tells me she's expecting again."

"Yes, she is, Nannie—I mean going to rest now, *and* another baby," Julia said; Nurse Mackenzie laughed.

"I'm thankful she is here, away from all that wickedness!" she said. "Shot at when she was standing still!—why, one wouldn't treat a grouse so," the Scotswoman added, in a comminatory tone.

H'm—so Élise had been talking! Oh well, here it didn't matter, thank goodness, Julia reflected as she went downstairs.

"Yes, she's going to have a nap," she replied to Edina's enquiry. "I thought we might try to get her to have tea in bed, and only come down for dinner."

"Yes, why not? There's a kettle and everything in Richenda's nursery, and you can get a tray from Nannie Campbell to take the things along on, or the Spanish girl can do it—what's this her name is?"

"Speranza—means hope."

"Oh well, I expect they'll soon be calling her Hope," Mrs. Reeder said cheerfully. "Philip's so sorry he pressed her about the partridges," she went on. "Mrs. H. says it was at a partridge-shoot that she got shot in the face."

"Yes." Julia passed on Hetta's account of this episode, including the heap of feathered bodies by the track, and the smell in the shooting-brake.

"Ugh! I can imagine it. I shouldn't think she'd ever want to eat one again as long as she lives."

"Well, tell her that. She was tremendously apologetic at having refused them, and hoped you wouldn't mind."

"I will. Did they get the man who shot at her? Mrs. H. didn't know."

"Nor do I—I made her shut up and go to sleep. But I'm sure she will tell me later; I think she's really longing to talk it all out."

"Best thing she can do—get it off her chest and out of her system. You'd better have your tea up with her, and give her a chance," Edina said.

"Right—I'll do that. Now, what can I do in the garden? I've got nearly two hours before I feed the creature again."

"Well, either the last dead-heads off the roses, or pulling out those eternal sycamore seedlings up the glen. I should do the roses, I think—that will finish them for this year."

"The seedlings we have always with us!" Julia grinned, and went off to get her basket and scissors. Snipping away in the soft autumn sunshine, she thought over this last talk with her cousin. Yes, it was going to be all right with Edina, she felt sure—and that was the important thing.

Some two hours later, after nursing her child in its own room, Julia collected a tray with milk and eatables in the main nursery, where the large party was already assembling, and gave it to Speranza to carry along to Richenda's quarters; there she switched on the electric kettle, and added cups and plates off the shelf—then she went and tapped on Hetta's door. Getting no reply, she went in; Hetta was asleep, but roused up when Julia partly drew back one curtain.

"Ready for tea? It's just coming," she said.

"Here? Oh, how nice. Is it tea-time already?"

"Yes. Have a good nap?"

"Oh, I slept *so* well!" She stretched out her arms. "I did not know one could sleep so in the day."

"You will here—it's the air." She drew back the other curtains. "Now I'll fetch the tea." She went and made it; then, giving the tray to Speranza, she went back and put a table and chair ready. Hetta was sitting up in bed; she had combed out her hair and put on a cardigan—she looked more refreshed and tranquil than Julia had seen her since her arrival.

· 244 ·

"You have it with me?" Hetta enquired, glancing at the two cups.

"Yes—Mrs. Reeder suggested it." She told Speranza in Spanish to go and have her tea with the others, and then poured out.

"She is *kind*. I shall be happy here, I know. Oh, I feel quite hungry."

"Good."

Over their tea Hetta, prompted by questions from Julia, did continue her account of what had happened when the Communists "came after her" to Gralheira: her suspicions of the three strangers, her crisis of conscience about them, and the awkwardness of going out with Nick and Luzia when she was afraid to walk alone.

"Oh yes, I saw in *The Times* that they had got engaged at last. How do Nick and the old Duke get on?"

"*Per*fectly! It is wonderful to see the good old man so happy; and he is going to do all sorts of new things at Gralheira, that Nick has thought of. I will tell you about that presently."

"Yes, do; I'm so glad it's being such a success. But now go on telling me about your three thugs. What *did* you do, in the end?"

"I went to consult Subercaseaux!"

"No! I thought you disliked him."

"Formerly I did not like him at all, but now I do—much more, at least." She went on to describe the excursion to La Trapa: the Monsignor's instructions about sending for Gil de Castelo Branco, and her interview with Father Martinez; then the man's attempt at suicide after the shooting, how she had sent for Father Martinez, and her struggles with Major Belmonte to ensure that the priest saw the assassin first—this made Julia laugh. Now and again she put in a question: when Hetta mentioned how craftily the little Father had passed her his notes in the book of devotion—"But he couldn't put down what he had heard in confession!" Mrs. Jamieson objected.

"Of course not. This was so fortunate, that the young man

thought himself too much of a Communist to make a proper confession—he refused outright to do that. So of course Father Martinez could record what he said, and this enabled the Spanish Security Police to find all the rest of the gang. But all the same the poor creature made a good end, and was given Christian burial," Hetta said calmly. Then she went on to tell Julia about the details of the plot that had been uncovered, as reported to her by Major Day.

"So after these people were caught, really everything was safe for this American Minister, and I suppose for me also; but Richard had got it into his head that *nowhere* was safe for me in Spain and Portugal. And I think the Ambassador felt the same."

"I'm not surprised," Julia said emphatically. "After two such escapes, I should have been petrified of a third try. And I'm sure it's far better for the child that you should come right away, to a place where you need have no anxieties."

"Yes, I think so. I feel so peaceful and safe here, and Julia, is such a luxury to have someone to whom I can talk *quite* freely! You may think this absurd, but you cannot imagine how *tiring* it is to have to be careful what one says all the time—especially when one's head aches," she said flatly. "Careful with Belmonte, careful with the old Heriots, careful with the doctor, careful with the Duke!"

"Why did you have to be careful with him?" Julia asked, surprised.

"The Monsignor thought he should not be told about the three men, in case he should do something impetuous before the truth about them was discovered. He was so cross when it all came out."

"I bet he was. Poor Duke!"

"And in Madrid also I had to be careful, with everyone, so that the real reason for our coming away should not be known. The Ambassador made up such a story about my wrist needing special treatment!" Hetta said, with a youthful giggle which Julia found very reassuring. "Physio-something; three

treatments every week, for months and months! *You* can perhaps give me this physio-whatever-it-is, Julia!"

"You silly!" Julia stood up and gave her a kiss. "But your
wrist is really all right now, isn't it?"

"Yes, only a little weak."

Julia gave her another cup of tea, and cut her a slice of the
immensely solid fruit cake, an invariable accompaniment to
Scottish meals, which she had brought from the nursery.

"Now that, I could not cut with my left hand," Hetta observed, as she bit off a piece.

"I should think not—it's all I can do to cut it with my
right!" Julia said. "Edina has to make these herself—it's the
one thing Olimpia can't do; they horrify her!" She sat silent
for a moment or two, while Hetta munched away, reflecting on
what she had heard.

"But surely the Americans must have known where the information came from, that enabled the Spanish police to catch
all those Communists?" she asked.

"Their Security people, yes—and I think possibly also their
Ambassador. But you see Walter Parrott, their Naval Attaché,
has a *very* silly wife, who cannot be prevented from talking
about everything she hears; so even he was told as little as possible. She is still lamenting that chauffeur of theirs, who organised the Toledo ambush of the Admiral, since she could
not be told that he had been deported."

"How very trying."

"It was." She went on telling Julia about her struggles with
Nell during the Admiral's visit, and with Luxworthy's daughter, making her friend laugh; she gave little thumbnail
sketches of the Admiral himself, of Lieutenant Ellington, and
of the Ambassador, to whom she was obviously devoted—
finally of Ainsworth and Major Day. Julia listened, amused,
but in the end astonished. How she had matured! Her assess-
ments of people and situations were so shrewd and balanced
—very different from the impetuous, violent likings and
antipathies of the little refugee, fresh from the wilds of Hun-

gary, whom she had known in Portugal only a few years ago, with her intolerance of social observances of any sort; but still the same honesty and warmth that had made her so lovable then. She thought, too, of what Hetta had been through: two attempts at murder; perpetually being discreet and, she was sure, putting a brave face on everything—and all the time anxiety for the child she was carrying.

They sat on, talking; Speranza came in and took away the tea-things, but still they kept at it, till at last a bell boomed out high overhead.

"What is that?" Hetta asked.

"Goodness, the dressing-bell already! I must go and feed that infant. Oh, there's time enough—dinner isn't till a quarter to eight."

"Do we dress very much?"

"No—just something simple; high, if you like. Have you got a frock out?"

"No—I will get one. They are in that trunk that Speranza has begun. Oh, how lazy one feels here!"

"Well, *be* lazy! Can I get you one out?"

"Oh, do—there is a red one quite near the top. And I will have a bath." She sprang off the bed and went and turned on the water in the bathroom. When she came back Julia was standing by the bed, on which a red silk dress was spread out; she was holding in her hands a little polychrome statuette of the Madonna, and gazing at it, absorbed.

"Hetta, how did you come by this? It was wrapped up in the dress—is that the right one?"

"Oh yes—Ellington only brought it just as I was leaving, so I rolled it up in the frock and put it in among my dresses, to be safe; there was no time to pack it properly in cotton-wool."

"But how did Ellington get it? It's *quite* exquisite; eighteenth century, isn't it?"

"The Admiral sent it to me, from America."

"Luxworthy? But surely it's Spanish?" She peered with her beautiful myopic eyes at some very faint gilded lettering round the base. *"Nuestra Señora de*—I can't read the last part."

"Socorro. Our Lady of Deliverance," Hetta said, with an expression of great happiness on her face.

"But how on earth could he get it over there?"

"Oh, Mama always says that there are very good antique-shops in New York—and Ellington said that he went up there and found it for me. You see we were together at Toledo, when the Communists had planned their first attempt, on *him;* and when he learned in Washington how they had tried to kill me at Gralheira, he determined to send me a present. Look underneath."

Julia turned the beautiful little thing sideways. On a piece of paper gummed to the bottom was written: "With heartfelt thanks. H.L." She stood the statue carefully on a chest of drawers, and went over and gave Hetta a quick kiss.

"I should like to meet your Admiral," she said. Then, as if to brush away the moment of emotion—"What shoes are you going to wear tonight?" she asked.

"Speranza got out those from my dressing-case," Hetta said, indicating a pair of black satin court shoes under the dressing table.

"Oh, but they have such high heels! Haven't you anything lower? Philip Reeder has rather a thing against very high heels."

"Yes, I have some silver sandals in that other case, with quite low ones."

"Well, get those out, there's a duck—or shall I send Speranza to you?"

"Yes, do; then she can find them while I have my bath." As she spoke she took a small vase of gentians off the dressing-table and set it down by the little Madonna.

"Tomorrow we will get Her some flowers of Her own," Hetta said. Then she went to have her bath, and Julia walked along the passage to feed her baby.